ESSENCE

A DIVINE DUNGEON Anthology

DAKOTA KROUT

JAMES AUWAERTER

RYAN BALL

ROHAN HUBLIKAR

RAYMOND JOHNSON

ALEXIS KEANE

DENNIS VANDERKERKEN

STEVEN WILLDEN

TABLE OF CONTENTS

ACKNOWLEDGMENTS

Thank you to all of the people that were excited to be a part of this process. There were a ton of amazing entries for this anthology, thank you all so much for jumping on board!

The stories in this book are from some very talented new writers, and I am very excited that I will be able to continue working with a few of them!

To the reader, thank you so much for the amazing enthusiasm you bring! We couldn't do this without you!

-Dakota Krout

Lion Start
By: Rohan Hublikar

Chapter One

"Your tea, milord."

Garron held the tray out, bowing his head. For a long moment, the rattling of the cups shaking in their saucers was the only sound in the room. Then the weight lifted, and he lowered his arms with a little breath of relief. Today was a bad day. He bowed a little deeper, feeling his bones creak with the motion and turned to go.

"Hold on, Gar." At the familiar voice, Garron felt a little smile creep on to his face...He smoothed it away.

"Yes, milord?" He hated how his voice sounded like an old man's, but he couldn't keep the rasp out today. And coughing would just make it worse.

"You don't sound too good today."

Garron looked up, straight into a pair of dark eyes framed by a face furrowed in concern. Andros had just hit his growth, and he looked like someone had taken the slightly pudgy boy Garron had known since birth and stretched him out until he was a lanky teenager. Long, black hair fell to his shoulders, and at the moment, it was matted with sweat and stuck close to his scalp, but even when it was dry, it always seemed messy to Garron. His mother had done a better job of cutting it.

"Do you want some of my tea?"

Before Garron could reply, the other person in the room spoke in a quiet voice that sent a shiver down Garron's spine.

"Don't be foolish, boy. That's Essence-infused. No sense wasting it on a fishy."

Garron remembered when Lord Tet used to sit in this room with Andros. He'd been a busy man, powerful and important, but he'd never said an unkind word to Garron. Or scared him. The same couldn't be said of Jackson.

After a moment of silence, Andros spoke again, a controlled rage creeping into his voice. "He needs it more than I do. I'll be fine, but he–"

"Wouldn't appreciate the *gift* he was wasting." Jackson's eyes flickered to Garron again, and his chest tightened. He'd never quite understood why, but Jackson had never liked him. When Lord Tet had left to go fight in the war and Jackson had become Andros' guardian as well as captain of the guard, it had gotten worse.

"It would still..."

"Not another word, boy. Just drink the infernal tea so you can get back to training. I want you on the verge of the C-ranks when your father returns. And *you*." Once again, his eyes rested on Garron, and this time, Garron could barely hold back a cough. Jackson kept his hair cropped close to his skull, though Garron had never seen his mother or anyone else cut it. It always had a singed look to it, as though he'd burned off the bits he didn't want instead of cutting them, but otherwise, his face seemed like a harder version of Andros', all sharp lines and deep shadows, the jaw just a little too long for the face. "Get going."

Garron bowed again, panic making him forget the pain. He hurried off.

"I'll have to have a word with Lord Tet about him. He's distracting you, but perhaps I won't need to, if..."

He made it out of the room, closing the door with a sigh of relief. It quickly turned into a cough and then a hack, and before he knew it, he was on the floor. It only lasted for a minute or so, which was better than that morning's fit, but he still grimaced as he struggled to his feet. Jackson's scrutiny was always a trial, but seeing Andros was almost enough to make up for it. He was almost sure that Hila had sent him to deliver the tea just so he could see his friend, and he was grateful to her for it. Especially since it felt like he didn't have many more opportunities left.

Stop being dramatic. Garron grunted, clearing his throat, and he shook his head. No matter how bad his illness was getting, he knew for certain that failing to get back to Hila in time would kill him faster. He started shuffling down the halls of the manor, heading to the kitchen.

CHAPTER TWO

"Took you long enough, didn't it?" the plump woman shouted over from the other side of the kitchen, her hands still working at chopping herbs as she looked over at Garron.

"You wanted me to spill the tea?" Garron smiled a little as he said the words, but he managed to keep his voice stern enough to match the cook's. Still, he couldn't manage to be as loud as the snort she let loose at his words.

"You're quick enough to swipe rolls from my oven, aren't you?"

She tossed the words over her shoulder as she swept the herbs from her cutting board into a waiting pot, stirring with one hand as the other felt at a passing tray of sweetbreads. She gave the man carrying the tray, a new hire, a nod, which he barely acknowledged as he continued on to the cooling racks. Garron caught the hint of a smile playing around her lips. The man was going to do well in Hila's kitchen. The smile was replaced by a scowl as she looked up at Garron for a moment.

"Jenny didn't make enough for seconds, you know." *Oh, right. The rolls.*

"I need to keep my strength up!" Garron put on a piteous expression, making a show of coughing into his arm. He managed to hold a real one back but only just.

His acting was only met with another snort. "Well, boy, you know what'll really keep your strength up?"

"Stew?" It *did* smell good.

"Exercise. Why don't you go on and see if those boys out in the east wing need help?"

"But don't you need a taste tester? I have a very developed palate, you–"

"Work on developing those noodle arms instead, why don't you?" *Ouch.*

"Hah! You'd better get going before she gets nasty, Gar!" Jameson called from his station where he was expertly breaking down and deboning a large fish for the night's dinner.

Garron suddenly remembered that there were at least a half dozen other people going in and out of the kitchen and considered whether or not he'd want to engage in a public sparring match with Hila.

"I'll see you all later then. Bye!"

Jameson's laughter followed him out of the kitchen, but Garron was still smiling. It vanished as he moved away from the kitchen and back into the claustrophobic halls of the Tet estate. He always breathed a little easier in the kitchen, though honestly, he did the best outside. He didn't really mind going out to the east quarter for that reason, though there was precious little he'd be able to do.

"Hey there, Garron."

Garron looked up into a pair of tired eyes, crinkled in a weary smile. The man had his guard uniform on, sword belted at the waist, but Garron could see that his tunic was stained with a viscous fluid.

"Hi, Ulysses. You've got something on your tunic." He gestured to the spot.

Ulysses brought a hand up to the spot, then winced as it touched the fluid. "Oh, right."

Tiredly, he reached for his sword and pulled out a little, embroidered handkerchief from between the crossguard and sheath. It was already stained with the fluid, and Ulysses spent a fruitless moment dabbing at the stuff on his tunic before Garron handed him his own cloth. "How's Myra?"

"Thanks." He took over the cloth with a sigh. "She's doing well, I think. Her stomach was bothering her a bit, though, and *she won't stop crying.*"

The last words were said with the sort of frustrated despair that Garron had only ever seen from new parents. Not that there were many in the estate, but there had been a few lower ranked guards like Ulysses—as well as kitchen staff or houseworkers—who'd come in and out, sometimes bringing families with them.

"That's rough." Garron patted his shoulder... the one not stained by baby vomit.

"Thanks, but Mylena's got it worse. I can't really complain. Just wish I didn't have to pull night watch, on top of–"

"*Ulysses!* Break time's up. Get back to post!" Garron winced at the voice booming down the hallway. *Abyss.*

"Oh, *you.*" As the man drew closer, Garron felt his chest tighten slightly like it did when he was around Jackson. In some ways, Lars was worse. Bigger than Ulysses, built like a block of stone, and loud to boot, and for some reason, every time he looked at Garron, his face showed distaste, as though Garron's face was painful to look at. Garron didn't think he was particularly handsome, but he wasn't *that* ugly. "Shouldn't you be doing something useful instead of standing around freeloading? You've got to earn your keep, you know."

Garron didn't point out that, like most of the senior guards, Lars did very little other than sit around 'gardening' or 'cultivating' or whatever they called it. He thought Hila did more real work than any ten of them combined.

"I'll get go–"

"I mean, not that you can really do anything worth keeping you around, but the boy won't let us kick you out." Lars' voice was edging toward spiteful now. "And after you spent all that time getting a world-class training with him for free, for no good reason."

Right, I'm so lucky. Garron barely remembered the 'training' Lars had talked about, but it hadn't seemed that exciting to him. He'd been Andros' sparring partner and done most of his exercises with him as well, but when Lord Tet went away, Jackson had refused to include him. Of course, his illness came in soon after that, rendering the point moot. He took a deep breath, trying to cool his annoyance. Then his breath caught in his chest, and he let out a hacking cough and another until he was doubled over, only on his feet because Ulysses was supporting him.

"You alright there? Do you need water or anything?"

Garron couldn't respond with anything but a cough, but Lars cut in over the noise, sounding even more disgusted than before, "Just get back to your post. Isn't like water's going to help him anyway."

"Yes, sir. I'll be right there."

Lars grunted, and Garron could hear the sound of his heavy footstep moving away even as he coughed. Ulysses still stayed until the fit died down, for which Garron was grateful, but he couldn't help being preoccupied with the knowing tinge to Lars' last comment.

When Garron finally walked out and around the estate to the east quarter, he was met with the sounds of stone grinding and men shouting. The construction work being done to build the new wing was frankly incredible. Jackson had hired a stonemason, a carpenter, and a few specialist builders for the task, but that meant much of the brute labor had to be done by the estate staff, including Garron himself.

He walked up as close as he dared to the construction site, where a pair of burly men were pulling a huge block of stone into place along the growing wall, scraping away imperfections and creating smooth joints in the process.

"Hey there, boy. You here to help?"

A man holding a stone tablet and a scrap of paper came over to him, eyes calculating. Garron liked the man, who called himself an 'engineer.' He claimed to have learned his trade from dwarves, though Garron wasn't sure he believed that, but he had to admit that the anchored pulley system that the man had built next to the wall was nothing short of amazing. Even now, there was only one sullen guardsman manning the rope which, after looping around a series of pulley wheels, held up the stone that was being added to the wall.

"Hm, why don't you go over and help out that fellow on the pulley rope? He says he can handle it, but an engineer always plans for the worst case. Remember that, boy." He tapped a nose, smudging it with dirt, before walking back to the wall.

Garron privately thought that 'engineer' was probably a made-up word, but he agreed in principle. The thing was, even if he wasn't exactly sure how Joris, the guardsman currently holding the rope, was managing to lift all that weight by himself, he was certain that his contribution would change absolutely nothing if something went wrong; although Joris was just as disdainful of Garron as most of the senior guards, he was at least quiet, and Garron found that being outside was helping his coughing a little. He managed not to have another fit for the rest of the day as he helped with the construction.

CHAPTER THREE

"*Gar.*"

Garron blinked sleepily, turning over on his pallet and nestling into the covers.

"*Gar.*"

Something *solid* nudged him, and his eyes opened. He shot up and knocked his head into what felt like a set of teeth. *Owww.*

"*Whoops, sorry about that. You okay? Never mind, we have to go!*"

Garron finally managed to struggle out of his covers and stand. He took a deep breath and noted with relief that it went in and out easily. Today was good, then. Now, what was going on? He couldn't see much of anything in the darkness, but he thought he recognized the voice.

"Andy?"

"*Not so loud!*" Andros' 'whisper' was quite a bit louder than Garron's normal speaking voice, but he ignored that.

"What are you doing here?"

A hand landed on his shoulder. "I'm here to save you, Gar. We have to go—now. I'll explain when we're clear." Apparently, Andros had also given up on whispering.

Garron sighed and began pulling on his boots. He didn't have a prayer of stopping whatever scheme this was. "Andy, if you'd just said it, we could have been on our way by now, whatever this is."

Silence. Then, "I've stolen some money and important supplies from the family repository. We have to leave and get you to a dungeon so you can swallow a Beast Core to fix your cultivation base, or else you're going to die in a week or two."

A cold feeling came over Garron. Most of that had gone straight over his head, but two things stuck. The first was that Garron was dying. A deaf, blind, old man with a drinking problem could have told him that one. But the second...

"You stole something from the *repository?*"

"*No time!*"

The hand on his shoulder gripped him with a strength that seemed out of proportion for Andros' size, and suddenly, he was in the hallway, stumbling along behind a shadowy figure, too startled to protest.

They were moving surprisingly quickly. Garron half expected a coughing fit to overcome him, but today seemed like a *really* good day. Except for the whole 'risking his life and possibly the life of his best friend' thing, but Garron knew all about appreciating small favors.

They took three turns, Garron moving under his own power but struggling to keep up with Andros. They were almost to the south exit now, the one Hila and the other cooks used for picking up raw ingredients. The kitchen felt eerie to him, barely illuminated and dead silent as it was, but they were through it in a flash. Only two more turns and...

"Hey! Who's tha–" The voice cut off with a choking sound, but Garron noticed that it had sounded... muted somehow. Almost like he was hearing it through a wall or something. There was a dull thud as a dark figure collapsed to the ground.

"Sorry, Ulysses," Andros whispered, tugging Garron along behind him. "You'll be fine tomorrow."

They moved past the still huddle of shadows, and Garron grimaced. *What are we doing?*

"Andy, why...?"

"Trust me. We *have* to do this. Now, come on. If Ulysses was there already, we must have missed our window. Thank celestial it was him on duty tonight. I wouldn't have wanted to run into Lars."

They made it to the exit, a large door set into a stone frame with a worn, brass handle sticking out. Andros grabbed the handle. Garron opened his mouth to tell him that it was locked, but before he could, there was a stirring of wind and a *click*. The door opened, and the sweet scent of the open air filled the room. And the chill.

"Andy, I don't have a cloak or–"

"I've got all that ready. We just have to get to it. I'm sorry." He *did* sound sorry, but he still pulled Garron through the doorway and on to the paved patio around the entrance. Garron sighed, only rasping a little, and moved to the path that would lead to the gate of the estate. Andros' hand stopped him.

"This way."

And so, wondering if he was in a very strange dream, he followed his old friend, ducking low and stealing across the perfectly manicured lawn of the Tet estate like an assassin from a bard's tale.

The estate was large, but the south exit was fairly near the edge, and soon, they found themselves in the light woods that grew on the outskirts. Garron was gasping, each breath only coming with a great effort, when Andros finally slowed.

"Alright, we're here."

It was an interesting feeling, working so hard in the cold. Garron's face, hands, and feet were all throbbing in time with his heartbeat, and he felt flushed, but whenever he sweated, the water grew cold against his skin and set him shivering.

"I'm so sorry, Gar. Here, put these on." Andros moved to the base of a tree, a young willow whose branches swayed despite the dead leaves, and rummaged for something. After a moment, he pulled something out and took a sharp breath. "Abyss, an animal must have gotten to it."

He was holding a tattered, brown cloak, just visible in the moonlight. It was barely holding together, and huge swathes of fabric had been torn away. "It got the food as well. Celestial feces."

Garron smiled a little, still shivering. "You left a bundle of food and clothes out in the woods without any protection? Nice one."

"Oh, shut up. I didn't think we had that many animals in the woods here." Andros' shadowed form hunched slightly, and Garron knew he was crossing his arms like he always did when he was annoyed.

"You're right. Animals in the woods. That *does* seem unlikely."

And then both of them were laughing. It lasted a good ten seconds before Garron started coughing, and Andros pounded his back lightly. It didn't help, but Garron appreciated the thought.

"What is this, Andy?"

Something settled around his shoulders. It was a smooth fabric, not too thick but certainly better than nothing. Andros' cloak. "There you go. That's made from Beast skin and fur. I pity the animal who tries to chew *that*. Sit over here for a minute."

Andros moved to a root that was protruding up out of a ground and sat. Garron did the same.

"So..."

"I'm sorry," Andros said again. "There wasn't anything else I could think to do. My father's away tonight, but he'll be back tomorrow, and I don't know if we'll have another chance before you..." He trailed off.

"What, die? I mean, I know it's coming, but how do you know when? And what does any of this have to do with that?" Garron kept his voice matter of fact. Plenty of people had tried to comfort him when it became obvious how bad his illness was. He'd gotten tired of it quickly and even more tired of consoling *them* about his own impending death. Being frank helped avoid that.

"Uh, yeah. Well, you know how I started opening meridians a few years ago?"

Garron shrugged. There had been a big party in the house; he remembered that much. He wasn't clear on why, exactly. "Sort of. I don't know what mandarins have to do with it, though. They're out of season, aren't they?"

"*Meridians.* Anyway, now I can see the Essence in the world and the corruption. And you..."

"What? And what do you mean, Essence?" Garron had heard that word, vaguely, especially back when he'd trained with Andros, but there were more important things to worry about in life than what Nobles babbled about. Even Andros could be a little silly sometimes.

Andros sighed. "We don't have that much time. They're going to find Ulysses if we don't get a move on. I can give you the memory stone later. The point is, I know why you're sick. I have something that can make you better, but we have to go to a place where you can take it safely. Or you'll die even faster."

Garron blinked. Then he blinked again. "You have... something that can *cure* me?" He reached a hand out, not really knowing what he was doing. "What–"

Andros grabbed his hand. "Let's start moving. We're close to the wall here, and I think I have enough Essence to get us over and make a break for it."

They began dashing through the woods, Garron shivering somewhat less under the cloak, and following Andros in something of a daze. He'd long ago accepted that he was meant to die young. It was simple reality, and honestly, he didn't mind so much. Fourteen years wasn't long enough to really know what he was missing out on, but now, there was a way to *live*. Somehow. He didn't know how to handle it. Except to try as hard as he possibly could to keep up with Andros.

They got to the wall in short order, Garron breathing much easier than he had all week. He looked up at the stone barrier with a numb sort of worry. He hadn't really registered Andros' words before about where they were going. What were they going to do about this?

"Alright, Gar, now it's time for the tricky part. I'm going to cultivate as much as I can before we go, but just so you know, I'm going to have to lift us over the wall, and then we have to *move*. The alarms on the wall will trigger when we get over it, and we have to make sure that we can get away before the guards catch us. I'm a higher rank than pretty much all of them, and Jackson's out doing his own training, so we should be able to get away before they can call him or Lars. But I'm going to have to do something a little, uh, painful. I'm not really the best with it yet, but there's no other way."

Garron frowned, considering Andros' form. His outline was rigid, almost thrumming with contained anxiety. He was terrified, but Garron heard the determination in his voice.

"Okay, Andy."

"Okay."

Andros took a deep breath and began walking around aimlessly, jumping occasionally. What the abyss? Garron kept his mouth shut, but he couldn't help but wonder if he'd taken a bad fall sometime the previous day. After all, he still wasn't clear on how Andros was going to get them over the wall, and now he was doing some sort of... dance? He was sure he'd just seen a pirouette. The wind stirred, then slowed. Garron noticed that the trees around them had stopped swaying so much, and he felt a familiar tightness close around his chest. Maybe it wasn't such a good day after all.

"That's enough. There wasn't much here anyway." Andros hurried back over, securing the little pack by his waistband, then spreading his arms out. "It's time now, Gar. We're going to go flying over the wall, but I'm not so great at controlling the way up yet. It's going to be rough."

"Uh, okay," Garron said. Uncertainly, he embraced his friend, and he felt long arms wrap around him very, *very* tightly. Too tightly. "Andy," he choked out, "you're..."

The rest of his words were ripped away as wind *gusted* all around them. Garron felt an immense pressure pushing on him, not from above but below, and when he tried to gasp, nothing happened. There was a rushing sound filling his ears, and abruptly, he realized that he wasn't on the ground anymore.

This was nothing like that bard had sung about. He didn't have time to appreciate beautiful landscapes or marvel at the freedom of the skies. He felt wind tearing at his body, his clothes began humming as the wind ruffled them. His cheeks were vibrating as well, and every inch of exposed skin felt like it was being pounded by a million little hammers. His ears popped and, a moment later, popped again. Suddenly, the noise, the wind, everything stopped.

"*Sorry.*" Andros' voice was muffled, but Garron hardly paid attention. *Now* he could see, and it was, well, strange. They weren't very high, but even so, he could still see most of the estate from this angle, and it looked so... small. The place he'd spent his entire life in wasn't even large enough to take up his whole field of vision. He could see tall, grassy plains where they would land, the dense forest nearby, and beyond it... were those mountains?

Then they started falling.

Garron was too surprised for a proper scream, and by the time he got ready for it, they were slowing down again, and his feet were touching the floor.

"That's done," Andros panted, shifting around but not letting go of Garron. "I heard the alarm go. They'll be on us soon. Actually, I think it'd be better if I lifted you."

Without waiting for a response, Andros scooped him up as though he were a baby. *What?* Yes, Garron was small for his age, but Andros wasn't huge. The other boy was holding him just as tightly as before with no apparent effort. *Celestial.*

"This is going to stink worse than a bucket of demon blood. Just keep your face against my chest, or you might get hurt." Garron opened a mouth already half-covered by Andros' chest, but in the distance, he could hear a high-pitched tone and, he imagined, men shouting. He shut it.

"Okay, we're lined up with Barry's Bellybutton and... let's go!"

The world became rushing noise and wind again, but this time, Garron didn't have the benefit of open air around him. He was being compressed, squeezed as flat as an apprentice cook's first attempt at breadmaking. He wondered, somewhere in the back of his head, why that was the only metaphor he could think of. Then another part of his brain pointed out that it was, in fact, a simile, according to Andros' old lessons, and then the silent screaming drowned out both voices.

It took far, far too long, and the worst thing was that they kept stopping and restarting every few seconds. The first dozen times, Garron hoped that it would end. Then he began hoping he would pass out. The only reason he didn't vomit was that he couldn't get anything out past the constant acceleration pushing his bile back. After a while, he retreated into his own mind and began thinking more closely about the situation. Had he really just escaped the estate with Andros? Jackson was going to be furious. Were they really going to cure his illness somehow? And was Andros really *still* going?

Finally, blessedly, they stopped. Garron tensed again, waiting for the horrible moment of acceleration, but it never came. Instead, the world spun, and he fell to the ground with a light *thud*. After a moment of just lying there, dizzy and confused with tears streaming out from his closed eyes, Garron began struggling weakly to his feet. He got to his knees before he vomited. Then he made it to his feet and fell over again, more bile spilling out of his mouth. On the third try, he finally stood, breathing heavily and painfully. He looked over to curse at his friend and felt his heart go cold. The light had started tingeing the horizon, and he could see that they'd stopped in another forest, much more unkempt than the one contained in the Tet estate. He could also see a gangly form laid out on the ground and a face framed by a mess of black hair. Andros looked as pale as death, and when Garron shouted, he didn't respond.

CHAPTER FOUR

"This had better work," Garron muttered in between gasps. He'd panicked for a few minutes, coughed for another, then vomited a little more. Somewhere in between, he'd thought about what was going on.

Andros had done impossible things that night. Leaving aside the flying and the infernal demon-running, he'd also managed to knock Ulysses out without touching him and unlock the door leading out of the estate with... magic? Based on the dancing in the forest and the way he'd felt the wind respond whenever Andros had done something impossible, he thought that the air had something to do with it. Andros had said something about having enough 'Essence' to make it this far. Maybe he'd been wrong.

So, Garron had to get Andros someplace with as much wind as possible and hope that would be enough to save him. In a forest, that was up a tree. Of course, Garron had about as much hope of carrying Andros up a tree by himself as he did of winning a footrace against a racehorse, but he'd seen the pulley system the engineer had put in place, the one that had let a single man do the work of ten. Garron didn't have the time or materials to set up a system like the one the masons used; he didn't even have a rope. But Andros had a knife in his pouch, and his cloak was made of *very* strong material.

Hand, hand, foot, foot. Or was it the other way? He didn't quite remember. It had been a long time since he'd had the time or constitution to climb trees. This one had plenty of little branches to make hand and footholds, but Garron hadn't done anything so physically taxing for *years*. It was a very good day, thank celestial, but that didn't stop the burning in his chest and the shaking in his limbs after a few minutes. He kept going, though. He had no idea what would happen if he didn't hurry. It had already been too long, and the air around where Andros was lying was completely dead. He was still breathing, but he hadn't recovered or roused at all, even when Garron tied the 'rope' around his shoulders.

Garron moved his foot, already getting ready for another torturous haul upwards, and he heard a *snap*. His cheap boot scraped against the tree bark, his knee smacking painfully into the trunk. His heart tightened in panic, and he held on to the other branches with a death grip.

Then the branch holding his *other* foot broke away.

There was a terrible moment of *wrenching* as his shoulders, then his arms took on the weight of his entire body. Then it got to his hands, and suddenly, his grip didn't seem nearly tight enough. His forearms started burning, and he held back a scream. He looked around wildly and spotted another branch right above his right hand. If he could get his hand there, maybe he could get his foot up to his handhold? It looked like it was just barely in reach. With only his hands supporting him, that might be too far.

As he *pulled*, a yell did escape him. His hand shot upwards, and fingers caught on the little branch stub. Scrabbling with his legs against the trunk, he managed to get higher and grab a good hold of the wood. Without pause, he *pulled* again, getting his leg up as high as he could. One advantage of being small and sickly, maybe the only one, was that he didn't have much weight to pull up, and he was flexible to boot. He got his foot on the open branch and breathed a shaky sigh of relief.

Garron took a moment, just standing there. He was high enough that a fall would have certainly broken bones and probably killed him. It was one thing to know that you were going to die of sickness in the near future and quite another to go out and risk your life for an insane plan that had almost no chance of actually working.

Is it?

He thought about what he'd seen in Andros just before they'd gone over the wall. Fear. Andros knew that he was risking everything to help Garron, risking truly angering his *Jackson*. He'd done it before, too, when they were both not even ten years old. He'd screamed for days and refused to eat when Jackson had tried to kick Garron out of the estate. Garron knew he'd taken a few beatings for that, probably more than he'd heard about. He owed Andros too much to give up out of fear.

So he kept going, the shaking worse than ever until he found a large enough branch and the cloak-rope started losing its slack. After a moment's consideration, he carefully took off a boot and rubbed it against the branch, smoothing out the wood as best he could before laying the rope across it. On the way back down, remembering the way the stone-workers' rig had been set up, he looped the rope around two more branches. Soon, he was pulling against resistance but not so much that he couldn't get anywhere. Thankfully, whatever the cloak was made out of, it was both strong *and* supple enough that it didn't get much resistance from the branches as it rubbed. About halfway down, chest heaving, Garron started leaning against the rope as a counterweight and began sliding slowly down the trunk, feeling the weight on the other end get pulled up at the same time.

When he reached the ground, Garron didn't quite know what to do except hold on to the rope for all he was worth. He could see Andros up there, dangling like a human scarecrow from the rope Garron had knotted about his shoulders. He was intensely grateful for the times he'd had to work with the stablemaster and to the man himself for taking the time to teach him all of those knots. Everything seemed stable; now, all he could do was wait and...

Coughing fits were never fun. Up in the tree, he'd suppressed a few out of pure terror and determination, but now that he was back on the ground, the infernal wrenching in his chest came back in full force. He coughed so hard, he was convinced he could feel things ripping in his chest. He covered his mouth and hacked away, the sound strangely dull in the life of the forest, for what felt like a quarter-hour. For a moment, the fit subsided, and he looked at his sleeve to see specks of blood combined with something... black. *What the...*

Then another great cough tore through him, and he reflexively brought his hand up to his mouth to cover it—the same hand that had been holding on to the rope.

Garron barely had time to realize what was happening before he heard a whizzing sound and a crack as the rope slipped off the first two branches. And then...

"*Ahhhhhhh!*"

There was a gust of wind, and something fell on Garron, not as hard as he would have expected but not gently either. He fell to the ground with a yell of his own.

"What the abyss!"

Andros wriggled, rolling off of Garron and trying to stand as Garron did the same. They both fell over when the rope tripped Garron up and pulled at the harness on Andros' shoulders. It took more effort than it probably should have to disentangle themselves, but both of them were pale and shaking now. Andros actually seemed worse off than Garron, which was, in some ways, a welcome change of pace.

"Are you okay now? I, uh, didn't really know what to do and–"

"I think you saved my life, Gar," Andros interrupted him, still panting with the white showing around his eyes. "There was enough Essence up there that my passive technique filled up my center a bit. Just wish you hadn't dropped me."

"Yeah, I don't know what any of that means. Maybe you should go dance around a bit until you're back to normal?"

Andros opened his mouth, then closed it and shrugged. He went off and started dancing again, eventually climbing up a tree with an ease that made Garron a bit jealous and hopping around the branches there. The whole while, Garron simply sat and tried to calm himself a little until finally, Andros settled down next to him.

"Okay, we've got to go. I have a feeling Jackson found out we left."

"What? Why?"

"Pillar of fire flared into the sky, down about where the estate is."

Garron felt his own eyes widen. "Celestial. Where are we going, anyway?"

Andros started frantically jumping around again, eyes going out of focus but voice still talking in a fearful tone, "Dad told me about it before he went away. There's a new dungeon up this way, but they couldn't set up Guild offices on it before the war started up. It's got an earth affinity, but there's a river running through it, so apparently, there's a good bit of water Essence in it too. It's not perfect, but it's the best option we have. And it's still young, so hopefully, we'll still be able to get through it and have you take the Beast Core."

Garron blinked, fear momentarily sidelined. "Wait, a new *dungeon?*" Even Garron had heard about dungeons. He'd wondered if they were real or just a bard's fanciful tale, but he'd reasoned that there had to *some* way Lord Tet could be as scary as he was. He must have been through many dungeons throughout his life. "I still don't get any of that other stuff, though."

Andros came to a halt again in front of Garron and started fumbling at his discarded pouch. "Wait a second... Okay, here we go."

He pulled out a stone that glimmered in the light of the sun peeking through the foliage. It was still early morning, and from its current angle, not much could make it through to the forest. Still, Garron could see that the little gem didn't quite match any of those in the fancy jewelry he'd seen on women who used to come to the estate for parties.

"I'm going to press this on your head, okay, Gar? It's going to feel weird, but just stay calm. You're going to learn a lot of information, so brace yourself."

"Wha—"

Knowledge *poured* into Garron's mind. Suddenly, he knew that Essence was the energy of the world itself and that corruption was the taint that it accumulated from the environment. He knew that humans held their Essence in their centers and that 'cultivating' was the word for pulling Essence into oneself and purifying it. He learned a cultivation technique that would let him pull in and purify Essence into a spiral in his center. And, most importantly, he learned how to perceive his own center.

If he'd had anything left in his stomach, he would have thrown up again.

From the gem—*memory stone*—Garron knew vaguely what Essence should feel like. He could barely perceive a hint of it in himself, but oh, the *corruption*. His center was a seething pit of foul earth and tainted water, like a forest gone to rot or a latrine pit that got too full, all bubbling and oozing through him.

He tried to move it like he'd just learned, but nothing happened. The corruption filling him seeped into every part of his body, and he could *feel* how it ground away at his being, holding him in chains of mud. Earth and water. A dual affinity, pulling in tainted Essence from the world around him so fast that it was a miracle he wasn't dead yet.

"*Why? Why didn't they tell me?*"

Garron gasped, falling to his knees. He knew the basics of what they were about to do. These were Andros' memories, he knew. He could feel the anger, the despair, and the pity that had colored his thoughts as he formed this stone. Not all of the information was clear. Some of it had been muddled in the making of the stone, but Garron could see enough.

"I..."

"...I know. It's *him*. But why?"

"I don't know, Gar. He hated that you were training with me. Dad was planning on letting you have a Beast Core when your mom died and everything, but when he went away, Jackson wouldn't hear it."

For the first time in Garron's life, he felt true, deep hatred well up inside him, out of his pit of a center. He'd been condemned to years of pain, *years* of believing he was meant to die, because of the indifference of one man. One monster.

He looked up at Andros, and he could see his rage mirrored in his friend's dark eyes. Now he knew why the other boy had looked so angry for the past year. He'd been fighting for Garron the entire time.

"Thank y–"

"Don't mention it, Gar. He's cost you too much already. You deserve this."

They embraced, and Garron felt his tears begin to dry.

"We have to go now, don't we?"

Andros nodded decisively. "We're really close now. My movement technique can get us there in a few jumps."

Garron felt the blood drain from his face. "Oh, *abyss*."

CHAPTER FIVE

Garron didn't really know what to expect from a dungeon, but once the tears cleared from his eyes and he got done dry heaving, he wasn't so impressed. It just seemed like a hole in the side of a grassy hill. They were on a slope, and the ground seemed muddier than it should... That must be the underground river Andros had mentioned. With his new senses, Garron could tell there was much more Essence in this place than anywhere else he had been—primarily earth but also hints of water. He could feel his center pulling in the power and the corruption, faster than ever.

Next to him, Andros winced. "You know, this whole thing has shortened your life span. You've been taking in more Essence but also more corruption. If you go to a low-Essence area now, you'd probably be bedridden."

Huh. Examining his new knowledge, Garron saw that he was right. It was a good day, but that was because of all the Essence he was pulling in. The corruption he took in along with it would stay behind and accumulate even more until it killed him. "Well, then we'd better get going fast, right?"

"Heh. I guess." Andros seemed... nervous?

"What's wrong?"

"It's just, I've never been inside a dungeon alone before. This one's only F-rank-seven or so, and I'm D-rank-three, almost four, so it shouldn't be too dangerous but... dungeons can be weird."

"And I'm..." Garron looked at his center again. "Actually, I can't tell."

"Neither can I. Somewhere in the low-to-mid F, I'd guess, but all the corruption makes it pretty immaterial."

Garron supposed that made sense, considering what he knew now. Andros really had put a lot of stuff in that memory stone: information about cultivation, a basic cultivation technique, and even some earth and water techniques he'd pulled from another memory stone. Those seemed interesting, but he'd save them for after he'd purified his center.

"Well, either way, we've got you, right? Let's do this."

Andros looked at him and took a deep breath before nodding. "Okay. I've already taken in about all the air Essence there was here anyway. Just keep safe. Hopefully, we can get some weapons or armor for you as loot."

With that, they stepped into the cave.

They walked down a winding tunnel in complete darkness for a bit before it started to lighten. A few moments later, the tunnel opened up into a dank stone cave, stalagmites growing up from the ground and stalactites hanging down from above.

"Wait, is it..."

"I don't know. Just call them pointy stone things."

Some of the pointy stone things were glowing with a soft light that nonetheless showed them that there was nothing to worry about in this room. Garron moved to take a step forward, and Andros stopped him with a hand. Without saying a word, he reached out with his own foot, and the stone below it crumbled away, revealing a pit lined with more sta– pointy stone things.

"I think we have to stay close to the..."

Garron nodded. "PSTs."

They began threading their way through the cave, always sticking close to the pillars of stone. Occasionally, a wrong step almost got Garron skewered, but Andros kept a tight grip on his arm as they continued forward. After a tense few minutes, they were clear.

"That wasn't so bad," Garron commented.

"No, but we haven't run into any mobs yet. Or loot. Actually, hold on a minute."

Andros went back into the stone room, moving carefully but much more swiftly without Garron to slow him down. He expertly threaded his way around the treacherous floor, using a leg to break away the false bits and reveal the pit traps below. Eventually, Garron caught the glint of something shiny.

"There we go!"

A few moments later, Andros was back at the end of the room, offering a slightly rusted metal sword out to Garron.

"It isn't much, but it's something at least. I'm a hand-to-hand specialist, so you should hold on to this."

Garron hesitantly accepted the sword, noticing that though the metal wasn't of the best quality, the edge was still sharp. "Okay. I can't say I'll be good at it, though."

"Don't you remember our lessons, back when we were kids?"

"Uh, most of those just ended with you hitting me with a stick."

"Huh. Fair point, I guess. Try your best, though. The next room will probably have mobs in it."

They continued on, the tunnel taking a sharp bend, and the smell of animal feces hit them. Andros took the lead, holding his hands up warily, and Garron awkwardly held his sword in front of him, trying not to accidentally cut himself.

They walked into another room which also seemed to have a forest of glowing stone protruding from its ceiling, with a floor bare except for dirt and excrement from some small animal. Garron stepped cautiously, but Andros motioned him forward after a bit of experimental tapping. They both looked around warily, wondering what the challenge here was supposed to be. Then something fell on Garron's face.

"Ahhhh!" he yelped, dropping his sword and clawing at whatever was on him. Sharp claws scrabbled against his skin, and he felt pain blossoming. There was a *wrench*, and he was free. He looked around wildly, scooping up the sword and looking to see what was happening.

Andros was wrestling with the shrieking, hissing creature now. It had dark fur with white and black markings around its eyes. A raccoon. Andros raised the animal up, clearly intending to smack it against the ground, but suddenly, his arms sagged, and he dropped the thing with a cry of his own.

The raccoon hit the ground with a solid *thud* that seemed out of proportion with its size, and four more identical sounds followed it in quick succession. It only took a glance to see that they were surrounded.

"Oh aby–"

A little monster jumped, quick for its size, and Garron took a clumsy swing at it, barely managing to aim it edge-on. He thought he would hit it, but right before his sword made contact, the creature suddenly dropped out of the air like a stone, landing with a thud in front of Garron and swiping a claw at his legs. Garron yelped and hopped back.

Behind him, he could hear the meaty sounds of flesh hitting flesh, the occasional crack of little bones breaking, and the yips of injured raccoons. Andros was busy, it seemed. The raccoon—the *monster*—in front of Garron snarled, and he swore he saw the skin beneath its fur lighten as it darted forward again. This time he was ready, though, and when it jumped, instead of trying to hit it, he just moved to the side as quickly as he could, sword slashing wildly at the same time. The raccoon did the same trick again, falling swiftly as soon as Garron's sword got close to it, and he took a swing at it on the ground.

The creature tried to dodge, but apparently, whatever it did to fall made it much slower because it failed to avoid his strike. His sword bit into the creature's hide, though not nearly as deep as he expected. Instead of cutting to the bone, he barely saw the blade penetrate an inch before the creature yipped, its skin lightened, and it darted past him. Garron turned to chase it, but he saw that it had lost interest in him. It was joining its fellows attacking Andros.

Garron's friend was being overwhelmed. Two of the little monsters were lying dead on the ground, but that left three who were all attacking him at once. They were jumping at him from all angles, and whenever he took a swing at one, it dropped to the floor, and one of its fellows took over the assault. Andros was dodging with exceeding grace, but he couldn't land a hit *and* keep himself out of harm's way. He needed help.

Another of the monsters dropped to the floor with a *thud*, and Garron took the opportunity to leap forward himself, sword flashing from behind. He just barely managed to keep from chopping Andros' leg off as the other boy took the same opportunity to aim a stomp at the mob. They both stopped short, and the creature scurried away.

"Watch out!"

"Sorry!"

"No, *duck*."

Andros shoved Garron to the side, and *another* raccoon jumped through the air where he'd been, only falling when Andros tried to kick it. This time, when the young Noble attacked the disoriented mob, it died, the wet crack accompanying Garron's rise from the floor.

Andros was already back to dodging, and when Garron spotted an opening, he tried shouting, "I got it!" before taking his swing. He'd swung down with all his might this time, and though the blade slowed quickly, the cut was still fatal. At the same time, another crack signaled that the final mob was dead.

"Phew. Those were a little tougher than I expected, but I'm glad I didn't have to use any Essence! There isn't much air Essence down here, so it's better if I save it for the Boss. And hey, check this out! I think I see a few silver here!"

Garron was breathing hard, intensely glad that he wasn't feeling the worst of his illness just then. "What *were* they?"

Andros laughed, gathering up the coins that had popped out of the monsters' corpses. There was no equipment, unfortunately. "Raccoons."

"Andy..."

"Well, they must have been soaking in the earth Essence from here. They had some sort of weight manipulation ability is all. Not a big deal on something so small."

Garron nodded slowly. "So, other mobs in this place might have the same ability or something similar, right?"

"Right."

"And do you think they'll be this small?"

"Not a chance."

In the next room, Andros was forced to use his demonic movement technique, carrying Garron again. Every time they took a step forward, a pointy stone... This was getting ridiculous; Garron decided to just call them spikes and be done with it. A *spike* would fall on the spot. When Andros sped them through the room, they suddenly found themselves at the end, and a line of stone shards was piled up in their wake.

"Hey," Garron asked as Andros released him, "how come you needed to cultivate after using that technique? The ones in the stone you gave me seem like they're supposed to loop back into you."

Andros laughed awkwardly. "Well, it's uh, something I made. I haven't really figured out how to do the 'looping' thing, and besides, it's worth the loss. It uses up my Essence to boost me forward really, really fast."

Garron frowned. "Isn't that bad?"

His friend shrugged. "I dropped a rank or two on the way here, but my cultivation technique is really good, so it's not much of an issue to fill my center back up. It's still a pretty insignificant amount of power, all things told."

Based on what Garron had learned, he thought Andros was underplaying what he'd done quite a bit, and he felt his respect for his friend increase even more.

In the next room, they found a different sort of challenge. Instead of raccoons, a trio of gray-furred deer was roaming about aimlessly. The one doe seemed fairly normal, though Garron had never seen a deer with that look of *hunger* in its eyes before, but the two stags had antlers that gleamed wickedly in the cave's light. They were made of stone and ended in multiple sharp points.

"You keep the doe busy, Gar. I've got the stags."

In a flash, Andros was off, jumping and executing a perfect kick on one stag's side. Both of the antlered monsters snorted and turned to charge him. Garron ran forward much more slowly and aimed an awkward slash at the doe's flank.

The mob *whipped* around, almost smacking Garron with its hooves before he stepped away. He held his sword out warily, and as the doe reared up, he moved to stab at it. He got a kick in the chest for his trouble.

Apparently, the deer's antlers weren't the only thing made of stone.

Garron fell back, losing his sword once again. The doe, graceful as any deer, gently laid its cloven, stone hooves to rest around him with a light *click*. Then she raised them up again, and with a yell, he rolled out of the way. His shout coincided with a dull crack of stone breaking from across the room. Andros was doing well it seemed. Now, if only Garron could survive long enough for his friend to save him.

No. Garron wouldn't rely on Andros for this. He could make do with what he had—his hands, his feet, his head, and a center filled with corrupted Essence.

When the doe came around to rear up before him again, Garron felt at his center and, pulling from the knowledge he'd gained from the memory stone, pulled at himself, gathering up the slow, disgusting power and *flung* it at the monster.

He wasn't quite able to see what happened, but he heard the wet *squelch* and felt the power rush out of him. It... didn't feel good. Vaguely, he heard a high-pitched snort, a little thumping. He didn't look because he was too busy shaking on the floor, overcome with coughing. A few moments later, he felt a hand on his back.

"Gar, just breathe. You're okay."

That gave him just the motivation he needed to control himself and sit up, chest still heaving, to look up in Andros' face.

"Oh... just... breathe? Thanks... for... the advice."

Andros' weak laugh brought a smile to Garron's own face. After another minute, he stood.

"That wasn't a great idea, Gar."

"I figured, but," he paused as another cough racked his body, "why? Those techniques in that stone used corruption."

Andros laughed again, stronger this time. "Those techniques are meant for cultivators with only a hint of corruption in their Essence. You just forced *so* much taint through your body and pushed out some of the Essence you have along with it. Look what it did!"

Garron looked. The doe was almost covered in a black, tarry substance that bubbled slightly against its fur. The creature was already decomposing, and the corruption was fading away, back into the surroundings. It wasn't a pretty sight.

Garron shuddered. "So, don't do that again, huh?"

"No. If you do, you'll probably just die. You don't have much more Essence left in your body, and you won't be able to get much more without purifying your center. Your whole body is backed up with taint."

Garron nodded, stretching his arms. Now that the coughing had subsided, he felt surprisingly... normal. Not much worse than he'd been the night they escaped. After thinking about it, he decided that was because of the amount of corruption he'd forced out—along with the Essence. It had balanced out, but he knew what would run out first if he kept it up.

They collected the loot, which included a well-made steel helmet that Garron jammed on his head, a knife that Andros laid claim to, and more coins, and they moved on. In the next room, they could smell the dampness of the river permeating the stone. There weren't any mobs or obvious traps...The only thing in the little cavern was a trio of simple boxes.

"Hm." Andros sounded skeptical as he stared at the crates.

"Hm?"

"I don't think this place is advanced enough for mimics, but I still don't trust it when there's loot without a challenge attached to it. They could be traps or something."

"Oh. Why don't we just skip it, then?" Garron suggested. Their primary goal wasn't to get rich, anyways.

"Good idea. It seems like we're close to the Boss as it is— if it's near the river."

They continued on, but instead of a simple open hole leading to the next connected cave, there was a solid, stone door built into the opening with a gleaming handle protruding from it. Andros tried the handle, and then the air stirred. And nothing happened.

"Celestial feces. It's not responding to my push, and this rock," he rapped it, "is too much for me to break and still take on the Boss. The key must be in one of the boxes."

Garron frowned. "Oh. So we're supposed to just pick one then?"

Andros shrugged. "I guess so. Hand me your sword?"

Garron handed the weapon to his friend, and Andros walked over to the boxes warily. Holding the sword out as far away from his body as possible, he used it to slowly open the leftmost box's lid. Three stone spikes shot straight up out of the box, clattering against the ceiling before landing harmlessly to the side. "Ha! Have to get up earlier in the morning to skewer *me*, dungeon!"

When Andros went to open the second box, the spikes shot out horizontally, straight at him.

To the young man's credit, he moved *fast*. With the grace of a gifted air cultivator, he twisted and jumped, managing to get his body out of the way a split second before the spikes ripped through him. The arm holding the sword wasn't so lucky.

"Abyss!" they both shouted it at the same time, Garron rushing over to his friend's side. The spike hadn't actually impaled him, thank celestial, but the other boy had a massive gash on his forearm, and the wrist hung limp.

Without hesitation, Garron took off his shirt and began binding the wound as best he could. Andros just stood, hissing through clenched teeth, applying pressure to his own wound as Garron worked.

"I deserved that one. Thanks, Gar."

"Don't thank me, how is it? Your wrist...?"

"Broken. It knocked into the last spike after the first one cut my arm, and I don't know *anything* about healing. Abyss."

Garron didn't say anything as he finished binding the wound. A knot of worry began tying itself around his stomach. Finally, when it was clear the bleeding would stop, he spoke.

"We have to go back, Andy."

"What?"

"If you fight the Boss injured, you might *die.*"

"And if I don't, you *definitely* will! Don't be an idiot, Gar."

"I made my peace with dying a long time ago, Andy. You still have a long life ahead of you."

The other boy hit him upside the head. Not as hard as Garron knew he could have, but it still hurt. "Still being an idiot. Nobody 'makes their peace' with dying when they're our age unless they're forced to, and my life isn't worth any more than yours. In fact, if one of us died here, it should be me. After all, you've been miserable the last few years while I've been cultivating. You should get a turn, if anything."

Garron thought about protesting. He opened his mouth. Then he closed it. Then he opened it again. "Neither one of us is going anywhere," he said, as firm as he could manage. "We're going to kill that Boss, I'm going to swallow the Beast Core, and we're going to go home carrying big sacks of loot over our shoulders."

Andros laughed. "That's the spirit! Now then why don't we get on with it?"

The last crate did contain the key, along with another, much better quality sword. After a brief debate, Garron took the weapon, leaving his rusty blade behind. Andros couldn't use the thing with his wrist and worked better without weapons in any case. Garron did the honors, sliding the stone key into the door and turning. With a grinding noise, the door unlocked.

"Ready?"

Andros looked over at him, and Garron felt the wind stir slightly.

"Of course."

Garron pushed on the door. Nothing happened. Then he cursed, Andros laughed, and he pulled the infernal thing open.

Garron had been thinking about what they would find in the Boss Room. It ended up being his first guess. Really, raccoons, then deer, and now...

CHAPTER SIX

"A wolf. Of course it's a wolf. You know, I was really hoping it would be rabbits."

"Rabbits as dungeon mobs? That would just be ridicu—"

A roar cut Andros off, and they got to work.

Garron moved to the side, holding tight to his sword. The monster's eyes tracked him for a second, and he felt shivers run down his spine. He'd never seen one of the things in person before, but he'd certainly seen plenty of dogs. Somehow, he didn't think that wolves were supposed to be his height at the shoulders with teeth set in stone and fur that glistened like crystal. For a moment, it seemed like the huge animal was going to pounce at him, but then Andros moved in.

He couldn't fight effectively, not with a broken wrist, but he captured the Boss' attention with a shout and a gust of wind straight to the face. He slammed a kick into the creature's side, which seemed to hurt him more than the wolf, and when the wolf pounced, he slipped out of the way. In a moment, he was dancing easily around ponderous claw swipes. The wolf was slow, thank celestial, but it was so heavy that the floor shuddered every time it landed from an attempted pounce. Andros was dodging fine, but the few blows he landed weren't doing anything.

"Get it while it's distracted!"

Right. Garron started moving in, raising his sword. The Boss was completely engaged with Andros, so he had no trouble landing a full-power strike on the nape of its neck. His sword connected with a crunch, and Garron saw pieces of fur break away as the sword continued to bite into the monster's neck.

It would have been much more impressive if the blade went in more than an inch.

With a roar, the wolf turned, taking a swipe at Garron. When he'd been watching Andros fight the monster, he'd thought it was ridiculously slow. He'd been somewhat mistaken. Andros was just *fast*.

The flat of the monster's stone claw caught him on the shoulder, sending him spinning away, thankfully failing to do any real harm, but the momentary stumble was enough for the wolf. Snarling, it bent its legs to pounce, and Garron was suddenly several feet away, next to the rushing river that took up the back half of the stone chamber. His head spun slightly, and Andros' tight grip around his waist told him what had happened. His friend had used the movement technique to get them clear for the moment. But the monster was still there, and it had already seen where they'd gone.

"Can't get through its hide either, huh? Abyss, I really wish I knew how to do lightning or something, but you need more affinities for that stuff."

Garron nodded. "This sword's not a good weapon for this either. A hammer or mace or something would have been much better. I can't get enough force."

"And I can't hold it because of my wrist. Look, it's coming."

Suddenly, an idea struck Garron, and he wriggled around in Andros' grasp, so he was facing outwards, turning them until his sword was pointing straight at the oncoming wolf's chest.

"Hey! What the–"

"Andy, I never thought I'd say this, but you need to use that movement thing, *now*."

"What? Oh, you want to–"

"Now!"

Wind rushed, the world shifted, and a massive force slammed Garron forward, sword-first, into the wolf. With a resounding crack and a flash of intense pain, he felt the weapon impale the Boss right through the chest. Then the rest of him smashed into the monster's body, and everything stopped for a moment.

"Gar!"

Garron tried to roll over. He had quite a large pallet. It used to be his mother's. He took a deep, sleepy breath and felt a twinge of pain. It wasn't going to be a good day, then, but he only had to worry about that in the morning. Maybe he could get Hila to let him work in the kitchen again.

"Gar!"

He groaned and opened his eyes. What was that sound? It sounded like... water? A river. Like the river in the east woods, where he'd liked to play with Andros. He'd always loved it outside, especially when his friend was there. Andros...

Andros slapped him.

"Ow!"

"Oh, come on. You were totally milking that. I didn't go *that* fast."

Garron grumbled under his breath as he sat up, wincing slightly at the pain. "Whatever. Is it dead?"

"About as dead as you're going to be if we don't get that core in you *right now.*"

It took a bit of help from Andros, but he managed to stand. Together, they made their way over to the river. Earth Essence permeated this room thickly, but this close to the water, he could feel his other affinity in almost as much abundance. At Andros' instruction, he drank deeply from the river until he was full to bursting and queasy. It didn't take too much; it was well past breakfast time, and his stomach was already complaining. The pure water made the feeling worse, mixing with his stomach acid in a thoroughly unappetizing manner.

"You know how this works, right? You swallow the core, and when I tell you, you start cultivating. You have the technique? The core's going to pull *everything* out of you, so we need to replace it with clean Essence, or you'll die. I mean, that's what I hear. I didn't really have this problem, but I've heard a few stories from Guild officers that meet with father, and I did the research, so I–"

"Let's get back to the part where I don't die," Garron interrupted him, trying to sigh and wincing at the pain in his ribs.

"Right, sorry. So, you cultivate, and then you have to throw up the core. I'm going to punch you a few times to make that happen, by the way. Is that okay?"

Garron shrugged. "Seems like you hit me enough as it is. Let's do this."

Andros nodded, suddenly seeming even more nervous than Garron. He pulled another gem from his pouch, one very similar to the memory stone, and handed it to Garron. Taking a deep breath, he realized that this would be the last time the air rasped on its way down, making him want to cough. One way or another.

He swallowed the core.

Garron had experienced a lot of extremely painful things in the last few hours–Andros' so-called 'movement technique', his disastrous attempt at using an Essence technique, and, of course, his recent high-speed collision, but this... His entire body, everything that was *him,* was being pulled into his stomach. Pain blossomed in a dozen points around his body, then a hundred, until everything was agony. He knew he'd begun spasming, but he had no control over his limbs. He could feel the dense, viscous, somehow *bubbling* corruption sliding inwards, some from his limbs but most of it from his putrid center. Then the sweet Essence, the dregs of pure energy he'd managed to retain despite the taint, vanished as well, all sucked into the core. And finally, the pain subsided.

"Now, Gar, cultivate!"

A large part of Garron was tempted just to glory in the bliss that was the absence of pain. He almost let go, but his words to Andros, his promise that both of them would leave this dungeon alive, came back to him. He remembered everything his friend had sacrificed for him, the risks that he'd taken, the blood that he'd spilled so Garron could have a chance at life. He began to gather the Essence, the power of the world itself, into his center.

Immediately, he knew something was wrong.

He was pulling at the earth and the water Essence around him, drawing them both into his center and refining the energy into threads that would go into forming his center, but something about the process felt... off. Incomplete. He was following the cultivation technique perfectly, but the Essence wasn't merging into his center properly.

"What the... Oh, *abyss.* You've got *another* affinity? But I've never seen you drawing in... *air. Abyss.*"

Suddenly, the Essence in the room blossomed, and a third type joined the earth and water, light like a summer's breeze. Garron acted on instinct, drawing this new Essence into his center and finally felt complete. He refined carefully but quickly, feeling his life force beginning to get drawn in by the core and rushing to replace the void with Essence. At the same moment, something hit his stomach *hard,* and his gag reflex, already on a hair-trigger from the day's activities, prompted him to vomit out all the contents of his stomach. The draw of the core vanished.

He continued cultivating, pulling Essence into himself from three separate sources, refining it, and using it to form a Chi spiral. There was a crunching noise from nearby and a few words, but Garron didn't hear any of it. All he could feel was pure *freedom*. He hadn't known what he'd been missing. It felt like he'd been mired in filth his entire life, and now, he'd bathed for the first time.

Eventually, he ran out of Essence to pull from. It was the water that went first, surprisingly. There was much less of the third kind—which he recognized as air—but he pulled it in at a fraction of the rate of the others, so there was a bit left over when he exited his trance.

"Finally, I thought maybe I should have been cooking us up some deer with how long you were taking."

Andros' voice sounded tired, and when Garron looked over, he saw that the other boy was a bit paler than usual. At his feet was a shattered gem, and there was still a bit of bubbling, black corruption fading away into the environment around it.

"The air Essence, was that...?"

"Yup. I'm D-rank-zero now. Celestial, Gar, *three* affinities?"

Garron felt a weak smile come over his face. "The air one is much weaker than the others, though."

"Believe me, I know. Only reason I didn't notice it. I pull in so much air Essence all the time, I never saw that you were doing it too, and all the water and earth taint masked it in your center. If I was better with Essence sight... I'm sure *he* knew."

Garron didn't want to talk about Jackson just then. He stood, and though his body still ached from the damage he'd sustained, he marveled at the way his breath came in so easily, without any tightness or rasping. He didn't feel like an old man anymore, and when he raised a hand to Andros' shoulder, it didn't shake.

"Andy, thank you. You saved my life. I don't know how I can repay–"

His best, oldest, and only friend hugged him, almost crushing him with Essence-enhanced strength.

"I've always known I'd need to get away from him eventually. I should be thanking you for giving me the motivation I needed to do it. There's no way I'm going back now."

They separated. Garron wasn't certain, but he thought Andros might have been crying. It was hard to tell through the blur of his own tears.

"So, what now?"

After another moment of standing across from each other, tears falling to the ground between them, Andros pulled the little knife out of his pouch.

"First things first, I need to cut my hair, and you need to get washed." He wrinkled his nose. "Then we'll get to a city with a portal and use all this loot to get passage to someplace far away."

"Where?"

"I don't know, but abyss if I'm going back to Jackson."

Garron looked at his friend, cradling his wrist but smiling through watery eyes. He took a breath and felt no urge to cough as he let it back out. He was finally free, thanks to his friend.

"Let's go."

LEGACY OF THUNDER
BY: STEVEN WILLDEN

CHAPTER ONE

Far above the city of Azguardia loomed the never-ending thunderstorm that made the city so famous. Lightning arced from cloud to cloud, from cloud to ground, and occasionally from building to building. Those last usually only occurred between the Conduction Rods extending from the roof of every structure.

The thunder was a constant rumble that *never* faded into silence. The populace of Azguardia enjoyed the comfortable presence of the light and sound of the storms. The Enchantments built into the city itself kept the thunder from being loud enough to interfere with conversation and sleep. However, only a stone's throw above the highest tower in the palace, the sound became deafening.

A lightning bolt formed as the connection between a low-flying cloud and one of the many Conduction Rods atop the palace grew strong. The lightning connected the Rod and cloud in a brilliant flash and was absorbed by the Conduction Rod. The power of the bolt traveled from the roof of the palace and into its walls.

Lightning came to a split in its conductive path. A portion of the power went deeper into the palace, and the remainder was shunted into a chandelier containing translucent crystals, the light of which brightened as the new influx of power entered the matrix of tiny Runes inscribed within.

The new pulse of light shone down on the faces of the royal family of Azguardia and several of their retainers. Perun, leader of Azguardia, worked ceaselessly at preparing his children and the children of his retainers. The Festival would start within the hour, and several of the children had yet to properly dress for the occasion.

Near one alcove of the chamber crouched eleven-year-old Jasper. He flicked his finger at a decorative set of plate armor in the alcove, causing a brief line of electricity to appear between his finger and one of the greaves. He repeated the flick every few seconds and maintained his expression of complete and utter boredom.

Jasper's younger brothers, Huginn and Muninn, were taking turns chasing one another around the chamber. Each held a rod made of hardened glass and a core of a copper alloy. Most children in the city referred to the rods as 'Giggle Sticks'. Each of these Giggle Sticks had a metallic sphere at the end, and with a minimal influx of Essence, the ball would gain an electric charge that would provide an amusing shock when touched against the skin of the unwary.

With a bit of practice, one could also project the shock from the rod to a target in the form of a tiny lightning bolt. The result of such a strike was nearly always the giggling of the assailant—hence the name. As the chaos of preparation continued, Huginn and Muninn held a whispered conference of war and decided to enact a temporary cessation of hostilities in favor of declaring war against their gloomy older brother Jasper. They each charged their weapons and sprinted toward their distracted sibling with weapons extended.

Jasper sighed as he heard his little brothers stumbling and laughing toward him. Without looking away from the armor he had been staring at for the last hour, he made a plucking motion toward his siblings, and the lightning Essence arced from the Giggle Sticks and into a tiny, roiling sphere that floated between Jasper's extended thumb and forefinger.

He rotated his hand and tossed the sphere back at the boys in one smooth motion. The would-be assailants tripped over themselves as their leg muscles spasmed. They began laughing immediately and then continued their game, leaving Jasper to his brooding. Jasper hid his grin as best he could.

A trio of servants shepherded Huginn and Muninn into the remainder of their festival-wear in time for Perun to clap his hands together and call for attention. "Everyone is prepared? Good. This year's festival is looking to be as memorable as always. The forecast calls for one of the largest yields of Essence flakes ever seen on Stormveil. This means that all of you children will have plenty of opportunity to collect Essence for yourselves."

"As always, we will be offering a bounty to any of the populace who wish to sell any flakes they find for coin rather than making use of the Essence within. However, this is an excellent opportunity for you to open up cultivation opportunities that might not normally be available to you. Hunt well and remember to be back before the storm resumes at sunrise. You already know your hunting teams. Hunt well and honor the bounty of the storms."

Jasper and his brothers were then led to a nearby spire. They took their position on the balcony near the top of the spire. All of the children of the royals and their retainers had positions at various balconies around the palace. Jasper, Huginn, and Muninn had the third-highest starting point, and that meant they would be able to start the hunt much farther away from the heavily populated city center.

While they waited for opening ceremonies to begin, the children waved at their friends on other spires and at the endless crowds in the plaza far below. The buzz of conversation from so many people blended together with the magically muted thunder in a way that was uniquely Azguardian.

The sun began to set on the horizon, and after several minutes of waiting, the crowd's buzz changed into shouts and cheering as Perun stepped on to the large, central balcony and waved to the people of the city. He was wearing his Stormveil armor, which meant that he was decked out in gold and silver and his armor was fluted and decorated in themes of thunder.

Armor like this was only worn on Stormveil. It had something to do with how the storm disappeared during the festivities, but the specifics were a closely-held secret. He made a small gesture with one hand, and air Mana suffused his neck and head. He made a second gesture, and the Mana extended from his neck and connected with a crystal built into the balcony. The crystal lit up as did an interconnecting series of crystals all throughout the balcony. When Perun spoke, his voice was amplified through each of the crystals, and his voice could be heard clearly throughout the plaza below.

"Greetings to you all on the eve of Stormveil!" The ensuing cheer from the crowd overwhelmed all other sounds for long moments. When Perun raised his hands for quiet, the noise died down to hushed whispers and the distant echoing of thunder. "We come together to celebrate our present and our past. We honor those who have come before us and forged this city into a magical wonder, we honor those who will sacrifice their Stormveil festivities to add to the Runes in the Stormbringer Chamber far below the palace, and most of all, we honor all of the good people of Azguardia."

The crowd cheered loudly as their ruler paid homage to his people. "Let us also remember the youth of our fair city. You are the future of Azguardia, and we honor you. As you hunt Essence flakes this Stormveil, remember to be honorable. Azguardia is not a city of thieves. We are a city of cooperation, dedication, and industry."

"The Essence flakes are a gift from our ancestors and should be treated with reverence. No other city can provide its youth with Essence in such a way. Let us be proud to be part of the only city on this continent that can boast that every single child has the opportunity to become a D-rank cultivator. With a little work, a little speed, a little luck, and a little cleverness, each of you children can become something more."

"As always, there are infusion stations placed around the city, and for the duration of Stormveil, their use is free. To you adults, please give the children first priority for enchanting their feet. They may have need of slow-fall during their hunt. Also, the royal household is increasing the bounty on Essence flakes to a full silver this year to help stimulate the economy. We appreciate your hard work and would like to continue to support you in any way we can. Now, who is ready to celebrate!"

The crowd went wild. Cheering went on for nearly a full minute before Perun stopped his voice-amplifying spell and flew gracefully up to the roof of the Prime Spire, the highest of the palace. The roof of this spire was flat and circular; around the outside of the circle were four metal rods pointing up toward the eternal storm. The rods rose to five times Perun's height and were spaced equally around the roof. Perun stood in the center and faced his people. He raised his fist toward the Azguardians, and they somehow managed to cheer even louder. Then Perun began to shape his Mana.

CHAPTER TWO

Jasper waited impatiently on his balcony. He just wanted the speech to end. The first few moments of Stormveil were his favorite part of every year. He glanced up to the Prime Spire where Perun was about to launch himself into the storm. Jasper could see arcs of lightning Mana shooting between the four launching rods and to Perun.

A pang of frustration ran through Jasper as he saw how effortlessly Perun used his lightning Mana to manipulate the magnetism of the rods. Jasper let out a little huff of annoyance as Perun shot into the sky so fast he could only be seen as a blur. He had yet to master the magnetism trick. It could be done with only Essence as long as you had the right kind of metal nearby, but he hadn't quite managed it yet.

He turned his attention to the built-in infusion station near the edge of the balcony. He stepped into it and pressed a finger to the activation Rune. Over the next five seconds, his feet were suffused with air Essence. The Essence wasn't enough to grant flight, but it was enough to grant slow-fall. Unfortunately, the effect only lasted about four hours.

The stations consumed a lot of Essence with each activation, but every cultivator in the city contributed Essence to the Essence-lines for the month leading up to Stormveil. The storage crystals in the bowels of the palace were brimming with Essence that had been saved up for use in enchanting the children's feet for Stormveil.

Huginn and Muninn took their turns at the station, and then all three turned their gaze up to the storm. Its churning clouds and constant lightning intensified over the next few minutes. The storm built, and Jasper could feel air Essence condensing all around him. He thought he could almost see an Essence flake forming up and away from the balcony.

The sun disappeared behind the horizon as the nine Mages of the Royal Guard flew out from the palace in a ring encircling the entirety of the palace and plaza. They used their Mana to darken the sky further with a dome that encompassed most of the city. Every Azguardian knew it wasn't wise to watch lightning for too long or else you would need a visit to a flesh mage. This darkness made watching what was about to happen safe.

Out of sight far above the city, Perun pulled the storm inward. The lightning stopped. The crowd held its breath in anticipation. The storm clouds fell in on themselves over the next ten seconds, their power seeming to increase the smaller they became. They roiled as they compressed and were forced inward, away from the margins of the city and closer to the point directly over the palace.

As the violence of the storm reached its zenith, the building electricity in the clouds formed into a single, huge bolt of lightning. It arced straight down and into the Prime Spire. Every light crystal in the city brightened to many times their normal intensity.

The light from such a massive bolt of lightning was dampened by the protective dome, but the people still squinted in reflex. Even the sound-dampening Enchantments on the city could not contain the crack of thunder to follow. Many Azguardians stumbled as the shockwave from the thunder hit them, though the Mage's dome protected them from the worst of that as well. After the populace recovered from the shockwave, they resumed their manic cheering as they watched the clouds.

The compressed clouds continued shrinking for another few moments and then took on a distinctively unstable look just before the entire cloud bank exploded in a burst of thousands of points of light. Each light shot out from the origin of the explosion and grew as it traveled through the Essence-saturated air.

Shining points of light grew larger as they took shape and grew into Essence flakes. Each Essence flake would have its own form, and no two were exactly alike. They varied in size somewhat, but most of them were about the size of a child's palm. Once the Essence flake had fully formed, it began to drift down toward the city and the surrounding terrain.

By tradition, the royal family sent their children outside the walls of the city in search of Essence flakes. They left the children of the common folk to hunt within the city walls where it was safe. Most children could not afford even a basic lightning rod, let alone the more advanced versions of Giggle Sticks.

It would be unwise to leave the protective walls during Stormveil without some means of both offense and defense. The saturation of Essence in the air during Stormveil had a tendency to attract a variety of creatures not normally present in the areas around the city. In fact, the cycle of Stormveil had been happening for hundreds of years. In the same way many birds fly to warmer climates in the winter, so did many types of creatures migrate to Azguardia in time for Stormveil.

As the flakes descended, Jasper tightened the straps on his backpack and checked the straps on his breastplate. He had only earned the right to wear the breastplate a year ago, and he still smiled every time he looked on the simple yet elegantly crafted piece of armor. His little brothers wouldn't earn their breastplates for two or three years.

Of course, that was why he was stuck with them during the hunt. By law, anyone going hunting outside the wall was required to do so in groups. The number in the group depended on the abilities of the children. Most children wanted to go in the smallest group they could manage. Each additional person in a group was one more person with whom you had to share your haul of flakes.

Each balcony had its own set of launching rods built in. Neither Jasper nor his younger brothers could make use of them on their own yet. However, they also had the ability to be activated and provide a similar propulsion to what Perun had used—if at a much-reduced capacity. Until you were able to strengthen your body through cultivation, the pressures of such an intense acceleration were severely damaging. The built-in launching rods gave enough acceleration that when used in combination with the slow-fall Enchantment that the children could make it safely outside the walls of the city, even without the ability to fly.

Huginn and Muninn checked their backpacks and feet and then stepped on to the launching platform together. Jasper quirked an eyebrow and said, "You are supposed to use that one at a time. You won't be able to fly straight if you go at the same time."

The twins just looked at each other and grinned. Jasper watched as they did something with air Essence. Jasper wasn't sure exactly what they were doing, but it seemed like they were intertwining their Essence somehow. When Huginn touched the activation Rune, tiny arcs of static appeared in rapid succession from the base of the rods traveling toward the tip.

Electric arcs traversed the rods so quickly it was difficult to track. The rods took hold of the boys by their specially crafted harnesses and launched them up and away. The twins soared in a long arc away from the palace and toward the distant highlands.

Jasper stepped on to the launching platform as his grin grew ever larger. He absolutely loved flying. He loved it more than anything else, even more than fighting. He checked all of his gear one more time and then pressed his finger to the activation Rune. Intense pressure pulled on the harness under his breastplate. His vision narrowed to a small tunnel of light as the forces of the launch took hold on his body. Jasper soared into the air with his body straight as an arrow with head tilted back and eyes forward. The thrill of the initial acceleration hit him, and his adrenaline surged.

For long seconds, he flew higher and higher. His ascent slowed, and he felt it when his upward momentum halted; for just a moment, he was weightless. Then as he began his descent, he shifted his body. He extended his arms out and forward as if grabbing the air in front of him. The air resistance on his newly extended arms and cupped hands caused his body to flip backward, around, and then upright.

Jasper rotated about forty-five degrees so that as the angle of his descent changed, his feet were pointed toward the ground. He was in a sort of crouched position with hands extended out and up. Jasper used his hands to stabilize his position, and the Enchantment on his feet kicked in.

Instead of continuing the normal arc of such a launch, the Enchantment slowed his descent considerably. With an effort of will, Jasper could increase or decrease the effect of the Enchantment as well, giving him that much more control over his path. As the air resistance slowed down his airspeed, he stood more fully erect. After half a minute, he looked more like someone sliding on ice than someone flying.

Ahead, Jasper saw his brothers touching down on a rocky slope. He angled his feet slightly to change course so he would land next to the twins. He could see as the twins turned toward their incoming brother, and he could also see that their Giggle Sticks were alight with electric charges and pointing directly at him.

CHAPTER THREE

When there were only a few body lengths between himself and his impending double shock, he channeled some of his air Essence into a brief but powerful gust of wind directed at the back of his right foot. The gust combined with the directional levitation of Jasper's feet and resulted in a looping backflip with a half twist.

This took him up and over his brothers instead of landing directly in front of them. He landed lightly behind his brothers' original position, and then the three were in a triangle. Jasper had deftly remained out of reach throughout. The younger pair seemed impressed with the last-second maneuver, and Jasper grinned as he drew his own rod and pointed it at the space between his brothers with a cocky grin.

The twins glanced at each other, grinned, and then activated their electric attacks at Jasper at the same time. Jasper infused his own rod with air Essence in the way he was taught would attract lightning. His effort resulted in two arcs forming between Jasper's rods and the rods of his brothers.

A contest of wills began between the three while the arcing continued. Jasper maintained his connection with each arc and then redirected each arc to pass through his rod and back to the opposite brother. Now, the electricity was passing from one twin, through Jasper's rod, and into the other twin's rod. This also freed Jasper from having to maintain the effort of keeping the incoming arcs away from him.

With his mind freed up, he launched his own arcs of electricity back at his brothers. As always, none of the 'attacks' were truly dangerous to them. His brothers were both in the D-ranks, and he was C-ranked. They also wore the bracers gifted to them as members of the royal household. Those provided hefty protection against air and lightning attacks.

However, when Jasper sent out his own attack, his arcs did not behave the way he was expecting. They shot toward his brother's rods and then connected the triangle between the twins. The three of them looked at the three lines of electricity, and all realized at the same time that the energy within the attacks was building with each attack.

Their hairs stood on end despite their protections, and the arcs grew larger and stronger. The energy built to a crescendo as a marble-sized sphere of ball lightning materialized in the center of the triangle. The sphere exploded in a crack of thunder. The three boys flew backward several body lengths and tumbled along the ground.

As they each regained their feet, they looked upon the area they had previously occupied. By the light of the nearly full moon, they could see the stone was scorched in a triangle, and at the center, the stone was glowing faintly red. Huginn shouted, "What in the abyss happened? Did *you* do that, Jasper?"

Muninn echoed him, "Yea, Jasper, what did you *do*?"

Jasper looked puzzled as he replied, "I just sent the same attack back at both of you. I don't know what happened. There is no way we should have been able to melt stone with three little zaps from a Giggle Stick. Not with the small amount of Essence we were using."

Huginn and Muninn looked at each other, grinned, and touched their left forearms together with exclamations of joy. After taking a moment to be impressed with themselves and their accidental accomplishment, Jasper ordered, "Come, it is time to hunt."

His brothers nodded and began running uphill. Jasper followed them, continuously scanning the sky for signs of

Essence flakes. There would not be as many flakes out this far, but those that fell out here tended to be more potent than those that fell in the city. Jasper had been too distracted since they landed and hadn't noticed any flakes falling, but Muninn insisted he had seen one land. The three set off to find their prize.

About ten minutes later, the group spotted a dim light emanating from an object up in the branches of a gnarled, old tree. As they drew near, they saw their first flake of the night. It was far too high to reach, but with air Essence, the distance was trivial. Jasper readied himself to shoot himself up with a gust of air. Before he could do it, Huginn said, "No wait. Let us do it. We have been practicing!"

Jasper shrugged one shoulder and nodded his assent. Huginn and Muninn stood under the tree and held hands. They each used a burst of air Essence directly underneath them, and they sprang up toward the flake waiting above. Their efforts got them most of the way up to the flake but not close enough. As their upward momentum halted and their enchanted feet kicked in, Jasper shot his own burst of air at them. This was enough to get them to their goal.

Muninn snatched the flake, and as their slow-fall activated, he looked toward Jasper and said, "No fair, Jasper. We could have done it without you."

Jasper replied with a wry, "Uh huh."

They pressed ever higher, looking for the tell-tale shine of the flakes. They found four more over the next two hours. Normally by this time of night, all three would be asleep. However, earlier in the day, each of them had taken a magically-induced nap for several hours to help them stay up late.

When the late hour eventually caught up with them and they felt the pull of sleep on their eyelids, they each had a potion in their packs that would help keep them awake long enough to get through the night. They wouldn't need the potion for several hours yet, but they were excited to use them. Children weren't usually allowed to stay up all night, even in the royal family.

The trio decided they could use a short break. They sat on a fallen tree and retrieved water skins and dry meat from their packs. Huginn and Muninn chatted amiably while Jasper quietly scanned the sky. That is why Jasper was the one that saw the glow of a flake swiftly moving through the air downhill and off to the side of their chosen resting spot. He said, "Look, that flake is moving!"

Huginn and Muninn looked in the indicated direction and confusion overtook their faces. After a few moments, the flake was near enough they could see it was being carried by a bird. It was difficult to tell what kind of bird it was in the dark, but when it let out a distinctive cawing, they knew it was a raven. Ravens were a common sight in the surrounding areas.

Jasper raised his rod and charged it with a small amount of Essence. He didn't plan to kill the bird. He just wanted to shock it enough that it dropped the Essence flake. Huginn and Muninn saw what Jasper was doing, and as one, they grabbed his arm and pulled it down just as Jasper let loose a shocking arc.

The energy lanced harmlessly into the stone a few paces away. As the raven flew out of range further up the slope, Jasper angrily turned to his brothers and said, "Hey, what was that for? I could have had him! I want that flake!"

Huginn replied, "We like ravens."

In a similar tone, Muninn said, "Ravens are good omens."

Jasper let out an annoyed sigh and said, "Fine, but I'm still going to go look for it. I want to get the flake before the raven can suck up all the Essence."

They gathered their things and continued the trek up the rocky slope. As they walked, the twins conversed. Huginn cracked a grin. "Wouldn't it be funny if ravens were fishies?"

Muninn looked at him in confusion. "Fishy like cultivators or fishy like swimmers?"

They laughed at themselves good-naturedly and continued by trying to decide what spells a raven cultivator would be able to use. The discussion went on for a time but was interrupted as they heard the cawing of a raven nearby. As the three approached the origin of the sound, they heard the flutter of wings and saw the raven fly away uphill still carrying the flake. The terrain leveled out a little but became more cluttered with stones.

They spotted the raven perching on a high branch in a dead tree. They didn't want to scare the bird away again, so they approached slowly and quietly. The raven occasionally let out a series of calls, but otherwise, it remained perched. They had walked half the distance to the tree when they saw another creature. A small, furry squirrel scrambled quickly across the ground toward the dead tree. It paused every so often and looked up, directly at the Essence flake on the branch next to the raven. The three children simultaneously let out groans of dismay. Jasper mumbled, "I *hate* Stone Squirrels."

CHAPTER FOUR

Jasper thought of his previous experiences with the squirrels. Being children in the royal household meant they had far more opportunity for combat training than the common folk, and in the case of young children, that meant hunting small creatures around the city. The higher-than-average accumulation of Essence in the air from the unending storms resulted in a higher rate of magical mutations among the wild creatures of the area.

Monster spawn rates weren't as high as one could hope to see in an actual dungeon, but mutations were much more common than in other lands. One such mutated creature was the Stone Squirrel. The children of Azguardia didn't like fighting them because most Azguardians focused on air and lightning. The Stone Squirrel was too agile for air to do much against them, and their stony nature negated most lightning damage.

The squirrel reached the tree and quickly climbed to the branch where the raven perched. The raven watched as the squirrel ascended; it didn't fly away as the threat approached it. Instead, it looked once directly at the three children and then back to the squirrel, which crouched and changed into its other form. Small, overlapping plates of stone forced their way out of the squirrel's skin and covered the small creature in earthen armor.

Then the squirrel pounced. The squirrel, the raven, and the Essence flake all fell to the ground in a tumbling chaos of scratching claws, feathers, and noise. The boys abandoned their attempts at quietly approaching and began to run. Jasper leaped on to a large rock, vaulted from the rock into the air, and used a blast of air to push him up and forward. His slow-fall

Enchantment kicked in, and Jasper made an effort of will to maximize the Enchantment. This put his trajectory straight toward the two creatures. His descent was slowed enough by the maximized Enchantment that Jasper bypassed the rough terrain completely.

Jasper charged his rod, but as he got closer, he realized he would probably only hurt the raven if he fired at the fighting animals. He saw that the squirrel had managed to pin the raven and was raking its reinforced claws across the bird's breast. The raven repeatedly bit at the squirrel's head, but the stone armor prevented any damage.

Jasper touched down several steps away, and his landing made enough sound that the squirrel startled. Jasper continued forward after his landing with a few quick steps and drawing back his right leg in preparation for kicking the squirrel. As Jasper's foot swung toward the squirrel, he was taken by surprise as the little creature leaped off the raven and on to Jasper's leg below the knee. The squirrel dug its claws into the leather of Jasper's boots, and then it bit Jasper hard to the side of his kneecap.

Jasper let out a loud curse and swung his rod like a club. The squirrel took the hit, but it didn't seem to bother the stone-covered nuisance. Dull pain in Jasper's shin told him he probably shouldn't try that particular move again when attacking a stone creature attached to his own body.

The squirrel's huge, *square* teeth were still buried in his flesh as Jasper began kicking his leg furiously to try to dislodge the nasty little thing. Just then his brothers came into Giggle Stick range, and each let loose an arc of electricity at the squirrel. Jasper never saw the arcs coming. He simply convulsed and collapsed to the ground. He knew immediately what had happened. No child in Azguardia grows up without being shocked a few dozen times at least. He shouted, "Don't shoot at the squirrel when it is latched on to me, moss-brains!"

He recovered enough to reach down and take hold of the squirrel. There was a little smoke coming out of the thing's mouth where it met Jasper's leg, but otherwise, it appeared unhurt. Jasper clenched his teeth and pulled with all his might. A painful tearing followed, and Jasper's eyes teared up. The squirrel made continuous attempts to scratch and bite its captor, but Jasper held it firm. He stood and said, "Absorb *this*!"

He threw the squirrel as hard as he could and then blasted it with the strongest, most concentrated burst of wind he could manage. The squirrel rocketed toward a large boulder and slammed into it back-first and spread-eagled. The impact left cracks in the stone. The squirrel slid to the ground and lay unmoving.

The twins arrived a moment later, and Huginn exclaimed, "That was awesome! Your air attack was so strong!"

Muninn gestured at Jasper's bleeding knee and said, "That looks like it hurts. Does it hurt?"

Jasper tested his leg by putting more weight on it and replied with tension and anger in his voice, "I am fine. Accursed thing deserves what I gave it."

The raven now stood upright but otherwise had not made a move to leave. It looked to be heavily favoring one leg, and one of its wings rested at an odd angle. The raven looked between the fallen squirrel and the humans several times before looking right at Jasper and tilting its head to one side.

Both the twins stopped paying attention to Jasper and approached the fallen bird. They cooed at it comfortingly and made attempts to tend its wounds. The bird allowed their ministrations. It didn't appear nervous at all. Then Huginn said, "Look, there isn't any blood!"

Muninn narrowed his eyes. "Strange. It looks like it has a broken wing, though."

Meanwhile, Jasper unslung his pack and withdrew a bandage. Each of the children from the royal household had one of these in their packs for the festival. The bandage was a one-time use item that magically sped up the body's normal healing. Such regeneration bandages were expensive, but costs meant little to children who grew up in a palace.

He wrapped the bandage around his knee and felt the flesh-magic begin to work. It would take hours for the wound to heal completely, but for now, the pain was suppressed. After securing his pack, he looked at the raven. Again, the raven looked toward the fallen squirrel, back to Jasper, and then tilted its head to the side. Jasper had the distinct impression the raven was trying to communicate something.

As Jasper considered the implications of that thought, he heard the faint sound of stone against stone. He looked to the place the squirrel had fallen and groaned. The squirrel was standing on all fours with its back arched.

"Brothers," Jasper said calmly, "it isn't a Stone Squirrel. It is a *Dire* Stone Squirrel."

The twins looked up in fear at the words, and all three locked their gazes on the threat. While Stone Squirrels weren't particularly dangerous to a D-ranked cultivator, a Dire Stone Squirrel was often in the C-ranks. The squirrel let out a horrible hiss, and at the same time, its stone armor grew sharp ridges. Then its eyes changed from matte black to glowing red.

Jasper snapped a command, "Form up on me, defensive tactics. It is weak in its mouth or wherever there is no stone."

The twins swiftly took positions to the left and right of Jasper and two steps behind, their feet settling into a stable combat stance. They drew their rods and charged them with

Essence. That was all the preparation time they had. The Dire Stone Squirrel charged.

The angry squirrel went bounding toward its prey with a terrible, growling hiss. As the creature neared, Jasper sank into a deeper, sturdier stance. The creature took one last bounding leap aimed at Jasper's neck, and just as they had practiced a hundred times, Jasper shouted, "Now!"

His brothers each shot a burst of air straight into the oncoming enemy. At the same time, Jasper launched himself straight up and over in a high front flip. The twins' attacks resulted in halting the squirrel's forward motion just as Jasper was performing his flip. About the time Jasper was a third of the way through his flip, he struck down on the nearly motionless target in front of him.

The sudden, energetic impact left a crack in one of the plates on the squirrel's back, and the force knocked it straight into the stone below. Jasper continued his flip around and would have landed cleanly as he had previously practiced. However, he forgot to take into account the Enchantment on his feet. He didn't normally have that kind of effect active, and so instead of the Enchantment helping and keeping him safe, it instead slowed his descent such that he over-rotated and landed on his back.

The squirrel quickly regained its feet and turned to his target that was now flat on its back. It immediately pounced at the downed human's face. Jasper didn't recover in time to defend against the attack, and as the squirrel raked its claws against one side of Jasper's face, he screamed in agony.

Huginn and Muninn thought better than to use their rods on the thing while it was atop their older brother, so they repeated their last attack, which blew the creature off Jasper's face. It tumbled over several times and came to a stop as it slapped into a nearby stone. Jasper was clutching his bloody face with his off-hand and backing away from the squirrel that was even now readying itself for another attack.

With disbelief in his voice, Muninn said, "Jasper, your eye is ruined! There's so much blood!"

Huginn echoed, "So much blood!"

Jasper, having regained his composure, stoically said, "I'm fine. Here it comes again. Hammer and anvil!"

Jasper retreated several steps, and his brothers advanced diagonally forward. He maintained single-eye contact with the squirrel the whole time, and it didn't change targets. It ran past the twins and launched itself at Jasper's neck a second time. Jasper shouted a wordless challenge and propelled himself forward and slightly upward through liberal use of air Essence. At the same time, the twins shot bursts of air at the squirrel's back, lending more speed to the squirrel's leap but also unbalancing its posture. The squirrel impacted against the center of Jasper's breastplate accompanied by the sound of stone cracking.

Jasper felt several stinging cuts underneath his breastplate where the ridges on the squirrel's plating had pierced the metal. It looked to be momentarily stuck to Jasper's chest, and so the young cultivator did the only reasonable thing he could think of. He shot himself several body lengths into the air and belly-flopped on to the flat stone below him.

The impact knocked the breath out of him, but a small smile crossed his lips as he heard the sound of more stone cracking. He felt the thing wiggling under him and heard its hissing. The spikes penetrating his armor had dug a bit deeper into his flesh.

Without thinking, he reached under him and grasped the squirrel's back as he had done before. Unfortunately, he had forgotten about the newly protruding spikes. Dozens of spikes dug into his hand, but Jasper held firm.

Still lying on his stomach, he used air Essence in a blast at the topmost section of the breastplate, just under his neck. The force pushed his body up and into a backflip that took him up off the ground, around, and back to his feet. During the flip, he tore the squirrel out of his armor with the sound of stone on steel.

He landed unsteadily on his feet. This time, only the slow-fall Enchantment kept him upright. With one eye ruined, he had misjudged the landing, but he steadied himself in a moment. He turned the creature in his hand so they could look each other in the eye. The thing made the same growling hiss, and Jasper replied with his own growling shout. He drew back his hand to throw the hateful creature into the air.

The motion of drawing his arm back gave the squirrel just enough wiggle room to get two claws into Jasper's arm, the pain of which caused him to loosen his grip. Instead of throwing the squirrel, he let go, and the squirrel landed right behind him. As the squirrel hit the ground, it took two arcs of lightning from the twins.

Neither appeared to do much more than cause it to convulse briefly. What the attacks did do was draw its attention away from Jasper. He tried to stomp the squirrel as it ran by, but he was too slow. It leaped at Huginn, who raised his rod reflexively to block. Muninn shot it with a puff of air that knocked it off its intended course enough that it only managed to tear at Huginn's sleeve as it flew past.

Jasper knew they had done some minor damage to this annoying foe, but he also knew their efforts were not particularly helpful. He was considering ordering everyone to retreat, but seeing the squirrel nearly hurt his little brother enraged him. He sprinted toward Huginn while the squirrel readied itself for another leap attack. Muninn couldn't hit it with any attacks without repositioning first since Huginn was now blocking his line of sight. The squirrel leaped, and Huginn attacked with another burst of air.

CHAPTER FIVE

The attack was mostly ineffective without the combined force of Muninn's attack. Huginn realized he was about to get mauled by a creature far more powerful than himself, and he raised his arms to shield his face and closed his eyes. But nothing happened.

Huginn could still hear the squirrel growling and hissing, but he hadn't been mauled. He opened his eyes and saw Jasper's off-hand reaching over his shoulder and grasping the squirrel. The problem with Jasper saving him in that way was the squirrel was now facing toward the hand that was grasping it.

The squirrel bit down hard on Jasper's thumb and began to grind. Jasper howled in agony once again but did not let go. He gripped tighter and tighter, but the stone plates prevented his grip from hurting the creature. The pain was so great that Jasper started staggering around as he tried to kill the thing. He pounded it into rocks as hard as he could to no effect. He looked around for a pool of water to drown it but saw none. The agony rose to blinding levels as the squirrel began cutting into bone.

Pain overrode his ability to think. He dropped his rod, grabbed the squirrel with his main hand, and ripped it away. His thumb went with it, as did his ability to do anything other than scream in rage. He threw the squirrel at the ground in front of him and increased its speed with a hasty blast of air. The squirrel bounced and rolled, all the while chewing on Jasper's thumb.

A flash of memory crossed Jasper's face. He picked up his rod in his bloody main hand, moved a few steps to the side, and shouted to his brothers, "Attack me!"

They looked at him in confusion, wondering if their brother had gone mad. He shouted even louder, "Hit me with your *Giggle Sticks!*"

Understanding crossed their faces as they charged their rods as much as they could manage at their rank. Jasper also charged his rod, but he could charge his easily ten times more than his brothers. As one, the three brothers let loose their attacks. A triangle of lightning formed between them with the Dire Stone Squirrel gnawing on Jasper's thumb directly in the center.

The power in the lightning was far greater than when this had happened hours before, blinding and overwhelming. The twins began convulsing as the lightning overcame the insulation on their rods. Then a deafening sound and blinding light were followed by silence and darkness.

Sometime later, Jasper awoke to something repeatedly poking at his cheek. He tried to swat it away, but when he moved his arm, he was jolted awake by sheer pain. He cried out, "*Ow*, that hurt!"

Then he startled; his hearing was damaged. Jasper could hear himself talk, but it sounded like his ears were stuffed full of beeswax. He opened his eyes, and his vision was also disrupted. He was confused for a moment and then remembered one of his eyes was ruined. There was a vibrant, white triangle in the vision of his remaining eye, even when he blinked.

Jasper slowly regained control of himself enough to be able to stand. As he got to his feet, his mind cleared enough to remember his brothers were also part of the attack. He saw them both lying there, unmoving. Both were much farther away from him than he remembered when they made their combination attack. He ran to Huginn and checked to make sure he was alive. Huginn's heart was pumping, and his chest was rising and falling. Jasper hurried to Muninn and found him to be in much the same shape.

He had seen enough people recover from thunder shock that he knew there was little to worry about. The bracers on their arms would have protected the rhythm of their hearts from being disrupted. They would both need to be examined by a flesh Mage, but everyone who went outside the walls on Stormveil was examined by a flesh Mage.

The remaining two regeneration bandages wouldn't help them recover from thunder shock. Jasper considered for a moment whether his brothers would be angry with him if he took their bandages from their backpacks. He decided they wouldn't be, so he took one out and wrapped it around the wound where his off-hand thumb used to be. He used the third and final bandage to wrap around his head and cover as much of his face wound as he could. The immediate reduction in pain caused him to let out a sigh of relief.

As he was tending to his wounds, he looked at the aftermath of their combination attack. As before, the stone was marred with scorch marks in a triangle, though this time the scorch marks were much darker and thicker. At the center of the triangle was a molten pile of stone vaguely shaped like a squirrel. A full pace around the squirrel's body, the stone was glowing red. It even looked like the squirrel's remains were sinking into the molten stone. There was no sign of his missing thumb.

Jasper sat on a stone, drinking water and thinking about Stormveil. Then he remembered waking up to something poking his cheek. He looked to the place he had fallen, and he saw the raven. It was staring directly at Jasper.

They continued to stare at each other for several minutes, Jasper occasionally drinking from his waterskin. The raven finally looked away and toward first Huginn, then Muninn.

Seconds later, both of his little brothers came to simultaneously. Jasper watched them as they reoriented themselves and came to grips with what had just happened. When they saw the molten squirrel, they cheered and hit their forearms together.

Muninn said, "Celestial skies above, Jasper. Look at that stone! It melted!"

Huginn added, "I can't wait to tell everyone about this!"

Jasper smiled and said, "Brothers, I hope you don't mind. I took your bandages."

They heartily agreed he was well within his rights considering he was the only one who had been injured. Muninn exclaimed, "Oh look, the raven is still alive! Hi there, mister raven. Will you allow us to tend your wounds?"

Then Jasper felt guilty about the bandages. He hadn't even considered saving a bandage for the raven, but even so, he didn't even know if it would work on a non-humanoid creature. To the immense surprise of all three hunters, the raven spoke, "There is no need, young master. I have seen to my wounds. Your kindness has been noted, however."

A long, motionless silence followed as the children stared dumbfounded at the raven. Then Huginn broke the silence with an abrupt laugh and said, "Ravens are the *best* omens!"

At that, the raven flew over and landed in front of the twins. Muninn asked it, "How is it that you can talk, master raven?"

The raven replied in its cawing tone, "I am a creature of counterpoint, a being of bane and boon. I bestow blessings or curses based on my mood, the day, the positions of the planets. You three have earned my blessing."

The twins exclaimed in delight at the prospect of getting some kind of magical blessing. Jasper had a suspicious look on his face and said, "Forgive me, master raven, but in honesty, I will admit I would not accept such a thing on your word alone. How do I know you won't curse us instead?"

The raven said, "Wisdom, it seems, you found when you lost your eye, your thumb, and curse you, do I, with the curse of the lost eye. Again and again, it shall vanish. May you gain wisdom many times to come."

Jasper sat up suddenly, and his hand moved to draw his rod. The raven hurriedly continued, "I jest, I jest. A boon you shall have. A protector and defender you look to be. Look at yourself, your blood, your wounds. Your little brothers have none. You put the safety of others before your own, and for that, I give the boon of life. An eye for an eye, when your two brothers die, their lives shall be spared but once. Your lives, one two three, are now intertwined. Both bane and boon bestowed."

With that, the raven took flight and left the children behind. Jasper watched as the raven left, and just as he lost sight of it, he could have sworn the raven's form changed into something else. He shook his head and attributed it to a trick of the eye. He couldn't wait to have a flesh Mage replace his eye.

The twins argued about what they thought the raven had meant by his words. Jasper let their conversation wash over him. He hadn't felt any different when the raven had supposedly bestowed a boon or bane or both. It was probably all just nonsense.

On the bright side, the raven had not taken the Essence flake when it had flown away. Jasper walked over and retrieved it. His Essence was quite drained, so he sat in the position Perun had taught him and meditated with the Essence flake on the stone before him. Over the next ten minutes, the Essence within the flake was siphoned into Jasper's center.

He felt refreshed and energized. That had been a strong flake. He was nearly at full Essence capacity after that single flake. The twins meditated together with a single flake between them. They each filled back up on their Essence over the next few minutes. The flake still had a moderate glow because it hadn't been fully drained. They stored the flake in their packs, and the three hunters continued their night hunt.

The rest of their Stormveil hunt was much less exciting. Their search led them to a mountain stream, and they followed its path uphill in their search for more flakes. They recovered twenty-two more flakes before it was time to return. They had encountered eight more hostile creatures.

Those were dispatched much more easily. They were all water-based, and lightning was particularly effective against them. There were dozens of other creatures that ran away as soon as they saw the approaching humans. Each Essence flake drew the attention of living creatures around it. Somehow, the Essence within was available for creatures to absorb, though they did it much more slowly than cultivators.

The sky began to lighten as dawn approached. The three had begun the trek back home an hour before and were nearing the city as Stormveil drew to an end. Jasper wished fervently for the ability to cast the slow-fall Enchantment, but it had worn off hours ago, and he had not learned how that particular Enchantment worked.

At least the walk back was entirely downhill. Even after drinking their potions of wakefulness, the boys were exhausted. As they came in sight of the walls, they could see hundreds of people lining the streets into the city. As the children came into view, hundreds of cheering voices erupted in a cacophony of drunken celebration.

It was a time-honored tradition for the townsfolk to get as drunk as they could on Stormveil while the children were out hunting. Most residents of Azguardia found it hard to sleep on Stormveil—not because of the unending noise of celebration but because of the lack of the sound of thunder. It just wasn't natural to sleep in a night without thunder.

The children entered the city and couldn't help but grin and wave. As was tradition, all the streets were lined by townsfolk cheering on the children returning to the plaza after the long night of hunting. Shortly after entering the city, a few town children dressed in rough wool clothing joined them.

As was tradition, all the children were treated the same no matter their station. The six children continued and joined with a group of five. The cheers continued as their exhaustion gave way to pride. Eleven became twenty-four, then eighty, then too many to count. The mob of children eventually made their way to the plaza.

The plaza was filled with merry revelers. The space in the front and center was left open for all the children. The noise was deafening as each child tried to tell the others about their adventures. Those that stayed inside the walls tried to get closer to someone who could afford to go outside the walls. They wanted to hear the tales of adventure and danger.

Jasper didn't bother telling any stories since Huginn and Muninn were talking enough for ten children. Jasper lost track of the number of times he was asked about the blood covering his clothing and armor as well as his missing eye. The magic of the bandages had worn off a few hours prior. He was no longer in pain, but he would need to spend a lot of time with a flesh Mage to replace his eye and thumb. The sun was just about to rise over the horizon as Perun stepped on to the balcony and activated his voice amplification.

CHAPTER SIX

"Hail to the valiant hunters, returned triumphant!" Perun's voice boomed through the plaza. The crowd went berserk. Jasper had thought it was loud when he was up in the balcony. Like every previous year, however, Jasper was surprised by how much louder it all was when he was down with the rest of the people.

After letting the cheering go on for long moments, Perun resumed, "Let us all give thanks for the work of our ancestors. It was they who provided us with this glorious city, and it is by the labor of their hands that we reap the benefits. Remember them. Honor them. For it is by their gifts that we can raise our children in such a magnificent city. Thus... Ends... Stormveil!"

As Perun finished his last word, he raised his hands high, held his hands in a grasping gesture, and then pulled downward. Something happened with Perun's armor during the gestures. Jasper didn't know what it was, but he could tell a large amount of power was connecting the armor with the sky. With Perun's motion came a bolt of lightning from a clear sky. Though this bolt was far smaller than the final bolt before Stormveil began, this one carried the promise of a year full of thunder.

Perun and the rest of the royal family descended to the plaza as the storm clouds reformed above the city, and the constant lightning and thunder resumed. Every Azguardian rejoiced as the familiar sights and sounds returned. The royal family exited the palace followed by a horde of servants bearing food and drink.

The royals mingled with the common folk of Azguardia and even handed out the Essence flake bounty personally to many of the children who chose to turn in flakes for coin. Those turned in for the bounty would be used to strengthen the children of the royal family and their retainers. The celebration went on for hours and would last all day and all night. Most people would sleep when they couldn't stay awake any longer and then resume the festivities as soon as they awoke. However, after mingling with the common folk for two hours, the royals returned to their palace.

The returned hunters all gathered in the throne room and stood before the throne, the older children in front with the younger fanning out behind. Beginning with his own children and going on in descending order of station, Perun asked for a summary of the night's escapades. All of the children had adventures to share but none quite so captivating as the tale Jasper recounted.

Many times, Jasper would brush over a detail, and either Huginn or Muninn would interject with a comment. When Jasper told of their first experience with the combined attack, Perun looked thoughtful. When he explained their more powerful repeat of the attack, Perun's eyebrows rose in surprise.

Perun slowly praised them, "It is truly rare for cultivators to manage such a feat at your age. Typically, such cooperative efforts require the use of Mana. Yet somehow, you managed with only Essence. Impressive. Jasper, I think it may be time for you and me to have a discussion about ideals."

The boys beamed at the praise, and Jasper was surprised to realize Perun meant to teach him about breaking into the B-ranks. That initial conversation usually didn't happen for another two years at least! He nearly burst with pride.

As Jasper told of the talking raven, Perun gained a worried expression. The change in Perun's demeanor gave Jasper pause, but he continued the tale. Jasper recounted the words of the raven as he bestowed the supposed boons and banes, and Perun gestured for Marilor, the court diviner.

Marilor and Perun had a quick whispered conversation, and the diviner looked at Jasper, Huginn, and Muninn in turn with eyes glowing white. After examining each, he turned and had a whispered conversation for another minute. Perun said, "You seem to have been... blessed. You are fortunate."

His words sounded positive, but Jasper couldn't help but feel there was much more Perun wasn't saying. He also noted a small pause between the words 'been' and 'blessed'.

After all the tales had been told, the meeting in the throne room came to an end. Perun approached Jasper and said, "Come with me. There is something you should see."

Perun took Jasper into a room adjacent to the throne room. Jasper had seen it before. It was a small room with a few shelves piled high with collapsible chairs. Jasper was beginning to think this was an odd choice of destination when Perun touched three seemingly random places on the back wall in turn.

The back wall vanished, and Perun gestured for Jasper to follow. "Come quickly. The wall will solidify again shortly."

Jasper followed Perun into a spiral staircase leading down. The staircase was well lit by periodic crystals powered by the storms. He looked back to the storage room before descending after Perun and watched as the wall reappeared in an instant. The stairs led farther down than Jasper would have ever guessed. They were probably twice as far below the palace as the Prime Spire was above the ground.

At the bottom of the stairs, Jasper saw a reinforced metal door. It seemed to have several ribbons of colored metals throughout the door. Jasper guessed those other colors were different types of materials with various affinities. That probably reinforced the door against different types of attack. Perun made several gestures with his hands and spoke four words Jasper did not recognize. The reinforced door opened inward on silent hinges. Perun stepped into the door and to the side to let Jasper see unobstructed.

The chamber before him was a domed structure approximately the size of the throne room. The wall, ceiling, and floor were absolutely covered with inscribed Runes. At the center of the room was a pedestal twice the height of Perun. The pedestal looked to be made of a kind of wood that Jasper did not recognize.

Atop the pedestal hovered the largest crystal Jasper had ever seen. It was easily large enough for Jasper to fit inside. It floated a handspan above the pedestal and turned ever so slowly. The color of the crystal was difficult to describe. It was both opaque and transparent but was definitely the off-white Jasper had come to associate with the storms.

Opacity and color both constantly shifted in the crystal-like, turbulent storm clouds. The entire chamber was saturated with air Essence. Finally, Jasper turned to Perun and asked in hushed tones, "What is this place?"

"This, young Jasper, is the Stormbringer Chamber. Normally, I don't bring a royal child here until they are thirteen years old and ready to transition to B-ranks. In your case, however... one out of two will do." Perun smiled as Jasper absorbed Perun's full meaning.

Before Jasper could respond, Perun continued, "Above the pedestal is the most valuable treasure in Azguardia. That is a luminous Beast Core. That means the monster from which this came was an S-ranked Magical Beast. By tradition, we do not teach the people about the Beast from which this crystal came. Its name was Ohd-ihn. It was a magnificent Beast that lived many hundreds of years ago. Its passage caused the ground to tremble, and its words caused the listeners to tremble in fear. It was a fierce protector and bringer of justice. It would travel to the ends of the world to pursue one that had wronged another. It was the absolute embodiment of vengeful justice."

"There came a time when Ohd-ihn tried to put an end to yet another war between celestials and infernals. The war had continued for decades and had destroyed almost every living being on the continent. Ohd-ihn's enemies decided to join forces since they believed the powerful creature would be their demise regardless."

"The forces of both the celestials and infernals combined their might into a single, terrible attack. The attack drained the life from every contributing participant. Unfortunately, the attack resulted in Ohd-ihn being poisoned by Chaos. Ohd-ihn was a creature of order, but it was wise enough to know that the Chaos within would destroy everything Ohd-ihn held dear. And so Ohd-ihn left behind the destruction from the Celestial and Infernal War. Ohd-ihn flew far until its strength failed, and it was forced to land. It landed here, on the slopes above. On the same slopes where you had your night's adventure."

"On the ground where Azguardia now stands was once a tiny, primitive village. The chieftain was a cultivator with a strong affinity for air. She fearlessly walked the distance from the village to the place where Ohd-ihn had collapsed. She called out to the magnificent Beast and asked if it needed aid. Ohd-ihn looked upon the chief and saw she was a good and honorable leader."

"Ohd-ihn could see the promise of order deep in her heart. Ohd-ihn said to the chief, 'I give unto you my power. I give unto you my soul. I give unto you the ideal of Vengeful Justice.' Sadly, the chief did not speak the language of the Beast. Despite not understanding the Beast's speech, the unknown words took root in the chief's heart, and over time, she came to know the meaning within her heart."

"As Ohd-ihn finished speaking its last words, its body dissolved into Mana and dissipated into the air above. The Mana caused a storm—a storm that never ends. Left behind after the body dissolved was this crystal, and it is with the power of this crystal that we give succor to the people of Azguardia."

"This chamber has been wrought over the years by members of the royal family. The Runes you see have been crafted carefully over centuries. Each year during Stormveil, the monarch of Azguardia comes to the Stormbringer Chamber and adds to the magic of this place. The magic inside these walls is delicate; the slightest error in Runic magic could result in the complete annihilation of the city."

"That is why the stone around this chamber is so heavily reinforced. You see, this chamber provides the royal family of Azguardia enough access to Essence that we have no need of our own dungeon. The downside to such an agreement is that such easily gained power is all too easily turned to sloth. This is why we expose our children to dangers so readily and so often. We wish you to become strong. We wish you to carry the heritage of Ohd-ihn with you. Now tell me one thing, young Jasper. Will you pledge your life to honor the ideals of Ohd-ihn?"

Jasper's entire body shivered at the power of Perun's words. He solemnly looked directly into Perun's stormy-gray eyes.

"I do so pledge."

FLIGHT OF THE GLITTERFLIT
BY: RYAN BALL

CHAPTER ONE

The adventurer began to squirm in pain. "Are you *sure* you're during this right? It hurts like the *abyss*."

Jack put even more pressure on the man's arm, willing the holy fire, a mixture of celestial and fire Essence, deeper into the wound. The wound slowly started to mend itself, but the man began to sweat profusely and started to moan.

"Please, is there another cleric who can help me? I'm not sure this is worth the pain."

"I'm sorry, sir. I'm the only one on staff today. Here, just sit still for another minute, and this will be over before you know it." Jack said a small prayer and felt celestial Essence flow through him. Unfortunately, as was his predilection, he also mixed in a healthy dose of fire Essence. The wound rapidly began to heal, but the man's face turned bright red as heat built inside him. He abruptly pushed Jack aside and sprang up from the cot he had been lying on.

"You're... you're doing this on purpose! You must get some sort sick of pleasure from this torture. I am leaving, and I am taking my offering with me!" He grabbed the bag of coins he had laid in the offering plate and strode from the room, letting the door bang loudly.

"But I didn't finish...!" Jack called out, letting his voice trail off. He looked down at his hands and sighed. No matter how he tried, he couldn't figure out how to apply only celestial Essence to his healing.

As a child, a dual affinity for celestial and fire had seemed like a literal godsend, and his parents had eagerly shipped him off to the Church, his future full of promise, but after he arrived, it quickly became apparent that he had a mental block that prevented him from using his main Essence types apart from each other. Over time, he still managed to reach the D-ranks, but his church superiors had grown exasperated with his limits. Eventually, they had thrown up their hands and sent him here—a mountain in the middle of nowhere—to work under Father Richard, a known outcast. In other words, he was a lost cause. He slumped against the cot, trying to repress the tears that welled in his eyes.

A hand gently rested on his shoulder. Jack looked up and grimaced upon seeing Father Richard. He had hoped to avoid telling him about this latest incident for as long as possible.

"Brother Jack, I assume from the shouting I heard that things didn't go too well today. Come, child, join me in my office."

Jack shuffled along after him, his spirits weighed down.

"Take a seat. Now, tell me about your troubles."

"Every time I visualize channeling celestial Essence, I feel compelled to add in fire Essence. I've gotten really good at using holy fire to roast those infernal-type dungeon Mobs, Impalers I think they're called, but for everything else, I'm terrible. I tried to form a barrier the other day and accidentally lit my party on fire."

Father Richard tapped his fingers together. "Hmm. Are you using a poor cultivation technique? If you're pulling in any celestial corruption, you may be subconsciously compensating for it by trying to avoid using celestial Essence."

"I follow the Church-approved technique, of course. I don't think that's it." Jack shook his head ruefully.

"How about your meridians? Let's see, looks like you have opened all but one. Your stomach meridian, huh? Usually, that's one of the first that people open. It's nice to be able to eat so little. Helps keep a trim waistline." Father Richard patted his stomach for emphasis.

Jack smiled wanly. "I've tried to open it, and I just... faint. Then I have a vision of fire consuming me, and when I wake up, the rug is burnt to a crisp."

"Well, there's your problem, my boy! Your stomach meridian must be the one primarily aligned with your fire affinity channel. Your body is so tired of fighting the blocked meridian that you're bleeding fire Essence into any other type of Essence you use."

"So how do I fix it?" Jack eagerly asked.

Father Richard scratched his head. "Well, I could force it open for you, but there's a chance that all that pent-up pressure might cause you to explode."

Jack's eyes widened. "Let's, uh, not do that then."

"Have it your way." Father Richard shrugged and pondered further. "Here in the Church, we believe the path of divine inspiration lies in doing good. Perhaps it would help you to get out of your own head for a while and go do something that helps others. That doesn't involve burning them up." He chuckled.

Jack stifled a groan. "Like what... uh, sir..."

"Actually, I've got just the thing. Yesterday, a group called The Collective stole a Glitterflit, one of those super speedy healing bunnies, from the dungeon. As you know, celestial-based animals are rare, and it's our responsibility to protect them. Your mission, should you choose to accept it—rescue the Glitterflit and restore it to the dungeon. I'll even pay you a few silver."

Jack contemplated the proposal. "Do you think this might help?"

"Probably not, but I can't have you scaring away any more adventurers. Unless they're more of those infected." Father Richard let out a belly laugh, clearly pleased with his own sense of humor.

Jack tried not to roll his eyes. Still, as annoyed as he felt, he kind of liked the idea of going on an adventure. Despite an overwhelming need for clerics in dungeon parties, most groups refused to bring him, especially after word got out about his little lighting others on fire episode. So it wasn't like he had anything better to do.

"Alright, I'll do it."

"Fantastic! Here, you'll need this." Father Richard tossed him one of the pendants the dungeon was known for giving out as loot. "By now, the Glitterflit will be pretty ill, having been away from the dungeon for so long. The celestial Essence that pendant exudes should be enough to sustain it for a while."

Jack hung the pendant around the neck, alongside the family heirloom necklace his parents gave him when he left home. "Any idea where to find The Collective?"

Father Richard shook his head. "Ask around a bit. They haven't exactly been subtle in their schemes, so I'm sure you'll find them easily enough."

Jack nodded and took his leave, a small spring in his step.

CHAPTER TWO

Jack surveyed the small, deserted warehouse in front of him. Nestled in a deep, dark corner of Mountaindale, it was the perfect place for a hideout—particularly of a group of low-ranked cultivators with pretensions of nefariousness.

He spied an open window and scooted up below it. He could hear no noises from within, so he decided to climb the wall beneath the window. Fortunately, the stonework of the warehouse lent itself to handholds. He unlatched the window, heaved himself through, and landed with a plop, releasing a cloud of dust.

The room was darkly lit, but he could make out some furniture, along with a board with various items pinned to it. One, a notice exclaiming, 'Beware: Little known group known as "The Collective" steals items from fishies'. Also, a few pictures of members, including one of a man attempting his best roguish grin, underscored by, 'Nick, Your Fearless Leader' written in capital letters beneath it. Jack couldn't help but chuckle a bit at the silliness of it all.

He glanced around but could find no sign of a cage or other indication of the Glitterflit. In the corner, a rug bumped up awkwardly. Pulling it up, he found a padlocked basement door outlined in the floor. A burst of holy fire later, the lock oozed off, and the door sprang open. He began to climb down a ladder, trying not to let his cleric robes get caught in the rungs.

Unable to see, he lit a flame in his hand. Boxes and stockpiles of items emerged into sight. He did a cursory search and found mostly low-level weapons, a few potions, and spare armor. He sighed in frustration. At just that moment, though, he heard a small squeak.

He spun around but couldn't locate the source of the noise. Taking a deep breath, he sat down in a meditative pose. He slowly pushed his aura out into the room, letting it expand to all four corners. At last, he sensed a faint beat of celestial Essence. Springing up, he heaved a few boxes aside until he found a small crate punctured with holes. Inside was the limp form of the Glitterflit, lying weakly on its side.

"Oh no, oh no. Please don't tell me I'm too late." He unlatched the crate and then hastily pulled the pendant off his neck and held it next to the Glitterflit.

The Glitterflit remained motionless, and Jack despaired. He couldn't fail this mission too; even Father Richard would lose faith in him. He desperately thought about channeling additional Essence through the pendant but feared he might accidentally burn the bunny to a crisp. Instead, he said a simple prayer to himself and clutched the pendant as tightly as he could. He felt a warmth seep from the pendant into his aura and gradually envelop the Mob.

After a few moments, the Glitterflit let out a small cough and nuzzled the pendant. Exhilaration raced through him.

"Hi, little buddy. You're alive!" He gently stroked the soft, white fur on top of the bunny's head. The Glitterflit ground its teeth slightly, sounding like it was purring. Jack took that as a good sign.

Leaving the pendant inside, he gingerly closed the crate. He cradled it in one hand as he did his best to climb the ladder without losing his balance. Reaching the top room again, he contemplated his exit. With a need to leave quickly, trying to scale the window was out of the question. Knowing his luck, The Collective would return right when he had his leg straddling the window ledge, his rear end hanging out for all world to see. So instead, he blasted his way through the front door, content with the benefits of his unique ability for once. Plus, it was nice to leave The Collective a little message. It wasn't exactly the Church's way, but Father Richard would likely approve.

He checked on the Glitterflit within the crate and found it hopping around, trying to bash the sides with the nub on its head. The little guy certainly seemed to have recovered his energy.

Strolling down the path to the dungeon, he felt happier than he had in a long time. He started mouthing the words to 'Killer of Her Loneliness', going so far as to mutter about how 'dangerlicious' he felt before blushing and checking to make sure nobody heard him. It certainly wouldn't do for a cleric to be caught singing along to a ribald tavern tune.

CHAPTER THREE

The dungeon loomed ahead of him. Jack always dreaded entering this particular dungeon. As a Church initiate, he had trained in the only safest, most predictable dungeons. This one was the opposite of that. Every day brought some new, crazy development that could kill you. The dungeon itself was rumored to be a devious mastermind the likes of which the world had rarely witnessed before.

He hoped to quickly sprint inside, find the Basher room, let out the Glitterflit, and then run back out. Since it was after dark, he didn't expect to run into dungeon parties but figured most would steer clear of him once they recognized him. Having a bad reputation had its uses.

He crept through the entrance of the dungeon until reaching the mining area. Seeing no one, he passed through the arch gateway and quickly dashed through the garden with the freaky mushroom creature with tentacles. Finally, he arrived at the Basher room. Not particularly eager to take down any of the Glitterflit's relatives in front of it, he lit up a holy fire aura, which he hoped would encourage them to keep their distance. He saw a few beady eyes peer out at him from the shadows, but not a sound was made. He breathed a sigh of relief, glad that all was going to plan.

He sat down the crate and opened it. The Glitterflit ran out, quick as a whip, making a few squeaks of joy. It circled the room, eagerly visiting with its fellow Mobs. Feeling relieved, Jack released his holy fire aura and leaned down to grab the crate and make his exit.

"Well, what do we have here?" A man stepped into the room, followed by a group of others. "A wayward cleric, holding a very familiar crate."

Jack recognized the man from the photo, the leader of The Collective named Nick. Nick took a step forward, his mouth twisting into a malicious grin, his squad shuffling awkwardly into the room behind him. "It seems somebody took an interest in a missing Glitterflit and decided to play the hero. The only problem is, he seems to have stolen our property."

Jack gave Nick his best flinty glare. "I'm here on official Church business. The Glitterflit belongs to the dungeon, not a bunch of thieving miscreants like yourself. Please, let me pass." He raised his right hand and lit up a blue, crackling flame.

"Oh, so you're the infamous Brother Jack? Perfect. Nobody will miss you when you're gone." Nick abruptly moved his hand down in a swiping motion, and an arrow was let loose from the back of the group. Jack felt a sudden, blinding pain in his side and collapsed to the ground.

"Pathetic. Enjoy bleeding out, if the Bashers don't get you first. Let's go, everybody. My appetite for dungeon diving is ruined for today." Nick gave him a swift kick to his bleeding side, causing Jack to gasp and see stars in front of his eyes. The group traipsed back out of the room, their laughs echoing as they made their way through the next few chambers.

Jack tried to sit up, but the pain was excruciating, and he briefly lost consciousness. Waking up again, he had a hard time thinking coherently. Maybe another group would come along and would find him, but he found it hard to believe that another group wouldn't just finish the job. Jack's general faith in humanity had been deeply shaken. He felt a darkness begin to close in on his vision as the pain gradually began to crowd out any other thought or emotion.

Just as Jack began to slip away completely, he felt a small tickle of fur and padded feet crawl over his arm and nestle against him. A bright flash suddenly lit up the room before coalescing into an intense glowing sphere. He felt pure celestial Essence emanating from the sphere, being driven deeply into his bleeding wound. His side became intensely itchy as his skin grew back and the organs beneath it reformed. His breathing stabilized, and the pain began to subside. The sphere dimmed, revealing the Glitterflit, looking tired but pleased with itself. It began to hop around Jack, chirping at him in encouragement.

Jack let out a sob of relief. He had just barely avoided death, all thanks to the world's fluffiest dungeon Mob. He gently stroked the top of the Glitterflit's head, trying to keep his hand steady.

"You saved my life, little buddy. It's been a crazy day for both of us."

He weakly stood up, patted the rabbit one final time, picked up the crate, and began to lurch towards the dungeon exit. It was time to get back to his room in the church, curl up, and sleep—and maybe spend some of Father Richard's prize of silver coins on a big mug of beer.

Just as he began to feel the rush of the mountain air again, he heard another chirp. Looking down, he saw the Glitterflit hopping along a few feet behind him. He frowned.

"You can't come with me, little buddy. This is your home. The Bashers are your family. Trust me, you're much safer here than you are with me."

The Glitterflit stopped for a moment and tilted its head to the side. It opened its eyes widely, and Jack swore he could see them glisten ever so slightly. He took one step towards the entrance, hoping the Mob would stay in place. Seeing its sad act have no effect, the Glitterflit chirped and hopped up past him towards the exit staircase. It quickly began climbing the stairs. Jack sighed.

"Okay, I guess I don't really have a choice. I suppose if you're coming with me willingly, the dungeon won't care." Jack peered around the room, waiting for some type of response. Seeing none, he shrugged.

He picked up the rabbit and cupped it in the palm of his hands. "I wonder what I should name you. How about Dusty, since I found you in a dingy, grimy basement." The Glitterflit heaved its shoulders a bit as if to shrug. "I don't really know Mob body language, but okay, Dusty it is! I also have no idea if you're male or female or whether those terms even apply to dungeon Mobs, but for the sake of simplicity, let's assume you're a boy. Is that okay?" The Mob looked at him and blinked, appearing not to comprehend. "Well, that's good enough for me!"

That evening, Dusty the Glitterflit lay on Jack's chest, a puffy furball of warmth. The two of them snored away, the fire in the hearth of the small bedroom slowly dying away. Jack slept soundly, even considering the traumatic events of the day. The Glitterflit let out a small sigh of happiness and snuggled deeper into his chest. A small halo of light shimmered into view and surrounded the nub on the Mob's forehead. A few seconds went by, and the halo released into a cascade of twinkly lights that floated off into the night sky.

CHAPTER FOUR

A few weeks passed before Jack noticed that Dusty had begun to physically transform. The first thing he noticed was that he was looking perkier, his fur having taken on a nice luster and tail having grown even fluffier. Even his funny rabbit buckteeth looked more uniform and straighter. Jack chalked this down to the Mob clearly reveling in his new home, even to the point of becoming the church's unofficial mascot. Jack was surprised that a dungeon Mob could so willingly make its home outside of its origin dungeon, but the Glitterflit was already unique as it was, and who was he to question the rules of dungeon Mobs.

Then Jack wondered if Dusty was starting to look, to put it politely, a little more rotund. It was hardly unexpected given the abundant amount of treats he and the other clerics gave the Mob daily. Typically, dungeon Mobs sustained themselves on Essence and so didn't have the need to eat, except for adventurer flesh when the occasion called for it. So, Jack hadn't expected the celestial bunny to consume so much. He had a voracious appetite for pretty much anything edible and the occasional inedible thing, which spurred a contest between the clerics to see who could be the first to discover something the Glitterflit refused to eat. One empty pantry and halfway through a storeroom later, Father Richard had proclaimed the contest over without a winner.

Still, Jack had a sneaking suspicion that something more was afoot. Sure, Dusty could just be a well-cared-for dungeon Mob, pleased with his newfound lot in life, or could he be about to evolve into something more?

Jack himself had begun to change as well. He began to feel more at ease when channeling celestial Essence, sometimes able to channel it alone for a few seconds before, inevitably, fire Essence crept in. Disregarding the random patches of burnt walls, Father Richard had given him encouragement that he was on the path towards a breakthrough.

Everything came to a head at once. Jack had taken out Dusty for a mid-morning stroll to the dungeon. He had no intention of going inside—the memories of his last visit still occupied his mind, and he also feared that Dusty would change his mind and decide to remain in his original home. He hated to admit it, but the Mob had given him a purpose in life he had never known before. Instead of waking up each day and focusing on everything that could possibly go wrong, taking care of the little creature gave him something fun to do and preoccupied his mind.

Arriving at the entrance, he stopped. The entrance of the dungeon looked odd as if no light was emitted from inside. A sign had been posted describing the new conditions that adventurers had found inside: mutated Mobs, impossible traps, and swarms of creatures that fought as if they suffered from no pain. Just at that moment, a group came running out of the entrance, shouting and screaming, their armor hanging from them by a thread.

One of them saw Jack and gestured as if to wave him away. "It's not worth it! The dungeon's gone mad!"

Jack shuddered. He had heard rumors that something was deeply wrong with the dungeon, even as crowds of adventurers still jammed its tunnels in search of huge loot rewards. Father Richard had returned from a few council meetings with a grave look on his face. When pressed, he simply shook his head, but the word was that the Mages of Mountaindale were contemplating intervening if the situation didn't improve.

He began to walk in the other direction when suddenly, Dusty's ears stood up, and his face became instantly alert. With a small screech, he leaped out of Jack's hands and ran as fast as Jack had ever seen him go. For a moment, Jack simply stared in awe at the sprinting figure. Was there such thing as Mob racing competitions? Maybe he could earn a little bit of money on the side...

With a start, he realized Dusty's intended destination. Of course, the dungeon. Letting loose a shout of frustration, he launched into a sprint of his own.

"Dusty, what in the abyss are you doing, you crazy dungeon Mob! Don't go in there, that's a dungeon!"

Jack fully realized how insane he sounded and was thankful nobody was around to hear him.

Try as he might, he couldn't catch up, and the little, white blur slipped into the darkness of the dungeon. Jack stopped outside, panting, a feeling of dread beginning to take over him. This was the last thing he wanted to do, the last place on this forsaken mountain he wanted to enter. Still, his loyalty to the apparently masochistic Glitterflit triumphed over his sense of self-preservation.

He crept inside, expecting to get attacked at any moment. He pulled out the pendant Father Richard had gifted him and waved it around, hoping to dispel the all-encompassing darkness. A few seconds passed. Nothing happened.

Jack exhaled in relief. Maybe the dungeon was taking a day off from its insanity. But then what explained the fleeing group from earlier? And where the abyss had Dusty gone?

He lit a fireball in his hand, hoping to light up the entrance chamber if even slightly. Again, it appeared deserted—nobody mining, no adventurers, no Mobs, just eerie silence. He moved into the herb garden, and the same type of scene greeted him. In a way, he felt more frightened than as if facing off against the usual set of Mobs. At least those he could predict and prepare for. Right now, he had no idea what to expect.

Stepping into the Basher warren, a grisly sight greeted him. Corpses of Bashers were strewn about, not yet reabsorbed. The few remaining alive appeared weak, some twitching when they saw him, as if to attack, before cowering in fear and running back into the shadows. At the center of the room, Raile lay on its side, its granite armor twisted into misshapen lumps and lesions covering the exposed skin. It wailed in pain, its eyes tightly closed and its body rocking back and forth as if listening to a haunting melody it couldn't put out of its mind.

Dusty was running in circles around it, letting out a stream of nervous, high-pitched squeaks. Jack recalled that the Glitterflit's original mission had been to heal Raile whenever it was mortally injured, the type of mid-fight surprise that could earn the dungeon a few extra adventurer deaths. Seeing Jack, Dusty jumped on top of the large Boss Mob and began to glow in its familiar, golden aura.

After a moment, the lesions disappeared, and Raile stopped performing its tortuous ritual. It gingerly opened its eyes and began to ease itself up into a standing position. At that moment, Dusty's ability expired, the lesions quickly reappeared, and Raile collapsed to the ground. Dusty jumped off and began running in circles again, waiting for its ability to recharge.

Jack was horrified. As far as he could tell, the two Mobs would be locked into performing this cycle for as long as the dungeon stayed mad. He knew it was up to him to somehow intervene.

He felt Essence flow along his meridians, only the stomach one remaining blocked. Dusty stopped its running and looked at him expectantly. It began to invoke its Mend ability again, and celestial Essence flooded the room. Jack concentrated as hard as he could on the blockage stopping the Essence from leaving his stomach. If he could just get past this one last hurdle, maybe he could save Raile and prove himself worthy of calling himself a cleric.

He concentrated deeply on the joy he had felt over these past few weeks, the compassion he had developed for Rusty, the purpose that his life had finally found. No longer was he just the child prodigy who constantly evoked disappointment in the eyes of his teachers. He was a cleric, for abyss sake. He had saved a vulnerable Glitterflit, and he would save its brethren too.

The Essence burst from his stomach, tracing along the affinity channel to his knee, then traveling up to his mouth, before down his arm and out from his palm. Celestial Essence poured from him, mixing into Dusty's aura and greatly intensifying the healing power. He also calmly cut off any fire Essence from leaving him. He found himself grinning from astonishment.

Raile lifted into the air, bathed in golden light. The lesions flickered and disappeared, and its armor realigned. Its eyes cleared completely, finally free of the endless song of insanity. It gently came to a rest on the ground again, then launched into a giant hop from excitement. Dusty did a little celebratory dance of its own before lying down in exhaustion.

Jack felt himself stagger, his body overwhelmed from having his final meridian open. A sudden upwelling of happiness overtook him. He really thought this moment would never come. Especially after healing a dungeon Mob Boss, of all things. Life could sure be surprising!

The thought of which should have prepared him for yet another development. With a startling snap, the nub on Dusty's head extended into a full-fledged horn. A foot in length, it was almost as long as Dusty itself. The Glitterflit's head sagged from the sudden weight, but Dusty gritted his teeth in determination and lifted its head up with pride.

Befuddled, Jack stared at the Mob, now a fascinating mix of rabbit and unicorn, the most elusive of celestial-oriented Beasts. He checked its abilities and found that Mend had been replaced with Salvation. He had never come across such an ability in his studies at the Church and had no idea what it meant. A problem to consult Father Richard on potentially. He scooped up the tired Dusty, reached out to give Raile a friendly pat before thinking twice about it, then strode from the room and towards the exit. His entire body reverberated with excitement and anticipation for his future.

CHAPTER FIVE

More time passed, during which Jack and Dusty both found themselves continuing to progress in new and interesting ways. Studying under Father Richard, Jack reached the long-awaited C-ranks and began training every day to catch-up on the techniques that had eluded him thus far. With a flourish, he could launch a celestial missile in one hand and a fireball in the other. Better yet, he could safely heal others and still wield holy fire at will. Dang, it felt good to be a cleric!

Dusty had yet to use its new Salvation ability, but he did seem to enjoy using his horn to great effect. When hungry, he poked you. When you came around a corner, and he was feeling mischievous, he tried to trip you. If you were a flying insect that buzzed around his head, you very much risked being gored to death.

The Glitterflit also seemed to a little bit smarter, as if fulfilling its mission one final time with Raile had allowed it to move beyond its original Mob instincts and begin to act more like a typical animal. He not only continued to eat everything in sight but would beg each morning for time to play, go on walks, and spend time with the other Brothers. He loved spending time bathed in celestial Essence and would creep and hide under the church's altar, often to the astonishment of parishioners. He even had a favorite spot high up on the mountain that made up the bulk of the dungeon's territory, where every so often the clouds would part, and sunlight would fall in a particular way so that the ground would sparkle and an energizing breeze would pass over and make the trees and plants whistle. Dusty would simply stand and soak it all in, while Jack would sit down to cultivate while he waited. Eventually, the moment would pass, and Dusty would jump into Jack's arms and demand to be returned to town. Whether by the position of his ears or twitch of his tail, Dusty never failed to communicate what he wanted.

One day, returning from a jog in the crisp, mountain air, the town came into view. Jack immediately felt within himself a sense of deep wrongness, his entire being weighed down by a heavy presence, and he detected a major uptick in infernal Essence. Conversely, celestial Essence seemed to be in retreat, fleeing from the onslaught of dark energy.

He noticed then streams of fire billowing into the air, appearing to come from a walking army of undead pouring through the town's destroyed gates. Someone had attempted to blast the undead with a firestorm. The skin on the zombies sloughed off into fetid puddles of miasma, leaving behind burnt, repulsive skeletons, which kept moving, undeterred from their march. Groups of cultivators gathered and began to combat the invaders and were able to do some damage to the weaker frontlines. However, the lockstep nature of the army demonstrated that a higher power was driving them, one that could brush aside the lower-ranked defenders without a second thought.

From his overhead view, Jack immediately searched for the church, positioned on the other side of town from the undead. He breathed a sigh of relief upon seeing it unmarked, a beacon of hope. Still, the settlement was barely a town, and it wouldn't be long before the church came under fire. He poured Essence into his legs, and he zipped forward as if propelled by the wind.

He reached the building just as the undead began to stream towards it. He quickly slipped through a side entrance, thoroughly locking the door behind him. Just then he heard a commotion from up the hall. One of the Brothers was berating a dust-covered man who stood next to a small hole in the building wall. Jack employed an invisibility aura and crept over to listen. He caught the tail end of the conversation, something about the Brother, who was a known stick-in-the-mud and someone who Jack routinely avoided, taking the man to see Father Richard. Perfect, that would relieve Jack of needing to go inform the church leader about what was happening if he didn't know already. Instead, he could see to his own matters.

He quickly darted to the cleric residential hall and ran to the end. The earlier sense of wrongness deepened, causing dread to overtake him. His bedroom door had been ripped off its hinges and hastily discarded. He could hear the shuffling of feet inside and low grumble of words, spoken by some sort of monster.

"Come here, my sweet. Don't want you a nice, delicious carrot?"

Jack burst into the room, channeling Essence into his aura to block incoming attacks and whipping up a lance of holy fire in his right hand. He faltered upon being greeted by the sight in front of him, though.

A bulky figure stood in his room. It appeared to be made up of body parts sewn together, each a different color of decay. Since they didn't match or line up well, the figure appeared monstrous with a domed back, one skinny, green arm, one thick, brown one, and legs that looked like they had come from wolves. Just the head still looked vaguely human, a mop of brown hair obscuring a pallid face.

On the other side of the room, Dusty had backed himself into the corner. He was shaking from fear but kept his horn positioned in front of him and wore an expression of defiance.

Seeing Jack crash into the room, the figure spun around and bellowed in rage.

"Stay out of this, cleric! I will slaughter all who get in my way."

Jack drew back his hand to launch the holy fire but stopped mid-throw. Now able to see the monster's face, he drew in his breath sharply.

"Nick...! What in the abyss happened to you?"

The figure snarled at first, but recognition settled on its face after a moment as well. The familiar roguish grin took its place.

"Well, who do we have here but our friend Brother Jack. Managed to survive our little ambush that one day, eh? In fact, you've even reached the C-ranks. If I didn't know any better, I'd say we might have helped you. What doesn't kill you makes you stronger, right?" He winked at Jack, the expression made grotesque on his inhuman face.

Jack attempted to repress the fiery anger that bubbled inside him. "Truly, I owe you a debt of gratitude. Thank you so much for attempting to kill me. Now, what are you doing in my room? And why do you reek of infernal corruption?"

"Oh yes, you do owe me, and I know just the thing you can give me as thanks. As for me, well, you must have heard of The Master by now. The most powerful necromancer on the planet, he who will sow the Earth with the seeds of destruction and give birth to a new order. I performed an errand for him. Not an easy one, I must tell you. He gave me this delightful form as my reward." He gestured all over his body with his green-colored hand.

"See, he killed me and brought me back to life, composing my new body of leftover parts from his experiments. Something about my old form being weak, prone to greed and jealousy. In this form, I only serve The Master. His will commands me." His expression had gone stoic, all traces of his formerly roguish personality wiped away.

Jack shook his head in astonishment before steeling his resolve. "Whatever it is this Master has asked of you, you can do it somewhere else. Now, leave before I force you to."

The thing-that-was-Nick let out a cackle. "Hand over the dungeon Mob, and I'll happily be on my way." He held out his other hand, dark and covered in fur. "The Master requests it. You will obey me or face the consequences."

A month ago, Jack may have run away. Or lit his robe on fire. Or mostly likely simply died in vain while trying to fight the creature. This version of Jack though, there was no way would he give up so easily.

He quickly pulled the blanket off his bed and channeled holy fire Essence into it, causing it to smolder and then light up intensely. He threw it over Nick and then leaped over to the corner with the Glitterflit. Scooping it up in the crook of his arm, he dove under the now-burning figure and began to haul his abyss-fearing butt down the hall.

An immense roar reverberated from his room, and barely a second later, a large fist connected with his back, sending him tumbling. He threw Dusty as far away from him as possible to keep from landing on the Mob and, most importantly, its horn. He heard a yelp as the Mob skid into the wall, its eyes dazed and confused by the rapid turn of events. He himself landed with a thud, face-down. Previously, such a punch would have wiped him out completely, but at the C-ranks, he felt ready to spring back in action right away.

Feeling a rush of air coming towards him, Jack shifted the Essence within his aura all towards his back. Nick's fist collided with the aura, which proved dense enough to stop the blow. Nick staggered back, caught by surprise.

Jack used both hands to push himself off the ground. Nick stampeded toward him, his face contorted with rage. Jack dodged, then pushed off the wall to position himself in Nick's blind spot. He quickly spun together a lasso of holy fire and tossed it around the monster.

Nick screamed from a mix of fury and pain, welts forming wherever the fire touched. Jack pulled the lasso tighter, doing as much as he could to immobilize him. He spotted Dusty and scooped him up again.

"You think you'll get very far? There's an A-ranked necromancer out there. He'll destroy you without a second thought," Nick managed to yell between gritted teeth.

Jack ignored him and fled the hallway. Emerging back into the main church, he could see the shambling forms of the undead surrounding the building. Clerics scrambled around the church, boosting the defenses and beating back any undead who broke through doors or windows. A few lay stunned on the ground, appearing to have been hit by enough infernal Essence to take them out of commission. Father Richard was nowhere to be seen.

Jack paused to consider his options. If he stayed in the church, he risked Nick getting free or the undead breaking through. Better to leave the building and hopefully find a safer place. That's when he thought of Dusty's favorite spot up on the side of the mountain. He figured none of the undead would make their way up there. Whatever their reason for being here, he doubted that kidnapping Dusty was high up on the list.

Jack found the hole made by the dust-covered man from before and squeezed himself through, then gently pulled Dusty through as well. The Mob had grown agitated, the loud bangs and yells of fighting startling him. He covered his eyes with his long, floppy ears.

"I'll keep you safe. Come on, I know just the place for us to go."

Halfway up the mountain, Jack began to feel the ground shake. At the start of the path was Nick, not only freed but appearing to have gone into some type of berserker mode, his eyes glowing red and the veins of his muscles bulging. The creature let out a fearsome howl, its mouth hanging open and panting. While the brown hair remained, the rest of the creature's face no longer resembled the man Jack remembered. It seemed as though its last remaining shred of humanity had been lost, and it was now fully consumed by an appetite for death.

Jack pushed himself harder than he ever had and sped even faster up the path. He had an idea. One of the first things they had learned as a new cleric was an incantation to turn undead. At the level they had practiced and so as to avoid using too much personal Essence, all it did was push the undead back a number of feet. With the right components to draw upon and the more powerful the cultivator, the incantation could be upgraded to have more effects, from paralyzing the undead to searing them. Pulling out his ever-handy pendant, Jack thought he might be able to take it a step even further.

Aware that he didn't have long but also that if he screwed up the incantation, he was likely to blow himself up, Jack strove for a balance between quickly and correctly making all of necessary gestures and words. He held out the pendant in front of him, focusing on its capacity to break infernal bonds.

The form of the creature began to come into view. Feeling his pulse quicken, Jack spoke the incantation's last word. He felt Essence rip out of him, flowing along his meridians and through the pendant, then giving shape to an enormous beam of light. The drain of the Essence started to become painful, and it occurred to Jack that he had overestimated his own power. He had no idea if one could drop down an entire rank and wondered if he was about to find out. As the pain began to become unbearable, he felt the familiar nuzzle of soft fur on his leg. A new source of celestial Essence poured into the pendant, quickly making up the difference needed to complete the incantation.

The creature crested the hill. Seeing the beam of light, it faltered, momentarily taken aback, but then the seemingly weak, green arm twisted in a gesture of its own and an array of black arrows materialized. The arrows sped towards the beam and collided with an enormous explosion of energy. A shockwave composed of chaos Essence spread and upon hitting Jack, immediately toppled him over.

Time passed by, during which Jack found it impossible to grasp any thoughts. Past memories would suddenly emerge into his mind, followed by hazy visions of a distant future. In between, he knew that he still existed in the present but had little awareness of his surroundings. All he could sense was the touch of soft fur. His thoughts became more and more distant, and the world steadily melted away around him.

CHAPTER SIX

Abruptly, the confusion parted. He attempted to open his eyes, but nothing happened. Instead, it was if he could feel the world around him directly. The rock beneath him, tasting of baked clay. The breeze, as crisp as ever, smelling of a distant, dying burning. A little splash of water below him, the Essence of which he... pulled... inside himself without even realizing it.

<What... happened? Where am I?>

"You're alive!" a small and slightly shrill voice rang out.

<Who are you? And what do you mean I'm alive? Of course I am. I was just... uh, my name is...">

"Give it a second. Your memories should return." All at once, Jack was flooded by an onslaught of images.

<Hold on, hold on. The last thing I remembered was the shockwave of chaos energy hitting me. Did something happen to explain why I feel so... formless?>

"That's actually the easy part to answer. You're a dungeon now."

Jack's stomach plummeted, or it would have if he still had a stomach. <Excuse me, what in the abyss are you talking about!? How can I be a dungeon? And who in the abyss are you? Tell me now!>

"You always did curse a lot for a cleric. First things first, stretch out your senses. You're only concentrating on your immediate surroundings. Focus on expanding until you reach the sound of my voice."

Jack did his best to follow the instructions, reaching out with his awareness until he arrived at a small form that was... furry?

<Dusty? Is that you? You're able to talk!>

"Right you are. I think I was already on my way to becoming a Beast, but that much chaos energy was enough to speed along the process greatly. In fact, I've already reached a high enough rank to be able to speak. Which is great for you, since you're pretty much helpless now!"

<Well, that's amazing! I always knew you were a special dungeon Mob, but now, can you explain how the abyss I got into this state?>

Although Jack no longer had eyes, he sensed the Mob blush. "About that. Let's see, after our beam of celestial light collided with the infernal arrows let loose by that hideous thing, the chaos energy shockwave created was so powerful that I think it permanently damaged your brain. You seemed to go in a coma, and I had no idea if you would ever wake up. So I used my ability, Salvation."

Jack felt the urge to rub his temples and rued his inability to do so. <Wait, so you're telling me that you turned me into a dungeon?>

The rabbit shifted uncomfortably. "I didn't know that would actually happen. I just thought it was an enhanced version of Mend and I could cure you of your sickness, similar to what we did with Raile. I think that is what should have actually happened, but the chaos energy interfered." He took an audible, rabbit-sized breath. "You see, when I used my ability, your soul began drawing from your body, and instead of being healed, it was directed into that necklace you've always carried around your neck."

<You mean my family heirloom? I thought that thing was worthless.>

"It most likely was, but again, the chaos energy seemed to have had an enormous effect on it. I believe it turned it into a soul gem."

<That's incredible! Except now I'm stuck inside a stupid stone!> Jack's moods whiplashed in his mind as he struggled to process all of this information.

"Listen, Jack. You're the first celestial dungeon to exist in decades. If word ever gets out, a lot of people will try to destroy you. I know this is all insane, obviously for me too, but we don't have much time to waste. We need to find you a home far away from this mountain, where you can become powerful enough to protect yourself."

Jack's emotional state stabilized as he began to ponder his future.

<You're right... My life, as I knew it, is gone. I'm an abyss-freaking dungeon now. Are you sure though, given all of that, maybe it wouldn't just be easier to put me out of my misery? You don't want to be stuck at my side.>

Dusty smiled his best rabbit grin. "I owe you everything, Jack. You saved me, and you took care of me. Besides, I'm just as much as an oddity as you are. Who knows what that so-called Master wanted to do with me or what others will try? I know dungeons are supposed to have wisps as guides, but I'd like to be yours instead. Between the two of us, we can find a reason to exist, maybe even thrive and be happy."

Jack pondered. Despite himself, his despair gave way to excitement. Sure, being a human was all he had ever known, but it wasn't as if he had exactly loved being a human, spending much of his existence trying to shrug off the mantle of failure. Maybe being a dungeon would allow him to do much more good than he ever could as a human.

<You know, Dusty, you're right. I'm not opposed to the idea. When I was lost my sanity before, floating in between the past and the future, I actually saw a vision—one in which the life-giving energy that you and I can provide can save this world,

banishing the darkness and leading to a golden age of knowledge, thought, and peace. Maybe we can help turn that vision into reality.>

The rabbit nodded thoughtfully. "I think you're on to something, my formerly human friend. Come on, let's find our new home."

With a graceful dip of his head, Dusty looped the necklace containing Jack's soul gem around his horn. He set off in a trot down the path, a sunset blazing behind them.

Splat!
By: Raymond Johnson

Chapter One

I cheered as the last adventurer fell over, his head hitting the floor a second or two before his body. The victory wasn't surprising; he wasn't supposed to be here. The adventurer wasn't ranked for our floor—neither were his buddies—but they came here anyway. Now, they are no more. The only truly surprising thing was that I got to observe a simultaneous double decapitation, as one of my Goblin comrades brought their sword blade up to and through the adventurer's neck as his ax cut off the head of his killer. That was why I was cheering; it was an impressive display of skill.

I would say that you don't see this sort of thing every day, but in this dungeon, it happens something like... oh, two to three times a week. Since no one else is around, the dungeon— the place I live—will absorb them and everything they own. I like to watch it when that happens. One second they're there; then they start to melt like snow in hot sunlight, and the next instant they're gone. The dungeon doesn't even burp afterward. It's probably the most impressive thing I'll ever see in my life.

Oh! Right! My name is Splat, and I'm a Goblin. I'm not an important Goblin like the Bobs. The Bobs are *essential* to helping the dungeon keep things running. They, the Bobs, are legion. There's just one of me. I'm a grunt, and I'm okay with that. I don't hold a rank, and beyond the basic transformation to Dungeon Goblin, I've never been upgraded like some of the others of my race.

Altogether, that means I'm comparatively weak, so they shove me into the front lines to greet all the dungeon divers. I'm surprised they don't call me entrée because the adventurers tend to eat me alive whenever we meet. Technically, I suppose I'm more of an amuse-bouche than an appetizer, let alone an entrée. I just make them hungrier for *more*. I rile them up, give them a taste for blood.

While this sounds... *dark*, it's really alright by me. *Somebody* has to take that first spear to the eye or sword to the throat. It makes me feel like I'm contributing to the dungeon in my own way. The life of a Goblin isn't all that bad, not down here anyway. I remember what it was like before we got here. I remember the hunger and the dying. I remember the disease and the fear. The Great Spirit—that's our name for the dungeon—makes sure we all get three meals a day, we all have a place to sleep, and we get clothing, weapons, and most importantly, a purpose.

I really like having a purpose, even if it is dying before everyone else. I get all the perks that the other Goblins get, which is basically I get to kill dungeon-delving adventurers on occasion, and I'm resurrected if I die. Beyond that, I have a lot of free time and get to do what I want—so long as I don't hurt the dungeon with my antics. But... I don't like free time. Free time bores me. I enjoy battling the dungeoneers! More to the point, I enjoy slowing down the adventurers by sacrificing my life so that my fellow Goblins can kill them.

You may be wondering why my name is Splat. That isn't the name I entered the dungeon with; back then I was called Kłótnia. I'm named after my grandfather's favorite uncle, or so I'm told. I understand that he was killed by a falling boulder, so I come by the name honestly. I kinda feel bad because I get to respawn whenever I get killed. Poor, original Kłótnia, however, only had his one chance to make a splatty impression. The others started calling me Splat after I was crushed by a falling tower wall, a stalactite, a giant warrior that I helped to kill who fell on me and killed me even *after* he died, and the last straw was when I ended up getting flattened by a giant warhammer wielded by a screaming barbarian. Personally, I think that they started calling me Splat just because no one could pronounce Kłótnia, but hey, if the boot fits... then you're not a Goblin.

It happened so often—my being crushed to death—that I asked the Bob that oversaw our battalion if I had offended the Great Spirit of the dungeon in some way. I suspected that I was the butt of some sort of dark humor, but Bob-thirteen assured me that wasn't the case and then gave me the *nicest* helmet to wear. It almost fits, too. The helm is made of bronze and carved with—what I'm told—is an engraving that looks like the dungeon's entrance from the outside world. It's my most treasured possession. I keep it on my pillow because I don't want it to get damaged by the next thing that smashes me flat or for an adventurer trying to claim it.

Losing it would just make me sad. It's so *shiny!* I spend most of my off hours polishing it. The others all wear their helmets, and it doesn't do them much good. Eventually, we all get killed by delvers. My helmet is pristine. It is probably the only clean and intact item on our whole level. Now, I don't want to talk too badly about the other Goblins, but they aren't very clean. I know for a fact that our sergeant has not bathed since the second day after he arrived here. He feels that he is cleaned up when he respawns, so why bother? His clothes are so stiff and inflexible that they now offer him extra protection as if they were some sort of leather armor. Actually, I have to admit that is pretty cool. I only wear a loincloth, and *no one* wants a stiff loincloth.

The other Goblins *really* hate the adventurers. That's okay. We *are* Goblins after all; Goblins and humanity have never really mixed together well. I'm not sure if we still qualify as just 'Goblins' anymore, though. The Great Spirit has changed us in lots of little ways; he knew he could rebuild us. He had the magic and the Essence. He made us better than we were... stronger... faster... smarter. I'd thought that it had cost the dungeon a lot of Essence to make us this way, but Bob said while he wasn't sure. He thought it was very cheap per Goblin; that makes us the best, most intelligent, and most Essence-efficient dungeon creatures.

I do have a secret, though. I'm not like the other Goblins. Big surprise there, huh? Technically, we are all immortal. Is that the right word? No matter how often we get killed, the dungeon respawns us. That means he remakes us. We just reappear out of nowhere as hale and hearty as we were before a dungeon party killed us. In general, our memories return up to our last respawn. Basically we don't remember how we died, or the people we were fighting when it happened. Sometimes, we get lucky, and one or two of will outlive the others, and they'll regale us of the glorious and gruesome ways that we expired. The others really cherish the storytellers; they keep us from having to read at night before bed. Ugh. Reading. It's better to have someone tell you the story. Trust me on this—you don't read for fun.

I'm different, though. I don't know *why*; I just am. I've been this way since the dungeon first altered us. See, I *remember*. I've never forgotten one second of my multiple lives. My recall is not only complete, but it is *total*. I not only remember each life, but I can tell you about every second that I have lived. I can tell you what color feather Gruntswick, my bunkmate, wore out to battle one hundred days ago.

Which is pretty annoying because Gruntswick has an atrocious sense of style, and I have to endure him wearing a leopard print vest while wearing a zebra-striped loincloth. You know when people see something so horrible that say they can never unsee it? They should bunk with Gruntswick for a week. That will clear their head of any other unwanted images. I'll tell you that for free. Of course, the memories it leaves you with will be the stuff of nightmares.

Roommates aside, I alone can also recall every time I was killed. My memories stop at the time of death and pick right up at respawn. I don't know what happens in-between. To me, it feels instantaneous. One second, I'm doing my best pancake imitation, a weapon being the last thing that goes through my mind, and the next, I'm perfectly fine and ready to face the next batch of adventurers. All in all, it is a pretty seamless transition.

Right now, you're probably thinking one of two things. First, you probably think that I'm not very good at keeping secrets since I just told you my biggest one and we've only just met. You've got me there. Thankfully, no one ever listens to me. Gruntswick usually knocks me out of his way or tells me what to do. He wouldn't listen to me if I told him he was on fire. In fact, I know he wouldn't because he let himself go up in flames after an adventurer tossed some oil on him. I told him not to grab a torch that they'd thrown at him, but he did it anyway, and he lit up the dungeon like he was a fire elemental drinking a cask of whiskey.

I do have one friend, Molbogious. He's actually my *best* friend because he doesn't yell at me to go away whenever I'm near him. I don't actually know if I am *his* friend; he *may* not know my name. I'm not entirely sure. It is about fifty-fifty either way on whether he knows I exist.

So, enough about me. This is actually a story about how I saved the dungeon.

CHAPTER TWO

Gruntswick's head slid across the dungeon floor like a curling stone tossed by an ogre. Yes, Goblins in the colder regions do curl for fun. Well, fun might be a strong word. They curl so they can forget that they are starving while also building some muscle mass. His head spun around three times, coming to rest directly at my feet. He had a vague but crooked, little smile on his face like he'd just heard the funniest joke ever told just before he died.

His eyes stared off into space, but they did that normally. The only time I ever saw Gruntswick focus on something was when someone slipped a plate of food in front of him. That might be why he lost his head so often—daydreaming about his next meal and what-not. He kept his what-not beside his bed and stored little knick-knacks that he'd taken from dead delvers in there. It's made of rough wood and is barely tacked together... but it's his. A good what-not is hard to come by in a dungeon.

Where was I? Right! As I said previously, decapitations happen pretty regularly around here. If the Great Spirit didn't keep absorbing all the loose skulls, we could build a pretty impressive pyramid of heads. Maybe even a wall of skulls to scare away our enemies. I heard that we weren't allowed to keep them for that purpose because we were awful architects; I suppose that's a fair assessment since Gruntswick's what-not was supposed to have been an end table.

I casually kicked the head aside and put on my artificial snarl. I'm not really all that violent nor am I intimidating, so snarling is hard for me and I have to fake it sometimes. One of the Boblins—that's what we call the Goblins named Bob behind their backs—used to tell us in training that we needed a War

Face. They would make us yell until we became hoarse and spit blood. I really worked on mine until the training Boblin said I should stop. I guess I have a face for armistice. If my mother had been alive, she'd have been so proud. I never thought I'd ever get an *army stance*! I kept practicing making my face and yelling until I would reflexively vomit blood if I managed a smile when I raised my voice.

This time, I succeeded in keeping my gorge down and didn't spew a sanguine spray all over my attackers as I made my angry face. I'm certain that they'd appreciated my courtesy because one of them said, "Thank the gods, I thought that little fellow was gonna puke all over us."

I thrust my spear forward, and it was easily batted aside by a big barbarian fellow. He was wearing a green fur cloak and verdant breeches. Strange what the mind focuses on, right? He laughed maniacally as he swung his huge, two-handed blade over his head in the process of deflecting my weapon. My spear arced through the air as if he'd aimed it right at his companion's foot, and the tip drove into his boot—nailing the invader to the floor.

Two of the barbarian's companions gave the barbarian the stink eye, while the human with the stick in his foot began to look woozy. I guess he was okay seeing other people's blood but not that of his own. A fountain of crimson juice climbed as high as his eyes, pulsing in rhythm to his heartbeat. The color drained from his face, and he feebly tried to pull the spear from his foot.

Molbogious took the moment of distraction to step from the shadows behind the barbarian. He drove his weapon forward, just below the barbarian's shoulder blade until it burst from his rib cage in a vermillion gout of viscera and body fluids. The sudden shower made me wish I carried a towel with me. The look of surprise that crossed the big man's face told me that

Molly had gotten in a very lucky shot because the light fled from the barbarian's eyes, and his mouth made an 'O' shape before he hit the floor.

Somehow, I managed to step out of the way of the plunging giant. His impact on the floor practically lifted me off of my feet. Unfortunately, I wasn't able to keep my feet beneath me, falling ass over tea kettle on to my rear end with a loud *wumpf*. Thankfully, my bottom already had a crack in it, or it would have split wide open.

The other dungeoneers weren't as unfocused as the barbarian—or their friend with a spear in his foot imitating a red water fountain—and in short order, they dismembered and eviscerated my good buddy before he could count to three. Granted, the last time Molbogious managed to count that high it took him an hour, and I'm fairly certain that he skipped the first two numbers. The point is, my good buddy wasn't going to be enjoying his victory with a hearty ale back at the fort this evening. At least not *this* version of him.

A duo of adventurers turned to look at me, dripping swords at the ready, and I realized that I was weaponless. It was a position that I often found myself in, and to be frank, I was stunned to have survived up to this point. I honestly thought the barbarian was going to fall on me when he went down.

Inspired by my roommate and bestie's foolhardiness, I stepped forth and grasped the shaft of my spear. My intent was to pull it out and make a brave show of things before I got squished. I managed to pull the spear back and towards me but could not dislodge it from the foot it now called home. This reminded me of a rumor I hear from adventurers, who often spoke of about some sword in a stone that was impossible to remove. Now I understood.

I simply lacked the upper body strength necessary to free the spear, and no matter how hard I tugged on it, the weapon would not budge. It was at that moment that a problem I have dealt with my entire life decided to raise its vile hand. Sweaty palms. I get them whenever I become stressed, nervous, tired, hungry, aroused, sick, angry, happy, or any other number of emotional states. The condition makes it impossible for me to hold anything for more than a second. Things in my palm just *squirt* across the room, as if they had been shot from a catapult when I get that way.

I had a tenuous grip on the haft of the spear to begin with, and in spite of my attempts to keep hold of the weapon, it snapped from my hands and sailed right into the spraying foot man's face. The shaft impacted with a terrible *crack* and a crunch of broken bones. The cultivator's eyes rolled in different directions, resulting in a reverse cross-eyed look, and he fell on to his back like a puppet with cut strings.

I was as shocked as the newly dead man, although my eyes didn't rotate around to look at each of my ears like his did. I couldn't *believe* that I'd actually killed someone, and naturally, Molbogious and Gruntswick were already dead and would never believe me when I told them what happened. My state of shock was overwhelming, and I was frozen in place until I heard one of the men say, "That little turd just killed Fezzeek and Ennigo!"

My head rotated involuntarily to look at them as they began to advance on me once again. My body refused to listen as my mind yelled at my feet to start running in the other direction. I find it ironic that my mind raced while I stood stock still. Desperately, I tried to think of some way to escape or defend myself. I played out a hundred scenarios in my head, and each of them ended with one of the dungeoneers stomping me to death.

The one on the right—a thin, willowy man of medium human height—carried his curved sword in one hand and a stiletto in his other. His black hair was long and stringy, matted to his head from exertion. I could see that he was missing a front tooth, and I idly wondered if he had *just* lost it or if it had been gone for a long time. I studied his face so that I would remember him the next time he entered the dungeon; I would use that knowledge to stay away from him. As far as possible. His companion was a tall, lanky man with curly, red hair, freckles, and had a part of the tip of his nose missing. He held a mace, and I instantly knew who was going to be the one dealing my death blow. He wore a malicious grin, which was intimidating enough that he might have some Goblin lineage in him.

That thought snapped me out of my stupor, and I turned to face them. I wasn't happy—since I kept telling my feet to carry me in the other direction for as far and fast as possible—but I was so scared that my nervous system was working in reverse. I don't mind dying. I do it a lot, but these guys looked like they were going to make my death take as long as possible. I could feel my ulcer rupturing, and my stomach contents begin to roil. It was not a pleasant feeling, so I did the only thing I could think of... I made my war face.

Instantly, a torrent of the foulest smelling, vile mixture of stomach acid, partially digested chunks food, and blood fired from my mouth and splattered into the red-headed man's mouth. He instinctively swallowed, but then realized what he was doing and tried to spit it out. Instead, he began to aspirate, choking on my stomach contents. He began to retch but could not get a clear path to his mouth from his stomach and so his own stomach contents shot out of his nostrils like a dragon breathing fire. All of his airways fully obstructed, he began to turn a pretty shade of blue that did not complement his hair.

I, myself, hadn't stopped the gorefest either. Unlike the human, I knew enough to let nature take its course and continued to hose the area down in a rapid-fire succession of one vile stream after another. Before the willowy man had taken more than two steps in my direction, I had already coated the floor with my vital fluids. It simultaneously made the floor slick, then sticky. I couldn't look at it; even Goblins have limits to what grossness they can endure. I *did* begin to backpedal away from my greasy stalker.

Seriously, I was a little shocked that the man didn't even try to help his choking friend. He just stepped over him *very* carefully with barely a glance to see how he was doing. The blue man's eyes were bulging, and his blood vessels looked like fat worms crawling just below the surface of his skin. The thought of worms made my stomach rumble. I had just vacated all of my tummy's contents, and worms were really tasty if you fried them right. Don't judge me. I don't look at you with sanctimonious scorn when you eat beef. Let's see how hungry you are after you just emptied everything you'd eaten in the last twelve hours. Fried worms are a delicacy.

It was then that I realized that I still carried my dagger, and I pulled it from my belt with a flourish. It wasn't nearly as impressive as his stiletto, but it could carve a rat up in a pinch. The cultivator peered past his stringy hair and eyed my dagger with disdain. I held the blade out towards him, pointing it right at his head. My hand trembled and shook beyond my capacity to steady it, and he could clearly see the blade wavering in the air. My arm vibrated so badly that it began to make a small circle in the air with my knife. I panicked, fearing that I was going to drop my only means of defense... so I squeezed even harder. At that moment, the shiv shot from my hand faster than a stone from a slingshot. Sweaty palms? It wasn't what I had intended, but I smiled devilishly as the blade found its way into his eye socket.

I hadn't killed him because the knife hadn't penetrated deeply enough to reach his brain or cut a vital artery, but it did blind him. He screamed in pain, dropped his weapons, and reached for his eye. In his haste to remove my weapon, he slipped on the gore on the floor and twisted his leg with a snap. He slid down the wall, agony etched on his face.

A wave of jubilance washed over me. I had not only *survived* the encounter but had actually managed to take most of them out! Besides myself, only Molbogious had managed to kill one of them. Gruntswick hadn't even managed to wound them, and I had *killed* two and wounded a third! Granted, I did so in the most gross and unlikely of ways, but I had still *done* it! Now all I had to do was to pick up one of their own weapons and kill the stringy-haired man with it. My eyes instantly fell upon the red head's mace, and I saw the irony just waiting to happen. I bent down, hefted the heavy truncheon, and took a tentative step towards the fallen warrior.

I struggled but managed to get the abyssal-dratted-heavy mace over my head and within range of his. He looked at me with his one good eye and glared. Had I not been in a position of absolute power, I would have been scared. Alright, full disclosure. I did pee a little but only a *little*. He was scary, okay? I'm not exactly known for my fortitude and bravery in the face of danger. I can barely withstand seeing the toenail of danger, and I am renowned for snatching defeat right out of the jaws of victory.

Before we came to the dungeon, I used to know this old, bat-eared Goblin named Murfee. He always said that if it was going to plan, then I would find a way to flub things. That is the censored version. Murf liked to use what is termed colorful language. His point might have been valid nine times out of ten but not today! Today, I was the one standing over the bodies of my enemies. Today, *I* was the one that would be lauded a hero. That was, of course, when I saw the greasy man had maneuvered himself beside a large, granite pillar, had braced his hand behind it, and was shoving hard enough that it had already begun to topple in my direction. I resigned myself to my fate and watched the nine-foot-tall, thousand-pound chunk of stone careen towards me.

The last sound I heard was my head going *splat*.

CHAPTER THREE

I awoke the next day hungry for some fried worms and wondering if wearing my helmet would have made a difference. Even if it would have, I wouldn't have worn it anyway. It would just be a piece of flattened metal now. I looked around and saw that Gruntswick was already dressed and getting ready for guard duty. He stared off into space, and I wondered what it was he wasn't thinking about today. I began to pull on my boots and wondered why I even bothered.

I never got stabbed, eviscerated, burned alive, eaten, or any one of a million other ways there were to die. I got *splatted*. No amount of armor was going to save me from that marble column that crushed me last night. Idly, I began to wonder where that column had come from. I have a perfect memory, and I didn't recall seeing it there before. In fact, I scanned my memories and saw that it hadn't even been there ten minutes prior to our encounter! Something strange was afoot. That was when I realized that Molbogious was in the room. The smell gave it away; his foot always smelled strange.

I said hello to him, "Hello, Molbogious."

Just like that. He *almost* turned and acknowledged me. What a guy! He'd come to get Gruntswick before they ended up being late for their patrol duty. He smacked my roommate on the side of his face, barely getting Gruntswick's attention. He grabbed him by one of his ears and led him away. I called out, but I don't think he heard me over Grunt's cry of pain, "So long, Molly!"

I slunk down on my bunk and began thinking. There had to be a way to *not* die every time I got in a fight. I began to review all of my deaths. Only this time, I paid attention more to what killed me rather than *how* I'd died. Slowly, a pattern began to form. I noticed that objects that had been used to crush me either seemed to appear out of nowhere when the fights began or moved from other locations without any visible means of assistance. I literally watched a huge flail appear beside the hand of a blond-bearded cleric who had been knocked over by a Goblin named Chadean.

The holy man had lost his weapon minutes before, making him my best-case option to earn a kill. As I approached him, he flailed about—the irony of the terminology does not escape me—looking for anything that he could use for a weapon. Lo and behold, his hand came to rest on a previously non-existent skull-basher.

I kept looking, and in case after case, I found rocks that hadn't been loose before suddenly barely able to keep from crumbling down until I got too close. Large and heavy objects would suddenly go from a stable position to being precariously balanced the moment I came into range. Over and over, weapons would move closer to my foes or would just magically appear from nothingness, only doing so in subtle ways that would not be obvious to anyone that didn't have perfect total recall. My secret suddenly became my greatest asset. I went through all two hundred and seventeen times I had died since I'd arrived in the dungeon, and in every single instance, my demise had been helped along by a mysterious malefactor. My head swam.

I could only come to two conclusions. My first supposition being that the dungeon was doing some sort of secret experiment on me. I was an unknowing guinea pig, just a pawn in the game of life, left spinning on some crazy water wheel that dunked me every so often. If it was the dungeon, then I couldn't complain. The Great Spirit had taken care of me and my people since the moment we'd arrived, and if he got his kicks periodically pounding me into mush, then I wasn't going to say boo.

We were all mooching off of him. It was the least I could do. I was happy to take one for the team, or as in this case, two hundred and seventeen for the team. Like I said at the start of my tale, I had already asked Bob if I had offended the Great Spirit. He'd been adamant in telling me he hadn't the slightest clue of what I was talking about, and by the way, who was I again? However, if I was wrong with that line of thinking, then it could only mean one thing.

Something was in the dungeon, and that something was stalking me. Not only was it stalking me, but it was also killing me repeatedly just like on Groundhogs Day—that day of the year where you just go out and kill groundhogs nonstop for hours until you feel like you've done the same thing over and over so long you go a little mad. It was just like that, but *I* was the groundhog. I didn't have a clue as to what could do that, so I considered going to see my Bob again.

After several minutes of deep thought, I decided against it. Bob would just think my brain had malfunctioned, and the dungeon would just reboot me into an earlier state. If that happened, I wasn't sure if I'd retain my memories or if I would lose them. I could talk to Dani the helpful dungeon Wisp, but she was often preoccupied with a little Wisp of her own and wouldn't have time for me. The dungeon itself wasn't an option.

So, I thought of our old storyteller, Parsna. Parsna was a wise and wizened woman who was old before our people knew what old was. She had become the clan's storyteller and surrogate grandmother for any younglings we had, and she had a wealth of knowledge packed between those ears with white hairs growing out of them. As storytellers went, she was the best.

She could practically make you see what she was speaking about, and if you talked while she was in the middle of a story, she would make you see stars. Her versatility was amazing.

It took me more than an hour to make my way to her. She was in another part of our level, so I meandered past several skirmishes between some Goblins I didn't know and some foolhardy D and F-ranked morons who got too big for their britches and decided to try their hand at taking us on. I kept well and clear of them, not for fear of becoming embroiled in a battle but because I suspected that my unseen enemy could only attack me if I was in the thick of it. I had nothing to *justify* that thought, but it was a solid gut instinct, and I followed it accordingly.

Parsna wasn't hard to find. She rarely left her cooking pot and could be found by its side at any hour, day or night. She sat there mumbling to herself and chewing on what looked to be the inside of her cheek. That was fine since she didn't have any teeth. I looked at her, and in spite of her frailness, I could see an alert and ready mindset well behind her yellow eyes. She spied me coming and spit out whatever she had been gnawing on out on to the ground. It looked like a baby rat. I didn't mind them, but they were a bit gummy for my palette.

"Whatcha want?" she questioned me without hesitation.

"Elder Parsna, my name is–" but she cut me off before I could continue.

Her voice sounded like wrinkled paper. "I know who you are, boy. You're Kłótnia, only you go by that ridiculous name of 'Splat'."

She leaned forward, squeezing one eye shut, causing the one looking at me to bulge out like a fish's eye. Parsna shook her head in disbelief and spit again. "Whatcha wanna ruin a perfectly good name for? You ashamed to be called by a proper Goblin name?"

I gulped. I could also feel water begin to drip down my hands. It was flowing like a waterfall, and even I was repulsed by how voluminous the sweat pouring from my palms was. It was now time for me to shake my head, "No. I am not ashamed. It is just that the others never even acknowledge me if I go by that appellation."

She snorted and then burst into a loud cackle whose sound swarmed around my head like a flurry of bats. Her laughter transitioned from a cackle to choking sounds, and soon, she was coughing up huge balls of phlegm. She casually wiped her mouth with the back of her arm and gave him a wink. "Boy, them others don't know you exist. Don't matter what you call yourself. They ain't never gonna know you is around them."

My blood froze in my veins. It certainly seemed like she knew something that I didn't. "What do you mean?"

"You are all but invisible to them. Your name was all that protected you, and you threw that out like a baby's bathwater." She leaned back into her chair and began to rock. Her face was a withered roadmap of suffering. She had lived a long and hard life before they had ever made it to the tunnels that led to the Great Spirit. She knew things that no other Goblin, not even the Boblins, knew.

"What do you mean, great mother?" My voice was more tremulous than I would have liked, but it got the point across.

"You are plagued by an ancient spirit. Your whole family has been. Kłótnia isn't a name. It's a counter curse."

My eyes widened in surprise. "You aren't serious!"

She burst out laughing, and I caught a glob of gloop right on my cheek as she laughed herself into another coughing fit. "Of course not, you idiot. Do you think so highly of yourself that you would actually believe that you were the victim of a curse that had transpired for decades?"

I numbly scratched my butt. That is a good go-to move to go to when you don't know what to say. It sort of feels good and often distracts the person you are talking to until you can think of something intelligent to say. In my case, it only came out as semi-intelligent. "Erm, maybe?"

Parsna waved her hand at me dismissively. "You *young* people. You take life far too seriously. You need to loosen up. Stop taking life so soberly. It's not like you are going to die tomorrow."

She paused at that thought. "Well, yeah. Y'er prolly gonna die ta-marra and the day after that and so on for a really long time, but the point is you won't cease *existing*."

I gritted my teeth and counted to ten. Thankfully, I am far better at counting than Gruntswick is, and I was finished in just under half a minute. Admittedly, I might have missed a number, but that's only because the number seven scares me. Know why? Because Seven carries a knife and doesn't care what the guard thinks. That's why. Calm once more, I did the unthinkable and asked her another question. It went against my better judgment, but I did it anyway.

"If I am not suffering from a family curse as you say, then how did you know that was what I had come to talk about?"

She stopped rocking and ran her wiry fingers through long, white and yellowed strands of hair. "Kłótnia, you die the same way every time. Over and over. Just like on Groundhogs day."

Excited, I quickly interjected, "I know, right?"

She chose to ignore me and continued, "The others ignore you, but Parsna sees. Parsna wonders for long time why you don't think to ask yourself this very question. I think to myself, this boy must be very dense, like a rock but less smart because you only think it is some kind of joke. Did it never occur to you until today that something strange is going on around you?"

I am ashamed to admit it, but she was right. I had never expended any kind of energy considering that the fact that I died by peine forte et dure occurred all the time. Oh, sorry. That's a Goblin phrase. It means death by pressing—in other words, being crushed to death. It had just seemed like a funny coincidence. I don't think it helped that the others had noticed me enough to start calling me Splat.

Abyss, I pretended my roommate even knew I was there and that I had a best friend that I doubted recognized me as even being a Goblin. All it took was for a few strangers to pick on me by making fun of my name to make me forget all the crap in my life. I hadn't been walking along with blinders on. I had stabbed out my own eyes and been *proud* to do so. That's how starved for attention I had been. If you had set a plate of attention beside a plate of fried worms, I would have wondered why you put the worms on a plate since everyone knows that they are best eaten right off the ground, but I would have eaten the attention first. It was only now that I realized just how pathetic I really was.

My ulcer burbled, but I told it to shut up. I didn't want to drench Parsna in my stomach contents if it could be avoided. I slowly let out a long and loud belch, making sure to keep the airflow constant and under control. I let the air out in a controlled stream that I sent into my nostrils. No sense of wasting a good smell on the storyteller. I was hungry, after all.

"That's right, boy. Ya see it now, don'cha? You've been a right proper fool." Parsna produced a pipe from the folds of her dress and struck a match with her thumb. She placed the flaming stick into the pipe's bowl and began to slowly puff and drag until a steady stream of smoke poured from her nostrils. At least I knew now why she coughed so much. She was clearly allergic to matches.

"Do you know what is going on with me?" I asked in earnest. I knew now that she wasn't to be trifled with and she didn't suffer fools. I wanted to get back to the reason I came here and see if she had any idea of what was on.

Parsna gave me a slow nod and motioned for me to sit. I looked around but saw no other chair or other item to place my buttocks on in order to relax and listen as she spoke. I began to point this out, but she made the sit gesture again. I soon found myself seated on the dungeon floor like a small child adoring his grandmother. I made sure my loincloth didn't reveal any of my dirty little secrets in front of her.

"You got a problem, boy. Yeh aren't cursed, but it would be better for ya if you was." Her yellow eyes pierced the veil of smoke that her pipe produced. "I think you are being fed on by a Paradoxen."

My mouth, quite involuntarily, twisted into a doubtful sneer, and my eyes looked at her questioningly. I suspected that she was pulling my leg, and her making me sit at the foot of her rocker was just icing on the cake for her. I suspiciously asked for more detail, "A what?"

Parsna rolled her eyes. "Feh. A Paradoxen. It is a sort of sickly Minotaur that is just out of phase with our time. It is physically weak, but it can slightly alter the flow of time around it."

I interrupted her, "What does that mean?"

"To put it bluntly, it can move items and things from one place to another. The Parad-ox chooses a victim, then leads them into danger, and does everything it can to kill its target. Once its objective is achieved, it eats the life force's potential that expelled at the moment of death. That's all the stuff you were gonna do before you died. That's not a lot of energy, and that's why Paradoxen are always half-starved."

"I am," Parsna paused, took a few puffs on her pipe, and spit; she continued with some saliva dribbling down her chin, "willing to bet that one was just passing through here when it stumbled on to you. There is something about you that draws it in and makes it want to kill just *you*. Otherwise, we'd never know it was here because it would just kill indiscriminately, and no one would ever catch on."

I nodded. She didn't say anything else, so I waited a little longer. Finally, I made the 'continue' motion with my hands, and she started speaking again.

"The Paradoxen can be stopped, but you're the only one who is going to be able to do so. That's partially because no one will help you if you ask—we're all pretty lazy when it comes to taking care of our own—and partially because those people who do recognize you don't like you."

A slow sigh escaped my lips. She was right. I was on my own. "What do I have to do?"

She gave me a look like I ought to just get used to being flattened, pulped, and crushed on a regular basis but said, "You're gonna hafta git inna fight."

CHAPTER FOUR

I hated to admit it, but the old woman had made sense. She had explained that I needed to get into combat with some dungeoneers, which would draw the creature out to feed. The Paradoxen, she said, fed off of your future selves. She had tried to explain it to me but, in the end, broke it down thusly. Time travel is possible. If the 'me' of the now goes into tomorrow, then the 'me' there is my future self. When I die, it eats him. She called it a probability field prolapse... or something along those lines. He got to eat the me that would never exist, and I got to die on a cycle of live, die, repeat ad infinitum. That's a Goblin phrase meaning a really long time.

So, I had to get into a kerfuffle—her word, not mine—with some adventurers. This meant that I had to *not* get killed by them as I looked for the time-traveling Minotaur. She'd said that the only way I'd be able to spot him would be to keep an eye out for any changes in my environment. So, while dodging swords, spells, and other sinister subjects, I also had to look for any change in the scenery.

"No problem," I grumbled sarcastically. Hunting down needles in a tornado is what I do on weekends for fun. In fact, I'm the two-time dungeon champion.

Here's the best part. Once I note the change, I have to look for an invisible presence. The Paradoxen is not immaterial when it moves things, and it actually has some low-level telepathy that allows it to send mental suggestions to people and animals, thereby dictating what it wants them to do. In my case, that meant having them crush me by any means necessary. That was pretty much why I always got squished. It was all by intelligent design.

Once I spot the jerk, I need to do some sort of quantum leap or something. Parsna is nice and very smart, but she's a little hard to understand. The gist of it is that I have to go from *my* time to *its* time by leaping through his pocket dimension directly to him. She had to explain to me that a pocket dimension did not exist in people's pants. Once I'm in his time, I can square off and fight him on even terms.

My only problem? Technically, I will not be in the dungeon anymore, and that means that if it kills me there, then I won't be merely dead; I'll be really most *sincerely* dead, as in completely and irrevocably demised. Deceased. Bereft of life. No coming back. So, I had to choose. Did I want to keep getting killed by this thing over and over again, or did I want to take a chance and try to get rid of it?

Anyway, that's how I found myself in the thick of battle with my companions Gruntswick, Chadean, Molbogious, and a few other Goblins. A large party of humans had strayed into our hexagonal section, and the boys were giving them what for. I jumped in like I always did and did my best not to die while the others attempted to kill one or two of them before succumbing to their opponent's superior strength.

One man in a blue and white cloth surcoat and chainmail pointed a finger at one of the nameless Goblins to my left, uttered a single word, and my brother in arms lost his head. A darker-skinned rogue in black leather yelled at him, "Way to go, Hunter!"

The Essence-thrower flashed a grin. "Thanks, Hays! Tell Willmarth to keep slinging his gray stones. He has their archers pinned down."

At that moment, a hulking barbarian with a beard that almost reached the floor appeared with a cask of ale in one hand and a hunk of bacon in the other. He tipped up the flagon—

which was thrice the size of his hand—and drained it in one go. He then shoved the bacon into his mouth, began foaming like a rabid dog, and his beard wrapped itself around Chadean. All that was heard for a long moment was the crunching of bones. The man named Hays shouted, "Get 'em, Lord of Beer and Bacon!"

As fascinated as I was by the power of the cultivators, I had a 'needle' to find. I began searching my memory for anything that was out of place. It took me about two minutes before I'd found what I was looking for; there was a huge chunk of the ceiling that was weathered and cracked. It definitely hadn't been that way moments before. That was two minutes of dodging, bobbing, ducking, and maybe even some crying before I had my target in sight.

I ducked an ax from the Essence-throwing cultivator and headed towards the strange crack. My eyes strained for the effort, but I could vaguely make out a humanoid form that seemed to be just behind a non-Euclidian angle. Again, I have no idea what that means. I just know that Parsna had used that terminology, and so I did too. Once you know what you are looking for, it's pretty easy to find, even if you have no idea of what it is. I bet non-Euclidian means it's similar to those non-Newtonian liquids Bob had us drink one time. At least the angles weren't going to give me the green apple splatters like those drinks did.

I told myself that this was it—I had a choice to make. Either risk everything or be a nothing. I didn't even know what I was doing until I had jumped at the monster. Without trying, I had entered his space hole. Yeah, that sounds gross. Sorry, but I was inside, and there was no going back. Either he died, or I did.

I pulled my helmet from my pack and placed it on my head while the stunned Minotaur started to rise. He was disgusting to look at. His skin was ulcerous with large, bare patches of missing hair. His body was emaciated, and I could see his lungs push out from underneath his ribs. The Minotaur's skin was paper-thin, and his hair was straggly and matted. The creature's eyes were sunken and yellow, holding no indication of life within them. The Beast's teeth were also yellowed and cracked; several were missing, and I could see maggots crawling along its gum line.

I almost felt pity for this monster. That was until I looked down and saw the remains of *dozens* of skeletons that were my size. In some cases, the flesh was still fresh enough for me to recognize my own face over and over again.

Something inside me snapped, and I drew out the crescent moon swords that I had wisely packed for this excursion. I slashed down at the fiend, fully intending to sever his neck from his shoulders, but he was *surprisingly* fast. His body might have looked sickly, but it reacted just as swiftly as he could think. Possibly maybe even a little faster. Granted, he didn't look all that intelligent, but the guy had some serious moves. I pulled my swords into a ready position and took a defensive stance. I'd seen Molly do that once, and it had scared some adventurers. *My* foe, on the other hand, looked unimpressed.

The Paradoxen snorted, and I *swear* steam poured from its nostrils. A few boogers, too and some snot that ran down his chin. He really needed to blow his nose; if we weren't in a life or death struggle, I'd have offered him a hanky. The Beast carried no weapon that I could see, but the moment he lowered his head, I knew I was screwed. His horns—the only part of his body that looked healthy and strong—were black, sharp, and glistened in the light. The Paradoxen's space hole—ugh—was small and did not leave me a lot of room to maneuver. If he charged, he was going to stick me because I couldn't duck, and I couldn't jump over him. It looked like my attempt to regain control of my life was over before it began.

The monster stamped its right foot and charged at me. Reflexively, I dropped my swords and grabbed the creature's horns as it came after me. I wrapped my legs around its shoulders and held on for dear life. I soon learned that it couldn't grab me while it ran, as it apparently used its arms for balance. This knowledge did me little good, however, since I couldn't let go of its horns or I'd drop to the ground and either get gored or trampled. I thought that we were at an impasse until I remembered that I was a Goblin. By nature, we do a lot of stuff that other races would consider gross. I'm one of those people.

So, I bit into his snotty, drippy nose... and tore off a nice chunk of meat. I *did* spit it out. I'm not *that* uncouth. Then I tore out another chunk and another. I kept repeating the process until I had worn away his upper lip and his whole nose. Blind with pain, the Paradoxen slipped from his interdimensional hidey hole, and we fell into the thick of the battle. We crashed on to the man called Hays, one of the emaciated Mino's horns piercing his chest when we landed. I rolled off of him and found my feet before he did.

I noted that Gruntswick was the only one of our group alive besides myself. He looked half-dead, but he always looked like that. It was just the way he stared off into space when he wasn't swinging a sword.

"Gruntswick!" I yelled, and he actually turned to look at me. I was so shocked for a moment I didn't know how to react. Thankfully, I regained my senses. I yelled as I pointed at the murderous, time-manipulating Minotaur, "Kill it!"

To his credit, Gruntswick tried. He stepped forward and raised his sword but was taken down by a sharpened beard-hair arrow from the man called Willmarth.

I sighed and ducked under an arrow aimed at me. The Paradoxen didn't seem to notice the battle raging around it, seeming more intent on getting back inside its space timey-wimey cubby hole, but he was still a little wibbly-wobbly from the fall. I wasn't having any of that. Lacking any weapons, I ran forward and kicked the bull right in his Mountaindale Oysters. The monster dropped like a sack of rotten potatoes to my feet, cradling his precious family jewels.

I scanned the area for anything I could use to finish him off when I realized that we were right underneath that shady chunk of ceiling he'd prepared for little ol' me. I dragged his body over until we were exactly dead center below the stone. I yelled, "Ironic justice!"

Then I thrust my hand into the heavy crumbling stone, just as he'd meant for me to do. It was a pleasure to feel my body squish between the Paradoxen and the ceiling with a sickening, but soothing...

Splat!

Alright, so maybe I didn't exactly save the dungeon as much as I saved myself, but I am a part of the dungeon, so I'm counting that as a save for the Great Spirit. Am I an unreliable narrator? I admit that I'm no Parsna, but I think I did pretty well for a nobody Goblin. Let's see how well you dictate your tale when you save a dungeon from the evil machinations of a murderous monster from outside of space and time.

I walk a little taller now and strut with something called confidence. I never knew what that was. I'm still not exactly sure, but I do know that for the first time since coming to this dungeon, I am well and truly free to just be a Goblin. My buddy Molly and I are going for some ale this evening after our shift. Technically, *he's* going there, and I'm going to mosey over and sit beside him before he notices I'm there, but that counts as drinking together. There are a couple of ladies that I've had my eye on for a while, and I think I just might manage to convince one to let me buy her a drink.

By the way, I am proud to admit that I was *stabbed* in the eye by a Dark Elf and died yesterday just like a normal, everyday Goblin. I have to say that death by stabbing is a tad overrated. It was not as pleasant as the others make it look. Decapitation and evisceration all look like grand fun when you are watching it happen to others, but it's all sprays of blood; then it takes some time to actually die. It hurts—a lot. I don't miss much about the old days, but compared to this... I'll take a good death by smashing any day of the week.

The Spirit Dungeon
By: Alexis Keane

Chapter One

Silas ran through the jungle, wiping sweat from his brow. Thorns tore at his feet, his shoes long since reduced to ribbons; branches whipped him, long barbs tearing away shreds of shirt and skin. Nonetheless, he ran.

The horde of demons and undead had razed his town to the ground, leaving his brewery in flames. His life savings hung from his belt, the thick felt bag swinging painfully against his leg as he sprinted through the thick undergrowth. Even knowing that the bag slowed him, Silas couldn't bear to leave it behind, as it was stuffed near to bursting with silver, copper, and a pair of gold coins.

It had to be the work of a necromancer, one who had gone down a far darker path than he had. Sure, Silas had a major affinity for infernal Essence, but there was a difference between an infernal affinity and a *necromancer*.

The Church held a dim view on infernal dungeons, destroying them when found, making it almost impossible for a newbie Infernal cultivator to keep on the straight and narrow. Because of the Church's actions, it was a self-fulfilling prophecy that people with access to the infernal became bad people. Silas, and many like him, had been forced to cultivate with one hand tied behind his back, siphoning energy from people if and when they died.

Obviously, doing so tended to cause issues. The loved ones of the recently deceased often took offense at a stranger siphoning the burst of energy from a corpse. Their anger would draw the Church, and soon, the cycle of hatred toward infernal users would be reinforced. It was no wonder so many Infernal cultivators resorted to dark deeds, simply to survive. Silas had been run out of town so many times when he was a younger man.

His brewery had changed that, had turned his life around in a way that he'd never expected.

But now... it was burning.

CHAPTER TWO

An uneasy twilight had settled upon the jungle by the time Silas found a well-worn trail. The trilling of parrots and buzzing of insects had fallen eerily silent, and even the roars of predators were muted. One of the only constants was the rush of the wind through the highest layers of leafy canopy.

Then something changed.

What started as a faint murmur in the approaching night soon developed into a chittering roar of squeaking and rushing wings. Bats flooded the sky, membranous wings eclipsing the evening gloom, hiding the world below from the last, hazy light of the evening. Millions of flying creatures, not an orderly flight but a frenzied aerial melee.

Fuzzy bodies slammed into each other, jostling for a position at the front of the swarm. A few spiraled into trees, wings bleeding and broken, but the majority always continued forward. A young raptor swooped toward the throng, talons poised to snatch a morsel from the mass.

It was not to be.

A battalion of black bodies split off from the host, intercepting the bird. The predator issued a screaming challenge, a vortex of air forming in front of it as it used its inborn abilities, eddies of air sharpening into cruel blades around its talons.

The bird of prey accelerated, the vortex manifesting into a drill of violently spinning air. Bats hit the Essence-enhanced raptor like a hammer, hundreds of them falling from the sky instantly, mangled bodies slamming through leaves and branches before thudding to the jungle floor like rain.

Hundreds became *thousands*, and for a moment... everything was silent. The rain of bats ended, and then the *raptor* was falling like a meteor, its body almost unrecognizable after being bludgeoned by thousands of furry bodies.

With no regard for their defeated adversary or even their fallen, the winged mammals that had split off to attack rejoined the colony and resumed their jostling for prime position.

Silas decided to check one of the downed bats. Creeping forward so as not to upset the bats, he was surprised to find that they were almost exclusively low F-rank animals. They were completely devoid of sharp talons, long teeth, or protective hides, and yet... through sheer force of numbers, they had overwhelmed a *far* superior enemy.

Silas didn't know much about bats, but he was nearly certain that they ate fruit, maybe bugs, and weren't overly aggressive. Even so, he'd just seen them take out a high D-rank, maybe even *C-rank* zero threat.

How? What in the *abyss* was going on?

***

Once the tide of bats had finally passed—against his better judgment—Silas started to follow after them. The path he was following was significantly easier on the feet than the dense undergrowth he'd left behind. His town-dwelling lifestyle wasn't all that helpful, but he recognized that this was probably a game trail.

As he walked, heady fumes began to assail his nostrils, weak at first but strengthening as he approached a verdant cliff-face with a gaping cavern in the center. Why was that scent so *familiar?*

Light spilled from the mouth of what must be a cave, illuminating a seething mass of bats wallowing in a gigantic hot spring that belched out from deep within the earth. That was no longer his greatest concern. He felt something; something that washed over him and filled him with hope and energy.

Infernal Essence was coming out of the cavern in great waves, *stiflingly* powerful compared to what he was accustomed to. The bats didn't seem to notice, and no predators or undead stalked the area. Yet, as the bats muddied the waters of the hot spring, bursts of infernal Essence blossomed from the churning bodies. Brief flashes of unexpected power, perhaps equivalent to the death of a chicken but nearly *constant.*

Silas struggled to think of the cause. This cave was obviously a dungeon, but, impossibly, that fact seemed to take second place to the mystery before his eyes. He crept forward, legs moving of their own accord, the memory of the unfortunate raptor scoured from his mind by a desire to *know.* What could release such potent necromantic energy? It *couldn't* be the bats... could it?

The fumes strengthened as he approached the springs, burning his eyes and nostrils. Still, he walked forward. Before Silas knew it, he was at the edge of the spring, the fumes so strong they were overpowering, yet filling him with a rapturous energy and enthusiasm.

Was that it?

More infernal Essence was released when strong emotions were experienced at the point of death. Were these bats feeling the same strange ecstasy he was? They certainly weren't acting the way they had before. Besides that, didn't bats *leave* their caves at night? Why did they come over here, just to enter *another* cave?

Gone was the mindless aggression they had displayed to each other as well as the threats in their path, giving way to something more... varied. Sure, *some* still hissed and snarled, trying to heave themselves toward him but unable to fly for some reason, but the vast majority seemed content to just float in the water with drooping eyes.

The final group was the most amusing; they *danced* through the water, musical squeaks issuing from their tiny mouths. One even managed to roll its way toward him, accelerating with half-controlled flaps of its wings, chirping like a songbird. Silas stood still, *astounded*, as the fluffy, little creature brushed up against his bleeding foot, serenading him with its piping cries.

"Oh, no *way.*" It all fit together. The bats' odd behavior, their aggression toward the raptor stalling their approach to the hot springs, the heady fumes, the dungeon, and the strange waters it produced. He'd finally figured out why the scent was so familiar.

The 'water' wasn't water at all, and unless he was getting something very wrong... the bats were drunk to the point that one was even trying to have intimate relations with his foot.

***

Once he'd removed the overly-friendly bat and returned it to the alcoholic pool—or maybe it was the pool of alcoholics— Silas edged around the hot springs, finally reaching the vine-covered cliff.

In the dark, it took him the best part of a half-hour to find an elevated ledge, the light spilling from the dungeon's mouth his only aid. He was tired, a fatigue that burrowed deep into his bones, but the current events were too exciting and opportune to miss.

For the first time in his life, Silas began freely *cultivating!*

The infernal Essence flooding the area had only thickened as more bats drowned in the springs or were poisoned by the vapors lifting off the hot surface. Their livers silently gave up as the emotions of their drunken stupor marinated their bodies in infernal Essence—Essence just waiting to be released and collected.

To Silas, it seemed wasteful. So much energy dissipating and washing out into the world. Yet, the more he thought about the situation, the more it seemed beneficial to the dungeon. While a strange truce blanketed the hot springs and the surrounding area, it did not extend to corpses.

Lured in by the promise of free food, predators arrived to feast on flesh steeped in liquor. In most cases, those same predators would bend their necks down farther to lap at the surface of the pool, already assured of the safety of the 'waters' by the edibility of the meat.

Creatures came from every direction, the darkness hiding hundreds of game trails that Silas was *convinced* led straight to this spot. Some, no longer content to drink from pools muddied by the bodies of thousands of bats, trudged inside. Inside, where hundreds of thousands more bats resided.

Many returned. Some—so Silas presumed—couldn't hold their drink and added to the flow of infernal Essence.

A different hunger drove him. He was unburdened by the animals' desire to return and sip from the spring once more; his hunger was to grow stronger. As his cultivation base swelled, that hunger grew. Like land starved of water, his parched Center became glutted with Essence, perhaps even enough to reach F-rank six.

He longed to enter the dungeon, where he was sure the true feast awaited him—animals and beasts, drawn from across the entirety of the jungle by the same urges that forced tavern patrons to always return for more.

The dungeon sat there, like a patient, silent spider at the center of a web of game trails. It felt like a trap; it seemed that at any moment, hordes of cup-bearing kobolds would spill out and drag him inside.

He knew that was unlikely, but at that moment, he *desperately* wanted it to be the case because the alternative was far worse. The dungeon had shown him the briefest glimpse of what it could give him, and he had sipped willingly.

Even so, with all the benefits this dungeon offered, Silas would leave in the morning to find an Adventurers' Guild in an undead-free town. He would claim the reward from finding a dungeon, and he would live a life of luxury.

Silas knew it wouldn't be enough. Eventually, he would return, walking happily into the spider's mouth.

CHAPTER THREE

"What do you want, necromancer?" the Guild clerk spat at him as soon as he walked in the door.

Silas nearly broke down in tears; it had taken a month of wandering to reach the nearest unburnt town. It was only extraordinary prescience, which had convinced him to take several braces of alcohol-soaked bats, that saved him from a painful, drawn-out death from starvation.

His clothes had long ago been reduced to ragged shreds, replaced with coarse sackcloth and the kindness of strangers who couldn't tell he was an infernal Essence user. That same 'kindness' had seen his life savings lifted from his belt by nimble fingers in the night.

When possible, he slept by abattoirs, breweries, and cheesemakers—an old habit of taking the opportunity to eke out pitiful amounts of infernal Essence by cultivating in their proximity. He avoided cemeteries by the same habitual token.

Some adventurers with a hero complex liked roughing up infernalists found near such places, and even going near abattoirs was cutting it close. Sadly, beggars couldn't be choosers, so he slept and cultivated where he could.

"I am *not* a necromancer! I just have a major affinity for infernal Essence." After a month of gnawing on bats preserved in liver-destroying quantities of alcohol, sleeping in the cold, being reduced to this state... the innate suspicion and hostility from the very people he'd come to see was almost too much to bear. Still, he pressed on. "I... I would like to claim the bounty for finding a dungeon."

"Oh, *would* you?" the clerk snarked, raising an eyebrow.

"Yes."

"Where is this... dungeon?"

Silas paused. "In the jungle near Viltras. I never asked its name. I don't think the locals knew... or cared. 'The jungle' was good enough for us."

"Viltras? The town that was burned by *necromancers*?" The clerk's voice turned sugary sweet.

Silas stiffened. "Yes... that's the one."

"How about you point to it on a map? Just wait a few seconds while I get one for you..." the clerk smiled nastily, "sir."

He sighed as the clerk left, wondering what horrible surprise the self-important desk-worker had in store. The clerk took a few minutes to return, spreading out a faded map with stained, moth-eaten edges.

"Now, where in..." the Guild official consulted the legend in the corner, "the Jungle of Toruk... did you find this dungeon?"

Silas took one look at the map, a singular smudge of green, before surrendering, "I have no idea."

"That's not very useful, is it? Any landmarks?"

"It's a large cave in the face of a vine-covered cliff. All the bats in the area fly toward it during the evening, and most large game trails lead toward it. The dungeon empties hot springs full of... addictive water outside the entrance."

The clerk's gaze turned piercing. "So it's expanded above ground then? Monsters too? Undead perhaps? Demons? Angels?"

Silas backtracked, "No, nothing like that. The water just flows out of the mouth of the cave, nothing more."

"Wait here. I'll get the Guild Leader of this branch." The clerk looked disappointed. More adventurers entered and exited the Guild Hall as Silas waited, some of them shooting him looks as dirty as his clothing.

***

"That's him. The only person to survive the demonic attack on Viltras, conveniently a necromancer. *Claims* to have found a dungeon," the clerk babbled excitedly, fawning over the Guild Leader, a swarthy human with a wicked-looking ax hanging from his hip. The Guild Leader glared briefly at the clerk, then walked over to Silas.

"Ah, so you must be the F-ranked necromantic mastermind behind the recent demonic invasion. At least, so my clerk tells me," the Guild Leader drawled, tracing a finger over his weapon. "We surrender."

Silas didn't know how to respond, so the Guild Leader continued speaking into the awkward silence, "We'll send a team to verify your claim, and you'll go with them. Payment of ten gold if the dungeon needs to be destroyed, five if not as well as an additional five percent of any income it produces. I'll give you my advice for a gold, though?"

To a normal citizen like Silas, a single gold was a fortune, and five was a king's ransom. However, the Guild Leader probably knew more about such matters, so he decided to take the loss and hope the advice was worth it. "Sure?"

"First off, ignore people like *that*. It'll get worse once people know an infernalist owns land around a dungeon," The Guild Leader jerked a thick thumb at the clerk, who paled. "Secondly, *buy* the land, as much as you can. You know where. Even if the dungeon gets destroyed for being infernal or celestial, you'll lose far more if it isn't. Take out a loan if you need to. I have *excellent* rates, for example."

The Guild Leader grabbed a random adventurer nearby, hoisting him into the air. "Don't I give great rates on loans?"

"Uh."

"Say yes."

"Yes."

The Guild Leader turned back to Silas. "See. *Everyone* agrees."

He released the adventurer, letting him fall into a quivering heap on the ground. "Third, get luxuries and transportation set up as quickly as possible. Adventurers are happy living in tents, less so in hovels. Owning expensive venues to eat, drink, and... platonically cuddle will vastly increase any profit you make. So, take out a loan. Did I mention I have *excellent* rates?"

"For platonic cuddling?" Silas asked with a straight face.

"That too." The Guild Leader smirked. "Fourthly, cultivate hard, train harder. You're inherently limited by your affinities, so make the most of your body and training."

He peered closer. "Major infernal, minor fire, minor water. Oof, that's a tough combo, but it could be worse. There'll be a lot of people out to get you, simply for your major affinity. I suggest you *platonically cuddle* them up before they *platonically cuddle* you up. Fifth and finally, you'll be traveling with an expedition party of adventurers—the only ones I can spare right now—to help them find the dungeon. That means you won't have time to buy the land. So, for a mere one percent of all income generated by the dungeon, in perpetuity, I can buy the land on your behalf."

"What's a percent?"

"An irrelevant detail, so yes or no?"

"Yes?"

"Wonderful. And will you be purchasing that land with your own money?"

"No?" He didn't like where this was going.

"Would you like to take out a loan? One thousand percent per annum."

"What's a percent, and what's a per annum?"

"A percent is the totality of a thing, split into one hundred parts. Every year the amount that you owe me increases tenfold, so pay me back quickly. Or slowly. Actually, I prefer slowly."

"That seems a little high?"

"Ah, you're a rare talent at negotiating. Three hundred percent then?"

"Is that good?" The Guild Leader nodded, grinning at Silas. "Okay then?"

Silas' head bobbed uncertainly.

"Wonderful." The Guild Leader clapped his hands, pulling out a roll of parchment. He waved it around. "This is a Mana-sealed contract; it'll bind us both to the terms of the deal. Just sign *here* with *this* quill and *this* ink. Don't ask how I knew you'd settle for three hundred."

Sure enough, even as he scrawled his name on to the bottom line, he saw the numbers for three hundred, followed by a strange squiggle.

It seemed like the right thing to do. Silas couldn't just let someone else snap up the land, but even as he did so, he felt as if he'd been conned.

"Ah, Silas, is it?" The Guild Leader took the contract, reading the signature at the bottom. The man scrawled his own name in the appropriate spot. "I'm Irwin. It's been a pleasure doing business."

He held out a pouch with four small gold coins inside. Silas took the bag, which was pleasingly heavy in his hands. Irwin continued, "However, you should be more careful in the future. Be very cautious when it comes to signing Mana contracts. You might just be making a deal with a demon.

"In this case, I am only bound to buying land on your *behalf* rather than land which you *specify* for me to buy *on your behalf.* Details like that can ruin you. Particularly if I decide to buy the entire jungle with loaned funds." Silas frowned at this terrifying thought.

Irwin laughed in response. "I wouldn't do that, *truly.* You can show me where you want me to buy in a bit. Anyway, four percent of a dungeon's income is a huge amount; food, drink, and *cuddling* venues pay themselves back quickly, particularly among adventurers."

"I'd like to pay off the first four gold's worth of debt." Silas handed the bag of coins back to the Guild Leader. After all, saving four gold now would cost him twelve in a year's time.

"Killjoy. Smart... but still." Irwin's eyes twinkled as he pocketed the coins. Then he stretched, his back clicking and cracking. "Well? Shall I introduce you to the team? You'll be helping them find their way there. They'll protect you if you get in trouble."

Or kill you first if you lead them into a trap... The words went unsaid, but the implication remained, hanging between them like a scarlet thread.

CHAPTER FOUR

It took a week before the charred skeleton of Viltras was visible on the horizon. A month and a week had passed, so there were no smoldering buildings belching smoke into the air like the last time he had seen the village. The demonic hordes were long gone. As they approached, the party saw no corpses littering the paths between the blackened remains of houses. Silas shivered; they'd probably been reanimated.

No crows cawed from the gibbet-like frames of houses that pierced the sky like a Drow's fingers. The fields stood silent, unharvested and untended; the hordes who descended on Viltras saw no use in the sustenance of the living, thankfully wasting no time in burning it either.

Silas dismounted his borrowed mare and stood in the ruins of his brewery; the stone tubs of mash tuns and fermenting vessels were sundered. Fetid muck, cloudy and dirt-filled, oozed out on to the scorched earth. The speedy fermentation within the liquid, once a welcome—if tiny—stipend of infernal Essence now gave way to the slower burn of rot and putrefaction.

It had been his way out of fleeing for his life. A surprise discovery that the yeast, which turned the sugary mash into beer, also released a trickle of infernal Essence. This was similar to the way the rotting corpses in cemeteries shed their necromantic energies into the surroundings but far less hated.

It was nowhere close to the Essence powerhouse of prayer on hallowed ground from the celestial end of the spectrum, but it had been *enough* for him. Somewhere in the back of his mind, more out of curiosity than anything else, he wondered if there was a similar yield of celestial Essence in the presence of rapid growth. Perhaps bamboo?

However, even the mare was getting impatient as he speculated, nickering and tugging gently at his shirt with oversized teeth.

The Jungle of Toruk loomed, beckoning them into the depths even from three miles away. To the spider's maw he walked.

***

The mare—indeed, all the horses—had to be left behind. The ruins of Viltras were the perfect location for them to rest. No insects, let alone predators, ventured into the place where they remained tethered. Two troughs filled with hay and water scavenged from the surroundings sat nearby. Still, nervous whinnying followed them as they walked away toward the trees.

The jungle was easy to run through if one was willing to risk losing skin and clothes to the thorny vines. Ironically, once sharpened steel came into play, progress slowed to a crawl, the jungle resisting attempts to proceed without intruders paying a heavy toll in torn skin and bloodied flesh.

Vak, the leader of the expedition, carved his way through the undergrowth. Sharp vines skittered off his plate mail, some even scoring small, white lines across the surface. His sword flashed left and right, severing the fronds of drooping ferns that blocked their path, leaving an echo of steel behind.

Finally, however, their small group attracted unwelcome attention. They spotted the creature at the last second, slipping through the trees like a wraith—unnaturally quiet despite its size. The gorilla lunged, a roar bursting from its lips; two massive fists crushed together to form a hammer of muscle and bone meant to smash the trespassers into paste.

Silas' eyes widened as the stroke fell toward him, blocking out his view of the leaves and sky. The right arm of the party's monk, Dexter, flashed forward. Fingers extended, thumb pressed against his palm, the back of his hand grazed the clenched fist of the massive beast.

Somehow, against all expectations, the gorilla's fist slid to the side, down Dexter's forearm, skating off his elbow and slamming into the earth in a tectonic eruption of soil and scattered leaves. A sense of impending doom sent Silas diving away, and not a moment too soon.

Stalagmitic serrations of stone stabbed the soil beneath where he had stood, extending in a line that sundered trees and boulders and sent splinters and shards of rock flying in every direction.

The gorilla gave a thwarted grunt. It stood hunched, both fists pressed into the earth as it glared at those who dared enter its domain. With a howl, it leaped forward, its arms flying out to either side, intent on sending its foes scattering like leaves.

Enora, a healer, ducked just in time, rolling beneath the beast's flashing limbs. Dexter, unbalanced from deflecting the gorilla's initial strike, took a massive forearm to the gut. He flew through the air, smashing into a thorn-covered shrub.

He hung from the side of the bush in defiance of gravity, hundreds of barbed spines poking through his robes and pinning him in place. The gorilla hooted in amusement, seeing its enemy hanging from the bush like some fleshy fruit ripe enough to burst with a single touch. Walking on its knuckles, it swung its body toward the imperiled human. It rose to full height, preparing to pulverize both Dexter and the shrub that held him with a single blow.

Vak's sword took it in its back. The blade traveled deep into the gorilla's body, piercing the mats of hair, gliding through muscle, scraping past ribs, and coming to rest within one of the creature's massive lungs. The forest was suddenly silent except for the whistling rattle that issued from the beast's mouth.

Dexter laughed weakly, and the gorilla spun with one outstretched arm, the rotation of its body tearing the blade from Vak's grip. A meaty hand slammed into Vak with the power of a charging bull, denting his plate mail and sending him flying through the trees, branches snapping before him as he tumbled through the air.

Vak landed in a heap, stiffly pressing himself to his feet and drawing a dagger from his boot. He spun it in his right hand, weaving a figure-eight of steel before settling on a reversed grip; blade pointing backward, pressed almost flat against his metal-clad forearm.

The gorilla charged him, no longer paying any heed to bush-fruit Dexter. Vak stepped forward with his left foot, right trailing back. The beast barged through trees like a juggernaut, roaring, intent on destroying the human who'd caused it harm.

Vak waited, wheezing from the strike the oversized ape had dealt him. The gorilla lifted logs and rocks as it ran, slinging them at the armored man. Vak swayed out of the way but otherwise made no effort to avoid the charging animal.

The world seemed to pause. Silas watched as the muscles of the gorilla's legs bunched beneath its mighty bulk. He could almost *see* the earth parting beneath its feet before rebounding like a wave, driving the ape forward with a strength and speed that muscle alone had no hope of imparting.

The gorilla shot through the air like an overweight javelin, seeking its enemy's life... and its enemy spun. Like a dancer, his balance shifted, and his footing followed. His dagger flashed. Once. Twice. Drawing blood each time. Then as the beast barreled past him, a second gauntleted hand seized the hilt of the sword protruding from its back.

For a moment, the sword resisted. Vak was pulled along with it. Then the weapon started to slide. With a spray of blood and gore, the blade tore cleanly through the gorilla's side, sending its vitality splashing to the jungle floor. Yet still, the beast lived.

Vak readied himself to hit the ground, tucking into a roll and holding his blades away from his body to avoid impaling himself. It was not to be. A tangle of low hanging vines *moved*. They coiled around his leg, snaring him, tugging him upward and leaving him dangling by a single leg.

Above him, a camouflaged pod opened, revealing a colorful crimson maw filled with thousands of backward slanting teeth.

He swung around, trying to hack at the tendrils of the Vine Horror that had caught him. In his panic, he almost failed to spot the eight-hundred-pound gorilla. Almost.

Like judgment from the heavens, the gorilla descended, blood frothing from its lips as it executed its final act upon the mortal plane, expecting that no living power would be able to divert or deny the coming blow. Vak closed his eyes.

Just then, a lithe healer tackled Vak to one side, sending the tendrils of the Vine Horror swinging away from the avalanche of muscle and carrying both of them with it.

Like thunder, the Beastly Gorilla impacted the earth, sending seismic shockwaves through the ground nearby. Hundreds of stone spikes erupted outward in concentric circles around its titanic body. Finally, the gorilla moved no more.

Enora plucked the dagger from Vak's grip and hacked at the vines encircling the man's leg. "No, don't!"

Too late. As the wounded Vine Horror withdrew with a rustling hiss, the man collapsed on to one of the spikes jutting from the ground, armor ringing from the drop on to the pointed stone, groaning in pain as he landed. Enora bounced, fortuitously, off his body and on to the cooling corpse of one of the jungle's former tyrants.

Sheepishly, she pulled Vak over to her, confirming that the spikes hadn't penetrated his armor. They both leaned back against the gorilla's body, breathless gasps broadening, giving way to slow chuckles and building into belly laughter that tore at their abused sides. They were *alive*!

A voice brought them back to reality, "Hey, guys. While it's fun *hanging* out up here all by my lonesome, do you think you could lend me a hand? I really need to trim my bush."

CHAPTER FIVE

"Oh, gods. Make it stop!"

"Please! No more. I'll do anything! Just don't *heal* me anymore."

Vak and Dexter squirmed as Enora moved between them, administering some much-needed aid. It seemed that being healed by an air affinity cultivator felt like being tickled everywhere at once.

Enora smiled innocently. "*Silas* could heal you instead?"

"No," the three of them chorused, Silas included in that group.

"Then be *quiet* and let mama give you your medicine." Enora beamed as she resumed the tickle-torture. It didn't help that she was covered in blood from digging through the gorilla's carcass to find a standard Beast Core.

Screams once again filled the jungle—at least not from pain this time around. As the laughter reached the point of maniacal, Silas struggled not to think about how much infernal Essence he could gain by tickling someone to death.

***

They found the game trail a few hours later. Anxiety about encountering another beast like the gorilla had slowed their progress to a crawl. However, once they reached the trail, the sense of excitement became tangible.

Silas felt an unseen weight of apprehension lift from his shoulders. The fact that a dungeon was producing alcohol seemed too absurd to take seriously. He hadn't even shared the specifics with Irwin or the expedition for fear of being ridiculed and dismissed as a drunkard.

But this was it. This was really it.

His way out.

A chance to grow without hurting anyone, without falling victim to the excesses of the Church.

He looked ahead.

A slow but constant parade of animals—all shapes and sizes—plodded toward where he *knew* the dungeon must be. The strange armistice seemed to be in effect, predators and prey walking side by side to the local 'watering' hole. Some things never changed. Some of his best friends had been celestial cultivators. When they weren't sober, at least.

The only exception to the rule was a family of tapirs, although that might have been because Enora had tried to snuggle them. Silas didn't exactly blame them for clawing her. If he looked that adorably ugly, he would have a problem with weirdos trying to cuddle him too.

The journey here had been uncomfortable, the party keeping communication with him to a minimum, but after the encounter with the gorilla, the entire team seemed to have loosened up. There was a lot more laughter and goofing off. Silas, for one, felt genuine gratitude to the gorilla for breaking down the barriers between them and giving them a common enemy.

"I could teach you if you'd like?"

Dexter's words made Silas snap out of the reverie of walking. "What?"

"Martial arts," Dexter continued as if the interruption hadn't happened. "I won't lie and say that we're not uncomfortable with giving you a weapon, but everyone deserves to be able to defend themselves, even infernalists."

"Oh?"

"We left you defenseless against the gorilla, and that wasn't right. So? Martial arts? I'm no master, but I could teach you a few tricks."

"I... *guess*?" He was non-committal at first, but then his mind went back to the image of Dexter deflecting the gorilla's strike. More firmly, he answered, "Sure. Yes. Thanks."

They lapsed into a friendly silence, continuing down the trail, seeing more and more animals as they trekked toward the dungeon. Birds called out from the trees, and colorful snakes wove themselves into knots among the branches, most avoiding the expedition but some creeping closer to watch them with glittering eyes. Curious or hungry? Silas couldn't tell.

Vak could. So, when a colorful songbird swooped down from the trees, heading toward Enora, *maw* opening wide—unhinging in fact—to reveal something... *other*... it was met with Vak's steel-clad fist to its otherworldly face, causing it to detonate in a flurry of feathers and meaty chunks.

Vak spat out a gobbet of twitching muscle that had flown into his mouth, and he grinned back at them. "Tastes like chicken."

He held one hand up, signaling everyone pause, then gagged, trying to remove the taste of the bird from between his teeth. They all laughed, except Silas. His body had stiffened as the wind subtly shifted. To the rest, the smell would be passed off as another oddity of the jungle; to Silas... it was unmistakable.

The faintest tang of the hot spring's fumes curled and twisted within his nostrils, and his lips curled to match it. "We're here."

***

Only a handful of bats splashed around in the alcoholic hot springs, the chiropteran equivalent of lunchtime drunks. The rest of the 'watering hole' was occupied by animals and beasts in various stages of inebriation, most either too happy or too drowsy to cause a ruckus.

Even the rowdy ones were relatively passive, content to growl and snap at those nearby, having quickly learned that a reckless charge through the alcoholic liquid—and the churned mud beneath it—would lead to a rapid and graceless plunge headfirst into the water as their legs failed them. The dungeon waited, massive above the hot springs. But of the tableau, it was the immediate foreground that held their attention.

"What in the abyss?" Vak muttered at the sight of the oddity of nature. Dexter shook his head, a look of baffled incomprehension on his face.

And then there was Enora, giggling quietly. A note of false reverence entered her voice, "Oh my god, it's a *spirit dungeon*."

***

It was far easier finding suitable ledges on the cliff-face when the sun was shining, at least compared to Silas' blind scramble in the dark. They set up their tent in a small recess, a curtain of vines and overgrowth muffling the noise of the springs below. A faint carpet of decaying guano covered the floor, a few groggy fruit bats flapping their wings as they clung to the roof, hateful eyes fixed on the torches that Enora brought out from her pack.

One lost its grip on the ceiling, dropping to the ground with a shocked *squeak*. It righted itself and stumbled around on the floor with ungainly little footsteps, one wing drawn over its face to block out the light. With a few more adorably irritated chirrups, a disastrous attempt at flight left it wedged in a tight hole in the wall. Enora rescued it, and the hungover bat curled up in the farthest corner using its own wings as blackout curtains. Then it dozed off, tiny chest rising and falling in time with its high-pitched snores.

The shadows lengthened as they observed the behavior of the fauna gathered around the main pool. Officially, it was for reporting back to the Adventurers' Guild, but it was really just an excuse to watch the animal antics going on.

Not that observations weren't made.

Enora nudged Silas. "Look at the pool. See how it's not infused with the dungeon's mana? That's strange. It goes against what you would normally expect. Dungeons typically go to great lengths to addict creatures with their Essence."

Silas stared at it. "I don't see anything?"

"Infuse some Essence into your eyes."

"How do I do that?" He had never learned; detecting the flows of Essence had never seemed particularly important since he'd never had any intention to enter a dungeon before now.

"Really? Your spiral is serviceable. You've got a decent amount of corruption in your Center, but your Chi threads are pretty pure. Someone's obviously taught you the basics. I'm surprised they didn't show you to pull Essence toward your eyes. That's normally the easy part. They didn't show you how to open your meridians either... You should find a better teacher in the future."

"Teachers," Silas corrected glumly. "I had an... unconventional... education. Few people want to take someone with only a major infernal affinity under their wing. I had to make do with plying low-ranked adventurers with alcohol until they were too drunk to care I was an infernalist. Not the best people to learn from. But I made do with what I had at the time."

Vak and Dexter nodded along, while Enora hummed little sympathetic noises.

"So, how did you get to your current rank? I would expect most necromancers to be starved of Essence. Not that you aren't a little runty already," Dexter added with a smile that defused what would otherwise be an insult.

"However I could. Cheesemakers, brewers, cemeteries, cesspits... they all release small amounts of infernal Essence. Cemeteries release the most, then sewers, but I didn't want to spend my life surrounded by the contents of either. So, I stole some money from a noble in the Phoenix Kingdom, not proud of it... well, *maybe a little*..." Vak snorted at the remark, causing Silas to pause before he continued.

"Then I escaped on the fastest horse I could buy, laid low for a while. Moved to Viltras. Built my brewery and used it to cultivate. I even discovered that adding more sugar helped increase my yields. And that's all there is to it." There was silence for a while. Enora shared a meaningful glance with her party, one hand resting on a pocket of her bag. Dexter gave a slight nod, rubbing his thumb and forefinger together. Vak shrugged.

Finally, the healer spoke, "How does a fresh start sound?"

CHAPTER SIX

Darkness had long since fallen upon the jungle. The bat air-force had arrived in spectacular fashion, sending all the other animals and beasts scattering into the trees or fleeing into the mouth of the dungeon.

The party of Silas' *friends*—an odd concept to him—waded through the heated main pool, trying to pack as many bats into the area as possible, torches raised high above their heads, turning insects that flew too close into short-lived meteors. Silas sat ten yards away, slightly tipsy from the fumes, singing under his breath. He'd never been particularly good at holding his drink; the irony never failed to amuse him, especially when drunk.

He began to stand, intent on grabbing a torch and helping the party corral the bats. They waved him back down with urgent gestures.

"Sit there, don't move. We don't want any accidents," Dexter called out, a trace of panic evident in his tone.

Once the bats had been packed as tight as they could go, the party pulled a bucket out of a bag by the side, carefully standing the torches in the ground. They filled the bucket to the brim with murky alcohol, flinging away a bat that decided to splash its way inside. It smelled foul when they brought it over, small hairs clinging to the surface of the churning fluid.

"Drink up." Vak grinned, enjoying Silas' discomfort.

"Do I have to?"

Vak smiled in response.

Silas gagged and retched as he grabbed the bucket and tipped it back, trying not to let the filthy liquid touch his tongue. He failed. The warmth of it made it *worse*—if that was possible.

Every time he tried to set the bucket down, Vak or Dexter pushed it back up to his lips.

Even trying to toss it didn't work, with Vak warning him in no uncertain terms, "Go ahead, we'll just refill it. You're draining the whole thing either way, and we need to get this over with before the alcohol starts affecting you."

Finally, he finished, trying desperately to quell the urge to puke. Without time to pause, Enora shoved the gorilla's Beast Core toward him. "You'd better pay us back for this."

Compared to the foul-tasting liquid, the Beast Core slid down his throat like greased butter. Enora continued, "Now, this is going to hurt. The pain will start any second now, but you *have* to pay attention. When Vak punches you in the stomach, *start cultivating.*"

"Punches me in the–?" Silas didn't have time to finish. The tingling he had felt tugging at his Center morphed into something awful as the Core *swallowed* him.

He was immersed in agony as a bright worm of energy devoured his hard-won Essence, eating at his flesh, rendering his tissues down to a cruel liquid that burned through his veins. Hatred given substance ripped through him with ethereal claws, shattering his bones and molding them into aching teeth that gnawed at his very being.

Silas writhed on the ground, wracked with unbelievable torment, longing for Vak to hit him—anything to make it stop, anything to end the siphoning of his self. Years of Essence drained over an impossibly long duration before, finally, his Center emptied, and the pain receded.

He looked up at Vak, nose running and tears streaming down his face. "Why didn't you hit me?"

"Don't worry, I wi–"

He didn't hear the rest.

New waves of agony erupted; he had nothing more to give, and still, the Core demanded to be sated. It tore through his veins like a rampaging porcupine, drinking up the empty space left behind, spines of anguish shooting through his tissues, sparing none of the corruption that resided within him from its hunger.

His heart pounded in his chest... then it *didn't*. The shock of feeling his heart stop drove away the suffering that came from the Core, replaced with a comparatively pleasant burning that radiated along the entire left side of his body—it felt wonderful, like being deep fried in magma.

Enora lunged toward him and impacted him hard, sending a jolt of airy Essence into his body and restarting his failed heart before he blacked out. Then Vak punched him in the stomach. "Cultivate! Cultivate now!"

That's when he realized the pain had *actually* subsided. Shocked by his heart failing, Silas hadn't registered his corruption emptying until it was almost too late. He drew in Essence like a drowning man draws in water during his final moments, but it wasn't enough.

There wasn't enough infernal Essence nearby to sustain them both. The pain resurged for a second, the Core's worm of bright energy gorging on the pitiful new influx, before fading as the Core sought his life.

"Darn," Vak shouted into the otherwise still night. "Dex, do it now!"

Dexter ripped a torch from the ground and tossed it into the pool. The flame sputtered... and caught.

The alcoholic watering hole went up in a wash of fire, although the flames refused to spread into the dungeon's domain. A wave of necromantic energies surged Silas' Center as he cultivated—first a trickle, then a flood. As if thousands of squeaking voices cried out at once and...

Suddenly, everything fell silent. The air whooshed past him; Vak grabbed him by the leg and ran, dragging Silas behind him. "Keep cultivating."

A tug of war occurred within his Center, the Beast Core devouring infernal Essence as soon as he acquired it. The worm of light continued turning back, approaching his life energies, but the density of infernal energy—from bats brought to the peak of euphoria, then burned alive in an instant—meant that as long as he kept cultivating, it wouldn't return to gorge on something far more precious.

"Stop," Vak ordered, "for just a second. Let it detach from your Center. Then resume cultivating."

Silas did as told, despairing as he saw the Core rush toward his vital spark, intent on consuming it. Then he cultivated like his life depended on it. Which it did. A hair's breadth from the point of no return, the bright worm turned back for a third portion of his Essence.

The fumes of alcohol above the pool decided they had reached a sufficient density and combusted. A hollow *boom* resonated in his chest, and the flow of air reversed, throwing him forward and bringing with it a new wave of infernal Essence. *Somehow*, Vak kept his footing and chose that moment—better late than never—to swing Silas by his leg into a small tree. His vulnerable belly hit the trunk so hard that the slender sapling *cracked*.

Silas retched once, heaving in air and emptying his guts on to the floor. What had once been a relatively bright, clear Core was now a dirty thing, containing an oozing, suppurating, *mass* of vile darkness splashed with just the faintest streaks of crimson and midnight blue.

Denied its meal, its strand of light flashed toward Silas, intent on getting its due. Vak moved quicker, dropping Silas' leg and bringing his booted heel down on the Core, *hard*, detonating it in a violent burst of black light. How *light* could be *black*, Silas didn't know. He didn't have time to care.

He puked again, his vomit pouring out in an endless torrent. As he lost consciousness to the sound of shouting, a single thought filled his mind.

Why was there so much red?

CHAPTER SEVEN

Silas woke to someone slapping him. He groaned. Why was it always the face? Sound returned, along with light.

The ground around him was splashed with fluids, more blood than vomit—all his. The trees around the crater of the watering hole were burning, the brightness sending hot needles through his pupils. He closed his eyes again, blocking out the sight.

Vak was shouting in his ear, punctuating each word with a stinging blow; Enora had both her hands pressed to his chest, forcing large amounts of air Essence into him. Funny... he couldn't feel the tickling.

The meaning of Vak's words caught up with him a moment later. "Cultivate. You need to cultivate. Your life energies are filling the empty space inside your Center. If you don't cultivate, you'll die."

The air was thick with necromantic energies, but in his delirium, it was like grasping at smoke. Silas pulled again, rewarded by a mote of infernal Essence filling his Center. His incoherence lessened as he drew on the energies of the world. Silas' first particle of Essence had been luck; his second wasn't.

Homing in on infernal Essence specifically, he began refilling his depleted Center. Out of years of habit—and with occasional input from the party—he swirled his accumulated Essence in a spiral, attenuating it into the thinnest Chi threads he could manage in his current state.

The fog over his mind lifted further and soon he was cultivating from a buffet of infernal Essence, ignoring the large amounts of fire Essence and the smaller quantities of earth and air.

Silas continued despite his pounding headache, not wanting to miss out on the cultivation opportunity of a lifetime. Blood still dripped from his nose, but his hemorrhaging was no longer life-threatening. His old supplies of Essence were fully exhausted, and he had no idea what cultivation rank he even was anymore, but it was a fresh start, just as Enora had promised.

Gone was the bubbling mess of corruption that clogged his Center, impeding his ability to cultivate and maintain a spiral. Nothing stopped the swirl at the core of his being from spinning, clean and clear of obstruction and complications.

Silas felt healthier than he had in an age, old aches and pains that he had forgotten even existed falling from his body. His spiral spun far slower than it once had, but that was to be expected. Once it built up some volume, it would accelerate. However, as it stood, the old rules still applied. Essence begets Essence. His previous cultivation base had been lost to the Beast Core and almost a great deal more, but he had gained significantly as well.

He wondered how many cultivators would pay for a second chance like this, to undo the mistakes and damage they had caused to themselves when they were still learning. Silas continued on for hours, trying to eke out as many gains as he could from the demise of the bats. It would be a long time before he had such an opportunity again.

Finally, however, the Essence levels had waned, diffusing through the jungle to such an extent that further cultivation was pointless. Regretfully, he stood, going to get some shut eye. It was just before dawn when the bats began to wing their way, uncertainly, out of the mouth of the dungeon, returning home— no longer flying in straight and certain lines, corkscrewing through the air and releasing whooping squeaks.

They flew higher this time, above the trees. No doubt cautious about colliding with the curving branches and the ground a short while after. It was the same horde of black wings and fuzzy bodies, but it lacked the same terrifying unity of purpose—getting hammered; now it was the lame—but continuous—departure of drunken partygoers, swerving their respective ways home, fewer in number than before.

Silas edged around them, still cautious of earning their aggression. Even unable to fly straight, tens of thousands of drunken bats making a beeline—or was it a *bat*line—toward him seemed a likely contender for the title of 'a bad time'.

The crater had already begun refilling, slowly but deeper than before. He supposed it only made it all the more deadly for anything that didn't float naturally. The sides would eventually collapse, flattening it out until it was level again, but until then it was just another hazard.

He heaved himself up the cliff-face, climbing under vines until he reached the recess where the expedition had pitched their tent. Dexter had promised to teach him some martial arts when he woke. Not that Silas needed any further incentive to sleep.

He dozed off on the floor as soon as he was sure he was safe, still wearing the same garments, though now caked in his own dried vomit and blood.

***

Silas woke to Enora burning his clothes. Apparently, they smelled foul; not that Silas could tell. His nose turned out to be filled with large, crusty plugs of clotted blood; it was only after *even the ashes* of his clothes had been burned that he managed to remove them from his nostrils.

Enora had him throw those into the fire as well. Vak had lent him some of his own garments, but they hung off his small frame like some sort of flag. A childhood spent without sufficient Essence had stunted his growth, so he cut a rather ridiculous figure.

Dexter returned from scouting out the area soon after. Without pausing, he tossed Silas a dagger. Silas fumbled the catch and picked the weapon off the ground. Enora snorted, then took a seat on an upturned bucket.

Silas looked at Dexter questioningly, to which the monk said, "Hit me."

Silas lunged at him with a half-hearted thrust. Dexter slapped away the strike with unnecessary force.

"Like you *mean it*." This was the first time Silas had heard the man raise his voice.

He lunged again, putting more weight behind his attack. Dexter swayed to the side, the blade carrying on past him. He grabbed Silas' arm, tugging him forward and tripping him over an outstretched foot as he unbalanced.

"Better. Again."

Silas picked himself off the floor, determined to land a strike on the man. Again and again, he was slapped away or thrown to the floor.

"Warriors obsess over weapons."

Smack

"Trying to find the sharpest blade," Dexter flicked the blade upward, ruining the strike, "or the strongest armor."

Dexter dodged to the side, sweeping Silas off his feet in the same motion.

"What they fail to realize," the monk slammed him into the ground, one hand pressed on his chest, the other immobilizing his knife hand, "is that we are already blessed with four weapons."

He head-butted Silas. "Maybe even five."

Dexter hauled Silas to his feet, then threw him toward the wall. "While a warrior focuses on mastering their chosen weapon. A monk focuses on mastering themselves."

Silas saw red, launching into an onslaught of steel, missing each time by the slightest of margins. The monk was moving imperceptibly each time, foiling every blow. "A monk rarely needs armor to protect themselves. Speed is our sanctuary."

Silas overextended, and Dexter slid behind him like a hungry shadow. "Our bodies are our weapons."

He raised one leg up and around, bringing it down on Silas' shoulder, sending him to his knees, the foot gone before the point of Silas' dagger could reach his sole. "A monk is always armed because he has *arms* or, failing that, legs."

He tapped lightly on Silas' back, overbalancing him. "A sword has a thousand ways to strike a telling blow, but by using it, you miss a million others."

Finally, he launched a brutal kick between Silas' legs, sending him groaning to the floor, curled up in a fetal position. With a featherlight touch, he worked the dagger free from Silas' nerveless fingers, tossing it to the side. Dexter sat down next to Silas.

"Some will tell you that martial arts are about self-defense. They are wrong. Martial arts are about ending fights; in a dungeon, that fight ends when either you or your enemy is dead. Martial arts let you choose who lives and who dies. You—or your enemy."

CHAPTER EIGHT

Dexter continued to teach him throughout the next few days, giving him exercises to improve his form and build muscle. As evening fell and after several rounds of healing from Enora, Silas began to cultivate the infernal Essence released by the bats as they swarmed and died.

He'd been allowed to pile their bodies on a nearby ledge, where their decomposition would provide a slow but constant release of infernal Essence. The result was a slow and steady accumulation of Essence in his Center, punctuated by the larger flares of several bats' death in the grip of intoxication.

Finally, a few days later, seeing nothing overly alarming, the expedition party took the opportunity to delve into the dungeon, not wanting to bring Silas along, particularly on a first dive when the threat level of the area was still unknown.

For his own part, Silas was happy to stay and cultivate, slowly working his way toward the next rank, his spiral picking up speed—although his progress was too slow to actually be able to see tangible results just yet. The thought of entering the dungeon only to encounter a beast like the gorilla sent shivers of dread down his spine. He was happier outside until he knew for sure what awaited him.

They returned, hours later, barely even panting, their arms filled with fruits and berries. They also seemed to be having trouble walking in a straight line. It took an age and several falls for them to work their way up the cliff-face.

Dexter, typically a poster child for balance and coordination, tripped on his way back to the tent, hiccupping. When he saw Silas looking, he stared back woozily. "Waddya lookie at? *Hic*."

One of the fruits, a peach, had fallen to the ground, and he looked at it speculatively. He struck what he thought was an authoritative and dignified pose.

"Ay will now *hic* teak youuu an impuhtant lessun. Your bod–*hic* bo– *hic* booty," Dexter frowned, wondering if he'd used the wrong word; then his concentration lapsed, and he continued, "is *hic* a weapon. Ay *hic* will now demon— *hic*–strate."

The monk bent down, berries and fruits spilling out of his arms in all directions. His teeth closed around the peach, and he gnawed at it violently, raising his head in triumph. Amber juice, thick as syrup, oozed out the sides of his mouth, and he had a look of bliss on his face.

Slowly, Dexter leaned down again, gathering up the fallen fruits before chucking them at Silas. "*Hic* Catch."

The peach dropped from his mouth as he talked, rolling between his legs out of sight; he scrabbled around, trying to find it. Only one of the projectiles Dexter lobbed actually came close enough to intercept, and Silas managed to snag it as it passed. It looked like an apple.

"Good. Now, *hic* demonstrate my tuchnique."

Silas took a small bite of the apple. His mouth was immediately filled with delicious cider, a perfect mixture of sweetness and tang, the burn of the alcohol masked by the cutting crispness of the fruit.

"Perfect, *hic* my uhprentice, Ay *hic* have taught yu *hic* all Ay have tuh teak. Like *hic* Ay did with my mas— *hic*–ter before me. Yu will now *hic* fight me. To the *hic* duff."

Without waiting for his response, Dexter surged forward, fists flying in an unsteady arc. He tripped at the last moment, giving Silas just enough leeway to jump back. Then it happened.

Silas wobbled, ever so slightly. The fruit was so potent and his tolerance for alcohol was so low that he became drunk immediately.

"Gotcha." Dexter had grabbed his leg, then slowly began to climb him like a tree. Silas reeled, falling backward with his arms windmilling. As he went down, his flailing knee caught the monk on the chin.

In the confusion, he managed to worm his leg free. The apple's juice had really taken hold by now. Silas managed to roll to the side and kept on rolling, and rolling, and rolling. Finally, he hit the wall, bracing against it to steady himself as he stood. Dexter had regained his footing as well, veering his way toward him.

He flung a fist at Silas' face, lightning-fast. An unsteady wobble sent Silas' left knee buckling before he could steady it. His body tilted in the same direction.

The fist shaved the stubble from his cheek as it passed, leaving an impact crater in the wall, radiating cracks in all directions. Silas stumbled forward, putting too much force behind the movement.

He rammed into Dexter, sending the monk sprawling onto his back. By some divine mercy, he kept his own footing, stepping on and over his downed teacher. He wobbled forward, unable to stop his momentum, mind bouncing down several flights of stairs before it reached the only obvious conclusion.

The fruit had given him superpowers.

He let himself tumble, falling bonelessly to the floor near a pile of fruit. Out of the corner of his eye, he saw Vak rummaging through a pack and Enora scribbling messages furiously—the 'screaming with rage' type of furious.

His questing fingers fumbled three fruits before he got a solid grip on one. Pushing himself back upright, he raised it triumphantly to his lips, taking a bite out of its tender, succulent flesh.

Silas felt the effects take hold, his vision blurring further and revealing dancing spots of blinding brilliance surrounding the torches. The fruit was unveiling the true nature of the world! This must have been what it meant to infuse Essence into his eyes! Just in time.

A blur, invisible to the naked eye, rushed at him. Fortunately, Silas' eyes were fully clothed.

He dodged to the side, Dexter's strike missing by a mile. He evaded the second, then a fourth, then a third. As he contemplated on the order of the strikes, he raised the fruit to his mouth for another bite.

The deeper mysteries of the world were revealed; Dexter's moves were broadcast by the incessant motions of the universe before he even made them. Silas switched to the offensive, fists, feet, and forehead flying forward, closing in on the startled monk with deadly force.

Thunder roared in his ears with the impact of the strike, a furious explosion of light bursting before his eyes, wind rushing past him. It was over. Dexter had kicked him over the ledge, out into open air.

The last thing he saw was Vak opening a cage, letting the birds inside take wing as he cried, "Fly, little carrier pigeons. Fly, fly, fly."

CHAPTER NINE

"Ow," Silas' eyes burned as he opened them, "my head."

His whole body itched and ached, so he did what any normal person would do. He scratched. The symptoms of the hangover were already dissipating, slowly, but he could feel them fading. The normal stomach ache he experienced during a hangover was absent as well.

What's more, he felt a creeping sense of refreshment flowing through his veins, a sharpness to his vision and increased ease with each breath he took. It was masked by the hangover for the most part, but he knew it was there because it felt so *different.*

There was a tickle beneath his nose; he scratched. His nose hadn't gotten any bigger... Instead, his fingers came away crusted in dried blood. He closed his eyes again, groaning.

What in the *abyss* had happened?

Suddenly worried, he checked his Center. His Essence levels had dropped *precipitously.* Something else was different. A fine thread of Essence had branched off his spiral, exiting his Center through a hole in its side and traveling straight to his big toe. It traversed the top of his foot, climbing from his ankle to inner thigh before dipping down to his groin and circling something that had *definitely* gotten bigger. From there, it moved upward, covering half the distance to his navel before veering off to his liver and gallbladder, suffusing every part of the two organs with a strand of Essence.

From the liver, the thread branched: one traveled beneath his ribs, up to his throat, then into his eyes before terminating at the crown of his head; the other headed straight for his lungs before rejoining his Center through another hole in its side and streaming back into his Chi spiral.

What in the world? Had he gotten so drunk that he opened up a new meridian straight to his liver?

Opening a meridian was quite dangerous, apparently, so it was worrying that he had done it in a blackout-drunk state. If he had been less fortunate, he might not have survived it. By the dried blood beneath his nose and caking his fingernails, it seemed likely that he *almost didn't.*

It was then that he realized his predicament.

He twisted his head around; he was hanging off the ground, suspended by a tangle of vines that had arrested his fall. Silas was grateful for the fact they'd caught him, saving him from a fall to his death. However, he now had a new problem. He was stuck.

"Hello?" Silas called out. "Is anyone there? I've fallen, and I can't get up."

Enora's head poked over the edge; she looked like rehydrated manure. "Urgh, why are you down th–"

She broke off, her voice suddenly rising an octave, "Did you *open a meridian*?"

"I was drunk. Don't judge me. It's your fault for bringing back the fruit, not mine." Silas shrugged helplessly. Karma took hold at the same time as gravity. The movement freed him from a restraining loop of vine, sending him tumbling to the ground.

It was fortunate that there were only three yards left to fall. By the time he hit the earth, Enora's head had disappeared from over the ledge, leaving Silas to climb back up.

Despite the state he was in, the climb was easier than it used to be, no doubt thanks to the meridian he'd opened... while drunk...

As he reached the top, he saw Enora rummaging through the bags, her muttering becoming increasingly frantic and shrill, "Where are they? Where are they?"

"What's the matter?" he questioned.

"*This*," She waved a sheet, filled with frantic scribblings, "*this* is the matter. I found this message, which I don't remember writing, and multiple pages missing from my bundle of papers. I'm really hoping the carrier pigeons are here."

Wait a second... hadn't they... "I think Vak released them. What's the problem?"

Enora's voice rose to a shriek, "Because I just sent an emergency message to every Guild Hall in four hundred miles that we discovered a Heavenly Spirit Dungeon."

***

It took a while to calm Enora down, by which time Vak and Dexter had recovered—the latter of whom avoided eye contact with Silas like the plague. Together, they explained the issue.

"Spirits are typically infernally or celestially aligned monsters," Vak began.

Dexter picked up where his leader left off, "Which means that any dungeon that can create them typically has an infernal or celestial affinity. Such dungeons can't survive without causing massive conflict."

"This normally isn't a problem." Enora had her face buried in her hands. "Dungeons can be destroyed, but a *Heavenly* dungeon of one of those types is a world-ending threat. They won't send a handful of adventurers. They'll send an *army* of them."

"So, when they find out that this is a mid-to-high D-rank dungeon—at best—with major fire, major water, and minor earth and infernal affinities, along with a talent for producing alcohol... they're going to be furious. We can't even stop them since we're fresh out of pigeons," Vak concluded.

"We'll become a laughing stock," Dexter stated heavily. "We're ruined."

***

"What can we do?" Silas looked at the despondent faces.

"I'm not sure there's much we can do," Dexter replied. "But we dragged you into this mess, so the least we can do for you is help you for as long as we're around. We'll continue training you, running you through the dungeon, all that stuff," he paused and considered, "on the proviso that you *never* talk about what happened last night."

"What happened?" To Silas, most of what occurred after the first bite of the apple was a hazy blur.

"Nothing." Dexter nodded quickly. "So, would you like to see what all the fuss is about?"

Silas laughed. "Why not?"

CHAPTER TEN

The air of the dungeon was rich and fragrant, like spicy bourbon. Stalactites covered the ceiling, dripping amber liquid into small puddles. At the center of the first room sat a bubbling spring, pumping out waves of alcohol from some unknown depth of the dungeon. The liquid overflowed, hot rivulets running down the slight incline into a pool contained within the dungeon—which, itself overflowed, draining out into the crater beyond.

Where the alcohol went once it flowed outside the domain of the dungeon was anyone's guess, but it was possible that the dungeon extended beneath that point, collecting the liquid as it seeped through soil and stone. Bats screeched overhead, and Silas kept an eye out as they soared uneasy spirals overhead, crashing into walls with adorable squeaks.

He'd been warned that while most of them didn't belong to the dungeon, a minority of them would sink strangely elongated fangs into any exposed neck, pumping pure ethanol into their victim's veins—alcohol poisoning at its finest. While relatively well camouflaged among their mostly harmless brethren, these bats could be identified by the slick hair covering their bodies—a result of the apparently delicious secretions of the creatures.

That raised a whole lawsuit worth of questions. The first of which being, *who* would ever look at some random bat and think 'I want to *lick* that and see what it tastes like'. Dexter had the good grace to at least look embarrassed.

The first Needlebat, as they had chosen to call them, swooped down silently on leathery wings. Vak's sword blazed a shining arc. The Needlebat fell in two halves, cleanly bisected by the weapon.

Soon, however, a storm of wings and sharpened teeth descended on them. One Needlebat managed to slip past Vak's sword, Enora's quarterstaff, and Dexter's flying fists.

It flew toward Silas, teeth glinting. He snatched it out of the air, his training with Dexter paying off. He wrung the vicious creature like a wet towel before letting it fall to the ground, neck broken. His fingers were stained with the oily substance on the Needlebat's skin.

He gave it an experimental sniff, taking in the heady but not unpleasant smell. Silas touched one fingertip to his tongue, eyes widening at the explosion of flavor that danced its way across his taste buds. Celestial! Dexter was right. Yum.

Soon, the last of the Needlebats had been slain. Silas sat down to cultivate the infernal Essence released by the bats' deaths before it fully dissipated. The death of a non-dungeon creature wallowing unseen next to the source of the spring also provided a surprising but welcome burst of extra energy.

The bats left behind their hollow teeth once they disappeared back into the dungeon. Useful to some specialized craftsmen, perhaps, but since no one wanted them, they just let them lay there. They proceeded into the next cave, but before they did, Vak taught Silas the process of infusing Essence into his eyes.

As soon as he did so, Silas spotted the problem. Two yards in front of the entrance sat a small patch of ground, which, to his Essence-infused vision, seemed to be pocked with hundreds of dots of lighter stone. Picking up a loose rock, he threw it at the area. As it landed, the circular coverings burst outward, clouds of superheated alcohol billowing into the confines of the dungeon.

They all covered their mouths, not wanting to breathe in too deeply. As it stood, the main trait the dungeon rewarded was proper liver function. The mobs didn't seem overly dangerous, but the constant onslaught of alcoholic fumes turned it into a test against one's own ability to keep a clear head as they descended into drunkenness.

The caves continued onward, the ambushes of Needlebats a continual distraction. Then one of the rooms changed. Dexter grabbed Silas by the back of his borrowed shirt before he continued walking forward. Rivulets of alcohol ran down the walls and ceiling in weird stripes, pooling on the floor before draining into the deeps. And there was fire. Burning at the far end of the cavernous room.

They stepped inside. Bats, large and ponderous, swooped down from hidden hollows, corkscrewing through the air in unpredictable directions.

Then one flew directly through the flames.

Squeee...

It was set alight, and a high-pitched whine erupted from its mouth. The sound increased as it burned, growing in pitch as it approached, suddenly flying at them unerringly. Enora stepped forward, quarterstaff swinging. The steel-shod end sent the bat tumbling away from them, its continuous squeak escalating further.

...eeeeaaakBoom!

The bat exploded, sending out a shower of burning alcohol that stuck to every surface it touched. One of the stripes of running alcohol that encircled the room went up in a flash. However, when the flames dissipated, the alcohol remained, seemingly unconsumed by the fire.

More of the... Fusebats... dove into the fire and flew toward them, flung back to the far reaches of the room by

Enora's staff before detonating. Once the Fusebats had been thinned out, they continued inward, stepping carefully over the streams of alcohol. More of the burning bats homed in on them, igniting the alcohol around the party upon their deaths.

A stray splash of sticky fire hit Vak's breastplate, burning for several seconds. When the flames faded, Vak was unharmed, but the steel in the affected area had begun to melt and run before resolidifying.

As the last of the Fusebats were dispatched, they reached the end of the room. The rooms before had seemed to be an extension of a natural cave; now, however, the walls slanted, funneling them down into a tunnel. The scent of the air changed from a spicy bourbon to a more earthy, bitter smell that clung to their nostrils.

Before them stood an orchard filled with trees, bushes, and oversized mushrooms. Fallen fruit littered the ground, fermenting even more—if that was possible. Wasps the size of deer munched on the rotting detritus, buzzing happily as they fed. Brightly colored frogs and toads hopped around, tongues occasionally flicking out to touch the surface of the mushrooms.

Dexter looked at the trees, longingly, "Would it hurt to–?"

"Yes," Enora and Vak shouted.

The monk then turned to look at Silas. "Stay close. Watch what's going on, but don't fight. You're not strong enough to damage those things."

They charged. The flying insects turned to face them, buzzing aggressively. The first monster reached them. The Giant Wasp menaced with its stinger, sharp and dripping with venom that steamed against the ground where it landed. Vak parried it like a sword, then slid his blade along the length of the stinger, cutting into its armored abdomen.

While the Giant Wasp was distracted, Dexter aimed an ax kick at its transparent wings. The thin membranes crumpled easily beneath the blow, exiling it to the ground. As it rolled to its feet, Vak took the opportunity to land another blow on its abdomen, this time slicing through its chitinous armor and revealing the monster's intestines.

A second wasp joined the fight, but Enora held it at bay, using her quarterstaff to press it backward, buying her team time to finish the first wasp. The wasp bit at Vak's feet, taking several stabs to the thorax before Dexter's foot left a crater in its head. The insect collapsed, curling in its death throes, stinger twitching to strike at the empty air.

They moved on to Enora's opponent. The second fight was far faster and far more brutal. Vak severed the monster's wings, giving Dexter time to pin the creature. As it lay immobilized, Vak and Enora each shoved their weapons through the wasp's glittering, compound eyes.

Moving through the orchard, the group systematically slaughtered the Giant Wasps that approached them. They sat down to cultivate for a short while, drinking in the Essence of the room—all except for Enora, whose affinities didn't align with the dungeon's.

For Silas, the rotting fruit provided a small stipend of infernal Essence, adding to the low concentrations that the dungeon pumped out into the air.

When they had finished, they proceeded to the next room. A massive toad sat at its center, surrounded by steaming vents that spewed alcoholic vapors. Just being in the room was enough to make Silas' head spin, even with his liver meridian open.

The rest of the party didn't seem to be faring much better, the high amounts of atmospheric alcohol taking their toll.

A rumble built in the toad's throat, the warty brown skin of its back and belly vibrating.

Then it burped.

A cloud of purplish haze burst out around it, thick and tannic, like wine. Its tongue shot out toward them, bulbous at the end, like a pink raindrop with a stretchy stem. They dove out of the way as the tongue shot past them, then retracted back into the toad's mouth.

Another belch sent a cloud of winey haze spewing into the air.

The monster hopped forward, purple mists parting behind it as it moved. Its head jerked to one side as its tongue shot out again, sending the long, prehensile appendage in a sticky slash toward the adventurers picking themselves off the floor.

With the exception of Dexter, they all dived back to the ground. The monk deflected the tongue with a deft flick. However, the action left a thick layer of slime across his knuckles. Dexter's pupils dilated, a silly grin on his face.

Suddenly, Enora burst out laughing. "It's a Toad Licker."

The Toad Licker burped in response, hopping forward.

It shot out its tongue again, intent on snaring the monk. This time, Vak's blade sliced at the bulbous tip, leaving it hanging by a tenuous string of sinew. Hot, purple blood oozed out, sending a blast of vineyard aroma into the air. The toad flinched back, retracting its nearly severed tongue.

Dexter, of course, bent down to sample the taste of the liquid. He rose, his fingers and lips stained purple. He had a manic grin on his face. "*Hic* Fight me, toad! You *hic* will not duhfeat me. *Hic* Ay am a master of the *hic* marital arse!" He charged forward, slurring, "Ay *hic* need no sword. My *hic* body is my weapon. Speed is my sanc—*hic*—tuary. Ay will drink yaw blood."

Vak shadowed him, trying to assist his teammate in his compromised state. The Toad Licker shot out its tongue again, but the tank was ready. Before it could wrap around the stoned monk, the sticky river of flesh slumped to the ground in a glistening coil, severed. Blood gushed out of the toad's mouth, and Dexter charged into the torrent, screaming in triumph!

The toad belched again, and Vak held his breath. Dexter didn't.

The monk sent a flurry of blows into the monster's fat, jowly face. Slurred drinking songs about martial arts filled the air, barely comprehensible. Silas stood at the back, shaking his head at the pandemonium, as Enora rushed forward, bringing her staff down on top of the Toad Licker's back. Vak circled around, hamstringing the oversized feet of the monster, while Dexter hammered blows into its toothless mouth.

Under the combined onslaught, the monster collapsed. Vak and Enora dragged the delirious monk out of the purple cloud, finally taking a deep breath. Dexter had progressed from highly intoxicated to nearly catatonic, repeating under his breath, "I don't know why flavor." Whatever that meant. Silas didn't know either.

However, as they returned to the orchard, ignoring the stairs leading down deeper into the dungeon, they all burst into laughter. It wasn't born of the humor of the situation but rather a deep comradery, of staring down death dressed in a clown costume and coming out in one piece, together. It was being alive with friends.

It was something Silas had never really experienced— being *comfortable* around other people. Of feeling *part of something,* anything. And at that moment, it was all that mattered.

Quietly, he spoke, "I think I might know how to deal with the army coming here."

***

Four hundred adventurers descended on the Jungle of Toruk, armed to the teeth. Mages of all abilities marched in the vanguard, blasting and burning a path through the trees.

There, at the mouth of a dungeon buried within a vine-covered cliff-face—a dungeon they had come to destroy—they met a team of smirking people.

The four friends who had been waiting for them smiled with bleary eyes and extended fruit baskets.

Hidden Lantern
By: James Auwaerter

Prologue

I had been hiking through the Phantom Mountains for nearly three weeks. My plan to travel to the new dungeon by foot was clearly flawed; the particular mountain housing the dungeon was even more remote than the clearly poorly-made and outdated maps had led me to believe. As it was, I probably would have gotten myself lost if not for the unusually thick Essence in the air and water pointing me in the right direction.

After sniffing my clothes, I grimaced and shuddered. I wasn't the only one who had noticed the Essence. Goblin scat littered the banks of the river down the mountain which this stream fed into, and even at a few days old, its stench had been almost unbearable. There were downsides to having every meridian open; while it meant my senses were nearly unparalleled by anyone who wasn't a Mage, it also meant that I had to suffer that much more around foul odors.

Of course, there were benefits too. Even without using active Essence techniques, my eyes were keener than a hawk's, my ears and nose superior to those of a wolf. Dangerous beasts of the mountains that could do me actual harm? I fled before they even knew I was there. Some cultivators might consider it cowardly to avoid testing their might in combat; I wasn't one of them. Even at the young age of twenty years, I'd encountered enough people and *things* capable of killing me with a casual effort that I had no illusions of my own martial prowess. Besides, I hadn't been sent here to act as a warrior.

A travel-worn road wide enough for a small wagon led up from the stream. It was the first sign of the town which had surely sprung up around the dungeon by now, though it still betrayed its probable origins as a goat path. As I began to climb, I heard someone shifting in place about one hundred yards away. I sighed slightly as I tensed up. This was *always* the worst part of any mission I was sent on—I was going to have to deal with people again.

CHAPTER ONE

"Name?" the guard threw out the question with the enthusiasm of a sewer worker scraping a turd off the wall, a bored expression on his face even as I approached. Even though his laziness benefitted me, I was still offended by it on some level. It wasn't like he was busy. I was probably the only lone traveler to arrive this entire day. Even most merchants would find the portal taxes cheaper than carting their goods across the rugged terrain. I had my own reasons for avoiding portals.

"James." True.

"Affinity?"

"Um, I think someone said I have an affinity for earth?" I said, sounding uncertain even though I knew that was the case.

The guard *glanced* at me with a flash of light outlining his eyes and nodded. He didn't seem to notice anything unusual. "Reason for coming here?"

"The dungeon." Also true, though somewhat circuitous and very incomplete. My oath to the Church forbade me from lying, and unlike some of my brethren, I didn't enjoy twisting words to mislead people. My orders, however, were clear.

"Mmph," the guard grunted. "It's a gold to enter the 'city'."

Even though he tried to remain nonchalant, I noticed the way his eyes narrowed just a little as he lied to me. Some cultivators learned to read auras to determine whether someone was lying or telling the truth, but I found that reading expressions was even more effective. Most cultivators learned to control their auras, but few paid much attention to their tells. I had made more than one sizable donation to my monastery's poor box after a night playing cards at the local tavern.

Given my appearance, there was no way that he could expect me to be able to pay that much just to get in. Revealing that I did, in fact, have several gold coins would draw attention, which was precisely what I was trying to avoid. My low opinion of the guard dropped even further, but now, it was time to see what sort of game he was playing.

"Oh *no*. I've only got," I trailed off, pulling out a small pouch and looking through it, "two silver and three copper in my pouch here. I've come all this way..."

I closed my eyes and did my best to look like I was trying to hold back tears. The guard lowered his voice and almost theatrically looked around. No one else was around. "Tell you what. I'll take what you've got and let you in anyway. If you get lucky on your first dungeon run, you might find a Runed pendant, and everyone knows Runes mean gold. You could pay me back then. Just don't let anyone else know what I did for you. I'd hate to see you get thrown out."

"Oh, thank you so much!" I handed over the pouch, doing my best to sound appreciative. Inside, I was burning up. I appeared young for my age—a benefit of effective cultivation— and I had bound my Chi spiral so that I'd appear to be in the F-ranks to anyone who wasn't a Mage taking an *extremely* close look at me. If someone with my apparent cultivation went into a dungeon without a strong team, it was the next closest thing to suicide. For now, all I could do was memorize his features. Hopefully, there would come a time soon when he would see justice.

"Before I go, I heard there was a church here? Can you tell me where it is? I wanted to pray before I went into the dungeon," I asked as hopefully as possible. The guard had already begun to lose interest in me once he had taken my pouch, and he gestured vaguely in a direction further up the mountain.

"It's that way. You can't miss it—there are only two buildings here, and it isn't the one that looks like a giant tree." He turned away from me to look down the mountain path. It was clear that the conversation was over, which suited me just fine. I began to walk towards the way he gestured until I saw where muddy footpaths had begun to form from frequent use.

Even before I could see the refuse, I could smell it. The best that could be said of it was that it wasn't quite as bad as the Goblin scat. Unlike most cultivators of my rank, I didn't have the option of blocking my senses with Essence either—another part of my oath. If the smell got any worse, maybe I could see if any of the other fishies were covering their faces to block it out. How could they not notice it? Maybe they had just gotten used to it, but I had to imagine that the only reason disease hadn't spread through the camps was dumb luck.

Well, dumb luck, and an extremely high cultivation base. As I made my way towards the church, which I could see once I climbed up a small bluff, I noticed that there were relatively few people still in the F-ranks, and most of them looked like they were locals who had come to the dungeon hoping to strike it rich. D-ranks were more common, and it seemed like there were even more Mages than C-rankers. I had been hoping that Father Richard was the only A-ranked Mage here, but my hopes were dwindling.

Thankfully, no one seemed to pay any attention to me as I walked into the church. It felt like it was almost literally *humming* with celestial Essence. There were a couple of other people praying quietly in the chapel, and while I would join them later, there was someone else I had to meet first. I was here for the man whose Mana I could now sense from a nearby room: Father Richard Demonbane.

Chapter Two

Father Richard was alone in the antechamber, which made my life easier. I didn't have to find a way to try to fit what I was about to say into a normal conversation.

"Father Richard, I was told that you needed a lantern for when the night is long," I announced softly. At least, I started to say the passphrase, but I had barely gotten past his name when he jumped in his chair and began to gather Mana. I threw myself to the ground, colliding with a small desk and knocking a bunch of papers and an inkwell on top of myself.

"A lantern for when the night is long!" I hurriedly finished in a far louder voice. The glow around him lessened. He had begun by shielding himself, rather than attacking me, but I hadn't expected him to be so easily startled. It took a moment—which felt like a very long time—before the Mana returned to its normal state. I remained still while he looked at me.

"I asked for a lantern. You don't look like one," he told me in a level tone.

"Is there a place we can speak, in private?" I coughed as I rolled to avoid the spilled ink. "I can explain."

Another moment passed, and Father Richard nodded. He held out his hand, and after, I figured out why; I stood up without his help.

"I'm sorry. I just don't like touching people," I told him sincerely. He nodded to himself again, and I got the impression that I had just passed a test. I looked down at my ink-stained clothes and sighed. At least I had avoided the *worst* of it. I knew that he wasn't going to like what I had to say, and a sloppy appearance wasn't going to make things any better.

"We'll go to the practice room. I've already tested it before. If they couldn't hear Dale yelling when I shattered his Chi spiral, then I... oh, I don't know how many people know I did that. Forget what I just said," Father Richard muttered as he walked farther into the monastery. "But before we go in, do you need to use the bathroom? We just had one installed. I can't believe I had forgotten about them before."

"Ah, no thank you." I blinked and thought about taking the chance to clean up, then shook my head. "It was a long walk, but I'm fine."

I knew I looked young, but really, I could handle my own bathroom habits. Wait, he shattered a Chi spiral? What?

Father looked like he was about to say something, but he held his tongue. Soon, we were inside a large room, twenty paces across. With a strength that belied his outwardly normal appearance, he closed the heavy granite door by himself and turned to face me. I let out a deep breath and relaxed as my Chi spiral unfurled into its natural shape for my C-rank. At the same time, I removed the Essence blocking my affinity channel for air.

"Junior Inquisitor James, reporting to Father Richard Demonbane as ordered by the Bishop," I gave him the full rundown, as was expected. Father Richard cocked his head and slowly walked around me.

"That... is a little impressive. I could tell you were hiding something once you entered the room, but I couldn't tell *what*. Are they teaching all Inquisitors that these days?" he asked as he stopped in front of me. I shook my head.

"I developed these Essence techniques myself. I had been trying to create a memory stone to help pass them along to a better teacher before I received this assignment." While it was possible for non-Mages to add their memories to a blank stone, it required nigh-perfect control of Essence and mind. Mana made so many things easier. He nodded, remaining silent for a moment as he gathered his thoughts.

"You're a C-rank and not just an earth cultivator but a horizon cultivator," he looked me up and down, and I winced. At least he managed to say the term without the mild disdain I heard from many clerics. While the Church didn't technically *require* its clergy to have the celestial affinity channel open, most did. As a horizon cultivator, I could cultivate anywhere with both air and earth essence, making it one of the easiest dual affinities to handle. I'd even heard that some people cultivated it by allowing themselves to be struck by lightning, though I wasn't about to test that method myself.

"Yes, and I know that I'm a Junior Inquisitor rather than the Inquisitor that you asked for." I took a deep breath. He wasn't going to like this. "The Bishop ordered me here to investigate your claims and provide an independent report."

I purposefully did not use the word 'unbiased', even if it's what the Vicar General had said, but it seemed the message came through anyway. I was right. He blew up immediately. I was just glad it was words and not Mana, even if some of those words were not the sort that most people would expect to hear from a cleric. Having been in the Church for several years, I was less surprised than most would be. Father Richard had a reputation, after all. He finally calmed himself down enough to speak to me rather than just yell.

"What part of '*my claims*' do they not believe? The dungeon's Essence? It's so pure, so... so *un-aspected*. This place is unlike any other I've seen." He grabbed my shoulders, and I couldn't help flinching. Even though his Mana was not associated with a violent concept, I grew even more aware of it when he made contact, especially when I knew he could probably tear me apart by hand if he wanted to. To his credit, he immediately let go with a chastened look on his face.

"It's simple, James. Infernal cultivators are going to be drawn here for the chance to cultivate. I need at least one Inquisitor here to find them. Some of them may be like Rose, but any who have advanced beyond F-rank through blood sacrifices and demon summoning... Those sorts of 'habits' taint the soul." I could feel a lecture coming on, which was a little ironic, considering that I was usually the one giving the lecture.

"Who is Rose?" I asked to try to head him off.

"Oh. A chaos cultivator," he told me that nonchalantly, but I had no idea *why*. I winced involuntarily; being born a chaos cultivator was basically a death sentence. As far as I knew, they didn't survive childhood unless they cultivated in a battleground dungeon before it was destroyed by the Church. If this dungeon was stable and not in line for purification, then it was even more important than I had realized.

"May I speak freely?" I asked. Father Richard shrugged.

"Why not? Everyone else around here does," he muttered the second half, so I wasn't sure if he meant for me to hear it, but he gave me the permission I needed.

"I was ordered to spend one week here to conduct the investigation as a hidden lantern. I don't like acting in secret, but the fact is that plenty of people hear 'Inquisitor' and think that I'm going to carry them off to some dungeon somewhere. Not like the dungeon-dungeon... Ugh, you know what I mean. The first duty of an Inquisitor is to seek the truth, not to smite heretics." I smiled as I said it, but Father Richard sighed as I continued, "But so long as I am here, I will follow your orders to the best of my ability."

"It's not *your* fault, James. If I hadn't witnessed all these miracles myself, even I would have questioned them, and my faith is strong. You saw that sheet of quartz that forms the floor of the chapel when you entered? It is what's collecting celestial Essence from the heavens, and it appeared overnight. As rare as they are, there's a *Silverwood* tree here, and it's growing hundreds of feet underground,..." he said. My eyes widened, and I couldn't help myself.

"A Silverwood tree! Did you bring that up when you made your request?" I interrupted.

"I know I had said something before." Father Richard frowned, though I couldn't tell whether the frown was at my interruption or difficulty remembering exactly what he had written. Cold sweat began trickling down my back. Silverwood trees meant Elves, and I had history with them. Two years ago, I had been the one who discovered the coven of Wild Elves summoning demons north of the Lion Kingdom capital. It was what drove me to become an Inquisitor, and it still haunted my dreams at times.

"If there's a Silverwood tree, then anyone who believes that Silverwood trees can help people move into the B-rankings is going to come here. I don't know of any trees that aren't controlled by High Elves or Wood Elves, and neither of them are big on allowing outsiders anywhere near the trees," I rambled on. Father Richard was right; this dungeon's lack of an affinity was attractive to infernalists, while the Silverwood tree was attractive to C-ranks and Elves. Put them together in a single location, and it was only a matter of time before infernalists or— even worse in my opinion—*Wild Elves* would show up.

CHAPTER THREE

Suddenly, the high concentration of Mages took on a new light. This mountain was disputed ground, and I had thought the Lion Kingdom and the Phoenix Kingdom were jockeying for control by sending Mages to influence the owner of the land around the dungeon. Now, I was beginning to think that there might not be enough Mages to defend it even with the two Kingdoms and the Guilds all added together.

"You didn't just want someone who could find infernalists," I parsed out my thoughts slowly to Father Richard. "You need more people who can *fight* them."

Father Richard grunted, speaking with a hint of bitterness, "If *you* were able to figure it out that quickly, then I shouldn't be surprised that the Bishop did as well. Is my sect still that much out of favor with him?"

I opened and closed my mouth, trying to figure out how to phrase my thoughts. "I do not think that it is the Bishop who dislikes your sect. I do not know whether he received your request himself. My orders technically came through the Vicar General, and when I spoke with him, he seemed to harbor doubts about the need for a full Inquisitor to be stationed here."

"That explains a lot, though I'm surprised that you would speak ill of him." Father Richard looked at me thoughtfully.

"I don't see it that way. He ordered me to serve you to the best of my abilities while I was here. I don't know if he really *meant* it, but it was a legitimate order. To me, that means speaking uncomfortable truths rather than trying to hide them." Father Richard chuckled at my words; then his face grew grim.

"This is what I get for trying to be clever." Father Richard sighed. "I hoped that the Inquisitor would understand what I've seen and call upon reinforcements from his own order. If not that, then at least be able to advocate for more clerics sent here without being accused of doing it out of a sense of self-importance."

"I may not be a full Inquisitor, but I've taken the same oaths every Inquisitor takes—to always use my essence to seek the truth, to always speak the truth, and to serve the Church with all my heart and soul. Already, as soon as I arrived here, I was extorted by the guard just to enter the camp."

"I saw one of the Inscribed pendants that the dungeon created, and your report said something about anti-demon Runes as well. I see their value, but one of the differences between a wandering demonslayer and the vicar of a location-based diocese is a focus on providing spiritual guidance to people..." I realized that I had begun lecturing Father Richard, and I had stepped well beyond my remit. I stopped abruptly and blinked, wondering how badly I had screwed up. The silence stretched out for what felt like hours but was probably closer to a minute. Finally, Father Richard spoke.

"James... would you pray with me a moment?" Father Richard asked as he began to kneel. Wordlessly, I kneeled alongside him, then bowed my head in prayer. Light shone down on us as the prayer concluded. I echoed his amen, then stood as he rose once again.

"Father, I did not mean to criticize you," I said as soon as I could. Father Richard held up his hand.

"You spoke the truth as you saw it. I fell into old habits. It's easier for me to destroy a hundred undead than to counsel people, to run the Church's bank, or do so many of the other things that are required of me. Things have grown more complicated since I sent that request a month ago. Let's sit down while I go over what has happened." The two of us walked over to a wooden bench along the walls and sat down facing one another.

"The number of people here has doubled twice in that time, which has put a strain on the Church as well as on things like cleanliness, as you saw outside." Father Richard raised a brow at that thought. "I don't have enough hours in the day to heal injured adventurers and preach sermons, let alone everything else. I've had to recruit other healers from outside the Church, but most of them don't have the celestial affinity."

That meant that the healing would be unpleasant at best or actively painful at worst. I had learned basic healing Essence techniques, but I was personally and bitterly aware that my own healing felt like being blasted apart by a sandstorm. It was better than letting the injuries fester until only a flesh Mage could fix them but only just barely.

"I can protect the people here against any reasonable threat that I can detect, but I can't be everywhere at once. A couple of days ago, something escaped from the dungeon and killed a few F-ranked adventurers. Before I even heard about it, another Mage caused it to flee back into the dungeon where it killed Dale, the owner of this mountain. Then—another miracle— the Silverwood tree brought him back to life somehow. Not undead, but alive." Father Richard paused for a moment to see how I reacted to that. For my part, I let it pass. That would be easy to verify—something that miraculous would have everyone talking about it. Seemingly satisfied, he continued.

"His body is fully healed, but I'm not sure how dying affected his mind. We closed off the entrance to the dungeon until we figure out what's going on. The leader of the Adventurers' Guild here, Frank, and some of the other more powerful Mages have already started discussing whether he's still fit to own the land," Father Richard said. "I've urged them to give him some time, but I think there will probably be a council meeting within the next week. Dale is the linchpin holding the two Kingdoms together. If one Kingdom breaks the land ownership contract and the other doesn't, it could lead to a war here with all the people caught in the middle. Even he does not understand his actual role in this situation."

"No pressure," I sarcastically agreed, then sighed. "It's fine. Being an Inquisitor was never advertised as being easy."

CHAPTER FOUR

The conversation didn't continue long after that. I had already spent more time near Father Richard than was wise if I wanted to hide my connection with the Church. Before I left, he was kind enough to use a bit of Mana to clean the ink off my shirt. At least when I left the church, I wouldn't be oddly stained.

As I walked out of the church, I began thinking about whether earth Essence alone could be used to remove stains. While ink was liquid, it wasn't like the water was the part that was staining the fabric, right? The challenge would be removing the fresh ink without removing all the other dyes on the clothing. It was an interesting idea, and it was enough to distract me. I put one foot down on the uneven ground and rolled my ankle, almost falling into the side of someone's tent. Even though I caught myself, the pain was bad enough that I sat down for a moment to catch my breath.

A shadow loomed over me, and I looked up to see a short man silhouetted by the setting sun.

"New here?" he asked, offering his hand to help me up. I hesitated, then took it. His palms were callused, but the calluses were those of a craftsman or miner, not a warrior. I let go as quickly as I could.

"It's my first day here," I admitted. He nodded sagely, then gestured for me to walk alongside him. I followed as he began to speak.

"My name's John. You came to run the dungeon, eh? You've got some lousy timing. They've closed it down until a wall gets built or something, but at least the Guild is paying for food in the meanwhile. Really, it's the least they could do. Well, let me give you some advice. Get your name on the list to enter as soon as you can. If you're lucky, you'll get a chance within a couple days once they re-open the dungeon, but it could be a week or more. If you're smart, you'll stick to mining—the upper levels may not have precious metals or Inscribed weapons, but they're safe, and I can introduce you to Tyler. He sells pickaxes, and he's willing to extend some credit if you seem like the trustworthy sort." John seemed to be a good person, and I listened as he kept on.

"If you fancy yourself a warrior, try to find a group that will take you with them. Some of them bring people to help carry out treasure. It doesn't pay much, but a good group will help protect you while you learn what's in the dungeon and whether fighting is what you really want to do." John paused, looking out towards where the sun was quickly dropping over the horizon. "There are plenty of people who came here dreaming of riches, but they died in that dungeon and didn't even leave a body behind."

"Let me show you where the mess hall is. There's a fancy restaurant for all the bigshot cultivators, but unless you've got more gold than you know what to do with, the cook at the mess hall will be your best friend here. Oh, that's another thing. If you're lucky, an adventuring group will enter the dungeon around the same time as you, and you can go gather some of the dungeon herbs after they've cleared out the rabbits. They're supposed to be delicious, but whoever was collecting them hasn't done so for a while."

"The rabbits?" Was he serious? John shook his head with a grin on his face.

"The herbs are the delicious things. I don't think... Oh, you mean that the main monsters are rabbits. It sounds like a joke, but it isn't. Imagine a half-dozen rabbits the size of a dog running into you, and some of them have horns. They stay out of the mining area, but between them and the plant monsters, it's not safe to go into the dungeon unprepared."

A line stretched out of a tent much larger than most of the other ones on the mountain. John and I stood at the end of it. Eventually, we passed through the entrance. A man behind the serving line looked over at me and chuckled.

"*Another* new adventurer?" the man's voice boomed out before he realized how loud he was being. His next words were a little softer, "They get younger all the time."

I bit my tongue. I had to keep telling myself that I didn't need to correct everyone about my age. John and I got a good portion of food and found a place at a long table to sit down. People were coming and going constantly, and John seemed to be done with speaking for the moment. Instead, he wolfed down his food quickly enough to impress even me. I had grown up in a large family where you had to eat quickly if you wanted seconds or even to keep all of your firsts, sometimes, but he put me to shame. The food was bland, so I didn't waste too much time savoring the flavor.

"I don't suppose you have a team I could work with, John?" John stopped eating for a moment, swallowing what was in his mouth, then shook his head.

"Sorry, but I don't have a team. I'm lucky if I can get hired on every other day. I guess some would call me a fool, telling you all this stuff—you're my competition now—but," he looked around the mess hall before continuing in a quieter voice, "you aren't one of the jerks from the Adventurers' Guild or one of those Mages. Us normal folks have to stick together some. Celestial knows that they don't give a hoot about us."

"Shoot, I didn't catch your name. What did you say it was?" John finally asked.

"James. Good to meet you, John. It's nice to know someone is looking out for the little guy." I paused, then steeled myself before holding out my hand. He shook it with a smile.

CHAPTER FIVE

The next couple days passed fairly quickly. John took me to a clerk with the Adventurers' Guild so I could have a chance to enter the dungeon when it re-opened, and he explained to me how to see whether I was selected for a dungeon run. Everyone in the camp would gather by the main Adventurers' Guild tent in the morning, about an hour and a half past sunrise.

A huge list would be posted, listing who was selected, whether they were part of a group, and what time they were scheduled to enter the dungeon. There was a clear divide between the members of the Adventurers' Guild and everyone else, and a smaller one between the locals and the miners and merchants who had—mostly—come via portal.

My efforts to try to find an existing adventuring team where I could work as a porter all failed. I knew I didn't look very strong, but showing off enough to prove otherwise would have risked revealing my true rank. Instead, I spent most of my time doing odd jobs around the camp. Merchants needed help unloading their wares, the mess hall needed dishwashers—though I resolved to never eat there again after I saw how some of the other washers just rinsed dishes out in the stream, downstream from where people washed themselves—and I even worked for the Adventurers' Guild for one afternoon.

It was somewhat grim work. The Guild was taking the extra time while the dungeon was closed to collect anything that the victims of the dungeon had owned and hadn't brought along with them. Of course, most people weren't foolish enough to leave anything too valuable in the camp—I had overheard plenty of people talking about thieves and accusing one another of being thieves—so that mostly meant things too large to easily move, like tents and cots. I got the impression that the Guild sold off their belongings to pay off any outstanding debts. Idly, I wondered whether Dale owed the Guild any money. I was sure they'd be happy to claim the deed to the mountain if he met with any trouble inside the dungeon.

The mountain, not very warm to begin with, was starting to grow colder as winter approached. I only needed an hour or two of sleep each day, so I spent my nights as active as I could and rested around mid-morning. It was strange to see how quiet it became in the early morning, just before dawn. Even if Mages didn't need to sleep, most of them still did. I could understand why; there is something about sleep that allows the body and mind to reset and recover. I just didn't want to go to sleep and freeze to death. If I hadn't been leaving in a few days, I would have seen about buying one of those tents myself.

On the third morning, I came across another early riser, about an hour before the sun would come up. Or maybe less; I was still getting used to how quickly the sun rose and set in the Phantom Mountains. He was moving slowly as he fastened up his tent. I paused for a moment. I knew that there were plenty of people who took some time to wake up in the morning, but his movements seemed shaky more than tired. Something about him seemed... off.

I looked around quickly—still no one else around. I relaxed, allowing my Chi spiral to unfurl just a smidge so that I could use a more powerful active Essence technique to enhance my senses even further. The dim moonlight became as bright to me as the noonday sun, and to my dismay, I could smell him; it seemed he hadn't had a bath in days. His body appeared almost skeletal, but that was wholly at odds with his cultivation. It looked like he was in the low D-ranks and... did he have every affinity channel completely open? My jaw dropped. Anywhere but here, that was a short ticket to an overwhelming amount of corruption. Even if the dungeon was as pure as Father Richard had said—and I knew I still had to verify that before I left—he wouldn't be able to cultivate anywhere else.

I had stayed in place too long. The emaciated man hadn't seen me, but if he caught me staring at him, I wouldn't have a good excuse. I started walking towards another rough approximation of a pathway through the tents, but some gravel crunched under my feet, and he looked over to me. I quickly dropped the Essence technique on the off chance he could sense it.

"James?" he questioned. I stopped dead in my tracks. The only people to whom I had introduced myself were the guard along the path, who looked like he was going to forget it as soon as I was out of his sight, John, and Father Richard. Oh, and that scribe working for the Adventurers' Guild for dungeon signups; she made my skin crawl for some reason. Even so, none of them should be spreading it around.

"Yes, I'm James. I don't think we've met. How did you know my name?" I asked politely. Now it was his turn to look confused.

"You sort of look like him, but you don't dress like him or talk like him," he muttered to himself. He looked straight at me. I had heard of piercing blue eyes, but this was the first time I had seen eyes so blue that Essence or maybe even Mana was involved. It felt a little unnatural, and I had to suppress a shudder. "So, if I said, 'get off my mountain', it wouldn't mean anything to you?"

As he said those words, out of the corner of my eye, I saw a faint line of Mana emerge from the ground and begin to twist itself around my leg. My foot twitched involuntarily—the resonance didn't feel remotely comforting like Father Richard's had. It felt imperious, like... like what a magically enforced landownership contract was supposed to feel like. Even when he didn't mean the words, it was still enough for me to sense what would happen if he had given an order. Pieces began to fall together.

"It would mean that you're Dale, the owner of this mountain. This is the first time we have met, but if you met someone who looks like me, it was probably one of my brothers," I decided to tell him.

"Oh, that makes... wait a second. You're James, and your brother, the portal Mage, is also named James?" Dale cocked his head to the side like a dog. I groaned inwardly. Of course, *that* James was the one who showed up here. I shook my head.

"Not just him. I have six older brothers, and *all* of them are named James. My father decided it was a good name, so we all ended up with it. You want to guess what his name is?" I heatedly asked.

"James?" Dale ventured a guess.

"No. Ian. *He* gets a unique name, while the rest of us all have to share one. By the time I was born, my mother was just calling us by number! Even all the way out here, I'm going to be 'the other James' now." I felt my childhood making my skin crawl. "Unless... did you actually tell him to get off the mountain? Is he gone?"

"I did tell him to leave, but I let him stay after he promised not to be an ass to everyone around him," Dale told me with a ghost of a smile.

"Actually, now that I think about it, he didn't actually promise..." he trailed off as he realized what had happened. I rolled my eyes.

"Neither of us are Mages, so trust me when I say that I know *exactly* what he's like to those of 'lesser cultivation'. He doesn't make an exception for family." I sighed. "If you aren't going to banish him, can you at least not mention to him that you saw me? I walked here instead of taking a portal to try to avoid him. I had no idea that he was actually out here already."

"That bad, huh? I won't let him know you're here. Anyway, I need to get something to eat. Goodbye, James." Dale's voice was surprisingly soft. I nodded in thanks. Dale shambled off, but before he got too far, I heard him mutter to himself, "At least there's someone on this mountain who isn't playing games."

He sounded exhausted. I thought back to what Father Richard had said a couple of days ago, and I had to wonder if the Mages he had mentioned might have been right. Dale sounded like a broken man. The question was whether he'd be able to put himself back together again.

The short conversation left me in a melancholy mood. I hadn't thought about my family for a while, especially my oldest brother. My family wasn't part of the nobility, but there were rumors that somewhere along the family tree was a noble's bastard or else a very successful thief. The Essence cultivation techniques my brothers and I had been taught from the family vaults were a lot better than those of most of the acolytes I had met after pledging myself to the Church. I had risen to the C-ranks faster than a lot of nobles' children, but breaking into the B-ranks meant developing an understanding of Mana, and that was as much inspiration as it was an art. Real nobles supposedly had a leg up on that as well, but so far, only two of my brothers had broken through the bottleneck, and neither of them was interested in helping out the rest of their family.

I had studied as much as I could. Most Inquisitors either bonded to celestial-oriented concepts like other clerics in the Church—things like 'justice' or 'mercy'—or else sensory concepts like what Spotters would do. Everyone said that you couldn't force an understanding of a concept, that it would speak to you, but all that did was frustrate me.

Until I advanced to the B-ranks, I would never be a full Inquisitor. The Mana-based oaths I followed were laid upon me by another Mage, but they would fade over time. Only once I could awaken my own Mana could I bind myself permanently and serve as I wanted to. On that somewhat depressing note, I walked off to see whether I'd be able to enter the dungeon today.

CHAPTER SIX

The third day was the same as the last two. I was kicking myself for walking out to this mountain. If I had taken the portal, I could have gone into the dungeon, felt the Essence for myself, and maybe even seen a Silverwood tree for the first time. Then again, maybe my brother would have been the one opening the portal, which could have revealed my identity to everyone from the start.

I had gathered a lot of information just by listening in on other people's conversations, including having verified that either Dale really had returned from the dead or almost everyone in the camp had been fooled into thinking so. I tended to disbelieve in massive conspiracy theories; it was too hard for someone to avoid bragging or slipping up some other way, but all of the stuff I overheard wouldn't substitute for first-hand knowledge of the dungeon's Essence.

John was just coming out of Tyler's tent when I ran into him. He had a small pickaxe, like what a prospector would use rather than the larger ones I had seen most miners carrying.

"Good evening, James. Still no luck with the dungeon, huh?" John asked sympathetically. He pulled a leather bag off his back and dropped the pickaxe inside. Most people would have found that totally normal, but I wasn't most people. The bag didn't deform as the tool fell inside, and I didn't hear it strike the leather. That meant that it wasn't a normal bag; it was a dimensional bag. There was no way that John could afford one of those—heck, *I* couldn't afford one of them even with all the money I had brought here—unless he was hiding something as well.

"No, same as everyone else," I said to him.

"If you're not doing anything tonight, maybe we could meet up after dinner," John said. He saw the expression on my face and immediately waved his hands in consternation. "No, no, not like that. I picked up an odd job, and I could use another set of hands."

"Oh, uh, okay. That's better. Sure, I can do that," I said. He nodded.

"My tent is on the windward side of the mountain with a blue circle painted on the flap," he said, gesturing vaguely. "We'll talk more there."

***

John pulled the flaps of his tent closed and double-checked the knot before sitting down on his cot. I awkwardly folded my legs underneath myself as I sat down on the floor.

"What I'm about to tell you could potentially get both of us into a lot of trouble. I hope that even if you don't do this job with me, you'll keep your mouth shut. Something tells me I can trust you, James," he said. I pursed my lips and nodded.

"I know how to stay quiet," I said. If he pressed me, I could promise to say nothing—I could write down something if I needed to—but I hoped he wouldn't make me resort to deceptive wordplay. Fortunately, that was enough for him. He nodded quickly.

"As you know, the dungeon entrance is walled off, but a rumor I heard is that there's another way in, farther down the mountain. If that's true, then we might be able to get in the dungeon, mine some gold, and get back out... all without paying taxes to the Guild. I'd like to have you as a lookout, so that nothing sneaks up on me while mining. I can give you a cut of the profits. Are you in?"

He had left a few things out. The dimensional bag, for one—given that he didn't have enough money to buy it, it meant that Tyler had probably loaned it to him, so he was also in on the plan. He also didn't say what cut of the profits I'd get for my efforts, but despite the way that John had literally told me how he intended to break the Adventuring Guilds' rules, I felt like I could trust him. What he wanted to do might be against the rules, but it wasn't immoral, which was my main concern. Besides, it might be the only way I could get into the dungeon to sense its Essence's purity.

"You got it," I said with a smile.

For the next hour or so, John and I went over the plan in greater detail. I'd take over mining if he grew too tired. We'd leave around midnight after we had both rested up and when the moon was at its peak. John was evasive when it came to where the second entrance was, but that was understandable. He did eventually let me know about the dimensional bag—though he still didn't mention Tyler by name—so at least I didn't have to pretend to be ignorant about that. Eventually, I left so he could get some sleep, while I tried to not think about all the ways that things could go wrong.

***

It was easy to leave the camp, even at the late hour. John led me to the stream near the camp, then started following it down the mountainside. I used a small amount of Essence to enhance my sense of touch further, making sure that we didn't step on any unstable rocks. By the time we had gotten near the base of the mountain, almost exactly where I had begun climbing the mountain a few days ago, John was openly wondering whether I was part mountain goat.

"This stream feeds into the river, and the river passes under the mountain. That's where the entrance is supposed to lie." He pointed. I looked back up the mountain, then over to John.

"How deep does the dungeon go? We are hundreds of feet below the entrance," I asked with confusion.

"Look, I told you all that I know." John showed his first sign of irritation. "Help me look for it."

He began walking upstream, stumbling much more now that I wasn't leading the way. I was seriously reconsidering whether this was just a wild goose chase, but then I noticed something. Compared to what I remembered from a few days ago, the Essence actually did feel a little thicker here. If the top of the dungeon was blocked off, maybe more of it was being forced out the bottom? John's cultivation was low enough that I wasn't worried about him realizing my rank, so long as I was somewhat subtle. I let my Chi spiral open up, then focused on the eddies of Essence swirling along the surface of the river. The water was definitely carrying stronger Essence from upstream.

I bounded past him, earning a muffled curse, as I followed the path back up the mountain again. As long as John wasn't too close, I could clear a path by uprooting brambles and pushing small boulders out of the way. It was a little fun, in a way. I hadn't had a chance to exert myself physically since I had arrived, and I could use the exercise.

Eventually, John caught up, and I had to slow down to keep him from growing suspicious. Even he could sense the Essence growing stronger, and his irritation had turned back into excitement. Up ahead, I spotted a small cave entrance which looked like it might be what John had heard about. As we got closer, however, a problem revealed itself.

"No. No no no." John pulled at his hair despondently. Though the entrance was large enough for a man to enter, the cave quickly narrowed to a much smaller tunnel no more than two feet around. I had used an earth Essence technique to map out the tunnel, and while it didn't grow narrower, it was significantly more twisty than I thought either of us could handle. On the other hand, I thought I could possibly validate the Essence purity, even after going through all the earth and water, but I had to concentrate all of my Essence to do so.

"This isn't a one-night job." I shook my head. "This could take weeks, maybe more."

"Forget it," he kicked a rock out of the cave. Something snarled at it. Wait, snarled? I hurriedly re-focused my senses.

Outside the cave were at least a dozen Goblins, brandishing an odd assortment of sticks, broken farming tools, and two pickaxes that looked like they were made by the Goblins themselves. Before I could figure out what to do, they rushed at us, screaming furiously.

CHAPTER SEVEN

I had never been in a fight before. Now, I was trapped in the mouth of a cave with nowhere to run or retreat, hopelessly outnumbered. I was bowled over by three of them, all of whom began to stab at me. Reflexively, I tightened my aura. The pain I expected to feel... didn't hurt? While their weight had been enough to knock me down, they were all as emaciated as Dale had been, and in their case, it translated into actual weakness.

More of them continued to pile on me, but I slowly began to stand up against their weight. Then I heard John scream, and I panicked. Goblins flew off of me, skittering away as they hit the ground. I looked around frantically, only to see John's head slam against the cave wall. Blood spurted from the wound, and he fell bonelessly to the ground.

I pushed with my Essence, and a gust of air threw the Goblins back three paces from me. Before one of them could smash John's head open with half of a garden hoe, I had already grabbed it by its slimy, flea-covered skin and thrown it away from me. John had several broken bones and the head injury that I couldn't do anything about.

"Get away!" I yelled. I didn't know if the Goblins could understand me, but they understood my tone. A few of them moved away, while others behind them prodded them to go back and attack me. I had to get out of there, fast. I grabbed the dimensional bag which John had dropped, then before I could change my mind, I healed him as much as I could.

I could hear his bones snap back into place, and the Goblins who had been working up their courage pushed themselves into the cave wall as he screamed again. At least the screaming meant he was still alive. Then I picked him up like he didn't weigh any more than the Goblins and ran out of the cave and back down the mountain.

***

I don't know how long I kept running. It was as though the thinking part of my brain had shut down. When I stopped, I was back to where the stream intersected the river. Breathing heavily, I put John back down on the ground. He was still breathing, though I didn't like his color. My healing, rushed as it was, probably didn't put everything back in the right place. I had to get him back up to the Church, but my adrenaline rush had finally worn out; all I could do was sit down and shake. I began to pray softly while I used a simple Essence technique to try to calm myself down. It was the first one I had learned when I joined the Church, a way to sense all creation around me. My heartbeat slowed, and I began to stand up when something else caught my attention. There were holes.

Not holes in the ground but holes in the space around me. Earth and air essence reached out from me, all around me, but... someone was hidden here. At least three someones, if I wasn't mistaken. I turned to the closest one, did my best to force down my fear, and said, "Who are you?"

There was no response. I looked at each of the other spaces, then back to the first one as it began to move. "I know you're there. If you want to kill me, go ahead and try." I meant for it to sound threatening, but it came out almost like an invitation. Finally, blessedly, something shimmered into place in front of me. An elf.

"Human. If I wanted to kill you, you would be dead," he told me disparagingly. "Our orders from IL-Anwa Essa of the

Huine nation, however, are to protect the tree, no more. You are no threat to it."

I didn't recognize either of those names, but that told me plenty. Wild elves didn't have nations, and we were far enough from the water that this probably wasn't a Sea Elf, so... Dark Elves. Only *slightly* better than Wild Elves.

"It could sense you. That is somewhat threatening," one of the still-hidden elves said in their native tongue. The one in front nodded, seeming to consider those words seriously.

"I mean no harm to the tree," I said in Elven. The Elf's gaze intensified.

"You speak our tongue... passably, for a human." He sounded just the *least* bit impressed. "If you tell me how you detected us, I will let you and your sick friend go."

I opened my mouth, ready to tell him, then closed it. I took a deep breath, then looked more closely at his cultivation. He was a Mage, which made what I was going to ask possible. Of course, it might just piss him off enough that he'd kill me anyway. I felt curiously calm as I spoke.

"I will tell you if you swear an oath on your Mana that you and the *Huine* nation mean no harm to those on the mountain. It would be better if I died than gave my people's enemies knowledge they could use against us." I could feel one of the hidden Elves raise an arm holding some sort of weapon. I wouldn't even get to see what was about to kill me.

"I swear, by my Mana, that IL-Anwa Essa and Dale of the mountain have been bound in oath, that we mean no harm to those on the mountain unless they threaten the Silverwood tree," the Elf spoke fluidly. "Now, human, my patience grows thin."

"The Essence here is thick," I said quickly. "You've hidden your Essence so well that you're emitting less than the surroundings. It was like a hole, an absence." I waited anxiously to see if my explanation made sense. Slowly, the two hidden elves faded further, and I couldn't tell where they were. The elf in front nodded.

"Acceptable. Now, move quickly if you want your friend to live." He then disappeared without a trace. I didn't hesitate, bending down to lift John and carrying him back up the mountainside to the church. Maybe Father Richard could do more than I could. If I broke my cover, then it was broken. Life came first.

CHAPTER EIGHT

If there was one good thing that came from John's injuries, it was that I had a reason to remain in the church while he healed over the next couple of days. I felt more than a little guilty thinking that way, but I knew that if I hadn't been around, he probably would have died at the foot of the mountain; never to be found again. If the Goblins hadn't killed him, then there was a good chance that the Dark Elves might have. I also returned the dimensional bag to Tyler. I didn't go into many details but let him know that John was badly injured and healing at the church.

I informed Father Richard about the Dark Elves as soon as I could. To my surprise, he wasn't as concerned about them as I had expected.

"Dark Elves aren't any more likely to become infernalists than humans. They have a reputation for being assassins, absolutely, especially the Moon Elves, but if what you say is true and they swore an oath to Dale, then," Father Richard sighed, "then I'd rather have them here on our side than worrying about Wild Elves. Did you get an idea of how many there were?"

I shook my head. "They mentioned that they were here upon the orders of Il-Anwa Essa of the *Huine* nation, and I detected at least three of them when I was in the dungeon, but there could easily be more."

"I am going to keep this a secret for now. If Dale recovers, he can explain why he took an oath from Dark Elves to protect the Silverwood tree. If he doesn't, well... we can cross that bridge when we come to it." Father Richard was looking at me strangely. "I know that look on your face. Sometimes, we don't always get a clear choice between good and evil.

Sometimes, it's just better or worse. These Dark Elves let you go when they could have killed you to keep their secret. I hope that is a sign that the Celestial is speaking to them in its own way."

I stepped out of Father Richard's chambers, much more aware of my own mortality than I had been before. In the back of my head, I knew that I could have escaped the dungeon's creatures easily if I hadn't been carrying John. Could I have left him there? I didn't want to think so, but between both of us dying or just him, I was afraid that I'd have taken the cowardly choice to save my own life. Even if I had done that, the Dark Elves could have killed me before I even knew what was happening. I could have died. I had a small inkling of what the adventurers went through every day, and despite their arrogance, I found myself envying their courage a little.

About thirty feet down the hall, I saw a dark-haired, young woman. She was almost my height, and even though she appeared delicate at first glance, the muscles along her arms and back made it clear that she was definitely an adventurer and probably an archer. A lot of people didn't realize how much strength it took to use a bow properly, but that only made her more attractive. I shrugged to myself. I felt a lot more confident trying to meet her in the church's building than I would if it were in a bar. I walked towards her, and she looked up as she saw me coming.

"Hello, there. I, uh... this is a nice church, isn't it?" That was the best I could come up with? I could feel my face turning red. She smiled politely at me. It wasn't looking good.

"You're cute, but you're a little young for me. If I started dating teenagers, I'd feel like Hans," she said with a shudder.

"I'm older than I look." I was somewhat affronted. I hadn't been a teenager for two years, and she didn't look that much older than I did. I mean, I still had a babyface, but that's why I had grown out my beard. "Who is Hans?"

"Hans is a man who is completely obsessed with me. He's old enough to be my grandfather. Possibly your great-grandfather."

She was teasing me. I sighed. This clearly wasn't going to work. Time to try to disengage politely. "Well, it was a pleasure speaking to you..."

"I'm Rose," she told me her name. I paused.

"That's funny. I had heard there was a little girl named Rose here as well," I muttered in surprise.

"Little girl?" Rose looked at me, almost *angrily*.

"Yes, she's supposed to be a chaos cultivator," I told her.

"Who was it who told you 'she' was a little girl?" Rose asked with a flat voice. As she spoke, something *chaotic* rippled around me. All of a sudden, I couldn't hold on to my Chi spiral, and it unfurled as I just barely managed to keep my air affinity channel blocked. Belatedly, I looked at her open affinity channels—celestial and infernal, chaos itself.

"Uh, no one." My mind was racing. All of the next sentences I could think of were not helpful. *I have never met a chaos cultivator who lived past childhood.* True, but nope! *I assumed...* Every sentence that started that way ended in bloodshed.

"Rose, is this boy bothering you?" someone said from just behind my shoulder. I jumped slightly and barely managed to avoid falling over. He sneaked up on me? I had noticed cloaked Dark Elves! Either the chaos that Rose released was still messing with me, or... yeah, that had to be it. I swallowed with an audible gulp before speaking.

"I am not a boy, and I was just about to leave after having inserted my foot in my mouth," I said to the blond man, then turned to Rose and said, "I apologize for having offended you."

"Sweet Rose, did he try to woo you? Impress you with his skill in cultivation? I assure you, just because he's also a C-rank..."

"He... is a C-rank." Rose looked at me again, and I felt like a bug being examined by a child who wasn't sure whether she was going to collect it or squash it. "You're right. He is. I would have sworn he was a fishy. He doesn't act like any of the C-ranks I've met."

"Oh, I get it." Hans started smirking at me. "He's a Flower."

"Flower?" Rose asked. I sighed, apparently loudly enough that she could hear it, as she turned to look at me rather than Hans. Actually, it was probably better that I explain it anyway. I spoke up quickly.

"It's a term—a somewhat rude one—for a person whose fighting prowess isn't commensurate with his cultivation. Like a greenhouse flower—beautiful but only capable of surviving in a protected environment." I winced at the term again; it was true. The explanation hurt all the more after what happened to John. If I weren't a Flower, I wouldn't have frozen, and he wouldn't have been hurt. Hans didn't seem to notice my guilt.

"Beautiful, huh? You've certainly got a high opinion of yourself. Personally, there's someone else here who fits the bill much better. Even her name is positively botanical." Hans turned to look back at Rose with a dreamy smile. She rolled her eyes at him.

"Didn't he just say that being a 'flower' is an insult?" she tossed in his face. Hans threw up his arms with a grand flourish.

"Ah, my dear, you couldn't be more wrong. The main difference between you and him—one of many—is that a Rose has thorns." Rose and I groaned in unison, but Hans continued to speak, "He feels like a low C-rank in terms of cultivation, but compared to you and me... heck, compared to someone like Tom or Dale, he's probably worse in a fight."

"Of course, if he becomes a Mage, all bets are off. The concepts that Flowers come up with to create their Mana tend to be... *interesting.*"

"I keep telling you, I'm not your 'dear'. I'm not yours in any way. I've had enough of both of you. More than enough. Goodbye." Rose walked away briskly, and while I looked away before I was caught staring, Hans had no such compunctions, clearly enjoying the view. After she turned the corner, he looked over to me.

"Wait... Hans. I know that name. You're one of the cultivators who was on Dale's team, aren't you?" Hans' expression didn't change, but his body tensed, and one hand dropped down to his side as if of its own accord. He had at least five daggers on him, and that hand was getting ready to draw one of them.

"Yes, I *am* on his team," he said bluntly, emphasizing the present tense. "Why?".

"If you're his friend as well as his teammate, you might want to talk to him. When I ran into him a couple days ago, he looked pretty out of it. I heard that some of the Mages here are concerned about him. Something about a council meeting?" Hans' eyes narrowed slightly.

"You seem to hear a lot for someone I've never seen before. You're telling me this out of the goodness of your heart?" He sounded incredibly suspicious of me. The irony was that *was* my motivation, but I knew if I phrased myself that way, he wouldn't believe me. Instead, I shrugged.

"Father Richard doesn't speak quietly very often. Though he's like a mouse compared to that cook at the mess hall... Anyway, I'd rather have Dale owning the dungeon than a fight between the Lion Kingdom, Phoenix Kingdom, at least three Guilds..." I cut myself off before I brought up the Dark Elves. I had no idea whether Dale had spoken to him about their presence here.

"Enlightened self-interest. Now *that* is a reason I can wholeheartedly understand." Hans looked to me with a sudden grin. "I had been thinking it was strange that he's been staying in his tent instead of resting in a comfortable bed in the church. Of course, I'll still verify what you said. If you were making it up..."

The grin stretched, showing surprisingly white teeth. Pointy looking teeth. I gulped. "Message received. But I wasn't making it up,"

I turned to walk away but looked back after a couple of steps. "By the way, she likes you."

"What?" Hans asked confusedly. I took a guilty pleasure in finally startling him. I might not be able to kill a dozen F-ranks with my bare hands like Hans seemed to be able to, and women I found attractive apparently thought I looked like a child, but I had my own strengths.

"Her pupils dilate when she looks at you. She can say what she wants, but the eyes don't lie." I tapped near my left eye with one finger, then continued to walk off. From behind me, Hans chortled with glee.

"I knew it!"

EPILOGUE

The last few days passed as quickly as the first two. I had considered keeping an eye on Dale while he convalesced, but I saw that Hans had already beaten me to the punch. Fortunately for me, keeping himself hidden from Dale meant that he didn't spot me. If anything, Hans looked impatient. Part of me pitied Dale. I didn't know which was worse—coming back from the dead or having to put up with a pissed-off Hans. I stopped to speak with Father Richard one last time before I left.

"Thank you, James. I can sense you've seen the same sort of things I've seen and that you know how important Dale's mountain will be. I promised him that the Church would serve as a place of healing, both physical and spiritual. I can't do that alone. You know what we need here now—not just Inquisitors but healers, preachers, and warriors too. My request didn't sway the Bishop, but maybe you can, now that you speak with the voice of *experience*." Father Richard sounded as serious as I had ever heard him.

Experience. That word struck a chord in me, and for a brief moment, I saw a vision of a pyramid ascending into the sky. A concept that transcended the senses, past memory and touching upon the soul. This was something to aspire to, but the concept required more than just the air and earth affinity I possessed. What else was needed? How strong did I need to become? Thoughts whirled around me.

"James? James?" Father Richard brought me back to reality.

"I am sorry, Father. I think that was the first time that I sensed ascension," I told him shakily. I wasn't ready for the concept. I felt flawed, incomplete. Unworthy. But I grinned anyway. That glimpse revealed what I could become, how I could serve as a true Inquisitor. Even if it took years, now, I had a goal to work towards. Father Richard looked surprised, then echoed my smile.

"Congratulations! It's like I said before—this mountain is full of miracles. If there's any guidance I can give you—if what you sensed relates to *Sonder*—then please come back when you can. It would be good to have you here when you didn't have to act as an agent in secret." The word in the middle echoed through me, and I felt it more than I heard it. The C-ranked Flower and the A-ranked demon hunter, seemingly as different as could be, but somehow connected in service.

"Father, I hope that one day I'll do just *that*."

BUTCHER BOY
BY: DAKOTA KROUT

PROLOGUE

"Are you *kidding* me? *Really?*" As these words entered Ramset's ears, his heart sank. His body felt numb, the blood draining from his face as he slowly turned toward the source of the accusing words.

Ramset looked at the girl standing with her hands on her hips, ample for a street urchin of the underslums. Ramset's hands clutched at the full loaf of bread that he had found on the street. It was only a *little* muddy, and if he had a chance to eat it... this would mark the first food he had eaten in three days. He had a sinking feeling that he wouldn't be getting that chance.

"You know *abyss* well that stealing from my territory is a death sentence, *boy.*" The girl started walking toward him, a feather hanging from a bandanna showing her gang affiliation. The 'Phoenix Feathers'. Drat. Today had started out so well.

Ramset shook his head empathetically. "I'd never steal from you! Or your area! I found this on the street, I swear!"

"And where were you *going* with it?" Her eyes blazed with hate as she looked over his skeletally thin form. "You think that *you* deserve that whole loaf of bread? Or *any* of it, for that matter?"

Other children were gathering around them, their bandanna and feathers marking them as more people that would participate in his impending humiliation. "You're just a *male*, after all."

"No! I... I was... there was no one around! I couldn't see anyone from the gang to give it to!" Ramset pleaded desperately.

She held out a hand. "Hand it over right now, and we won't leave you *dead* from the beating you are about to get."

Ramset instantly obeyed, placing the loaf in her hand. His trembling hand betrayed him though, and he released the bread before her hand had fully grasped it. The loaf *plopped* to the ground... and the group went silent. Ramset dived for the bread, catching it on the first bounce and handing it to the gang's leader. She took it from him with her left hand while the right fist connected solidly with his cheek, knocking him to the ground. He sprang back up, knowing better than to stay on the ground where people could easily kick him.

"*So* disrespectful," she stage whispered, shaking her head. "Well, I *tried* to be merciful. Kill the male."

Ramset had started sprinting away as soon as he saw the set of her jaw. The others were surprised by his initiative, which was the only reason he made it out of the closing ring of bodies.

"Hey!"

He didn't bother reacting to the yelling voice, making for the main streets. He would have made a clean escape, but a stone from a sling caught him on the spine, making him stiffen and stagger. The people giving chase gained enough ground to begin pummeling him. Some used their fists, but most had at least a board, brick, or eye-poking stick. The leader had a length of chain on her and landed a solid blow to Ramset's side as he regained his feet and continued running.

The filthy mob of screaming children spilled out on to the poorly-maintained streets, chasing Ramset as he freely bled from multiple welts and cuts. He poured on the speed, ignoring subtlety in his need for distance. He sprinted straight down the street, passing into the next district. The screaming began to draw guards, but even they simply giggled at the sight of a filthy child being chased by more of the same. The guards only gained serious looks as the mob approached the next city district, nearly ten minutes of continuous running later.

Ramset kept running even as guard whistles started shrilling. The other children dispersed as guards moved to block them, but Ramset's mind was clouded by exhaustion; he ignored the warnings.

Simple words drifted to his ears, "You're *dead* the next time we see you!"

He kept running, ignoring all cries and curses, losing himself in unfamiliar streets. A scant ten minutes later, he stumbled and fell on to a patch of grass. His mind fled, and he was unconscious as soon as he landed.

CHAPTER ONE

Ramset woke up with a groan as he huddled away from the hobnailed boot that had just impacted his side. His dry eyes cracked open, and he looked up at a powdered, well-dressed man.

"If I ever catch you on this property again, I will *not* bother to wake you myself. I will leave you to the Lady's guards. This is your only warning." A snooty, cultured tone reached Ramset's ears. The tonation of the voice made it obvious that he didn't mean the Lady's personal property but the level of the city he was laying in.

His mind caught up, and Ram realized he was being spoken to by the personal coachman to the undercity Lady. Ramset began shaking, breaking into a nervous sweat as he realized where he was laying. He tried to leap to his feet, but the bruises and malnourishment combined to ensure that he could only get up at a speed an old, dying man could outpace.

Ram tried hard to remember the male version of 'My Lady'. He almost couldn't remember, but it flew to his tongue as he spoke. "M-my Lord, please forgive this one. This one regrets his impertinence. He had not realized he had fallen on the property of the esteemed Lady."

Ramset tried not to panic as the coachman obviously wavered between calling the guard or simply getting on with his day. It seemed the subservient bowing was all that was required, for the coachman grunted and shooed him away. Ramset took the opportunity to scramble away as fast and far as he could go.

Living at the lowest caste of society—and a male to boot—Ramset could easily be killed and his body dumped into the trash without a person breaking a single law. He hurried into familiar territory, slipping from the undercity into the overslums when the guards were looking away. As he left the whitewashed walls behind, he cast a wary gaze back into the richer part of the city. Ramset cringed and even his dreams of a mythical 'someday' withered as he saw a troop of burly, curvy guards walking along the street.

As a male in the Tigress Queendom, Ramset's options were exceedingly limited. He didn't even have the option of military service to allow him to escape the slums, and he was too weak and slow to be a good thief. He also couldn't *leave* the city without written authorization, so there was no way for him to escape into the countryside and find a way to work for food. He began to see red as tears threatened, but he held them back as per usual. Water was a precious resource to him, as he wasn't allowed direct access to the city wells without a female's permission.

Ramset thought about his destination—or lack thereof—and started to slow down. What was the point? If he made it back to the area of the underslums he came from, some group would likely kill him. The week before, he had tried to beg for food near merchants without permission from the local gang, and when they caught him, they had beat him mercilessly. Add on the 'theft' of bread yesterday, and his options were simply gone.

Thanks to malnutrition, Ramset was small for his ten years of life and too weak and slow to be a messenger for even the worst gang. They had threatened him in a way similar to the coachman, warning him about showing his face in the area. He thought about what he should do, scoffing at his overreaching daydreams.

The underslums were the territory of the gangs and formed a ring around the extreme outer edge of the city. The only thing between them and the countryside was a twenty-foot-thick, forty-foot-high, smooth, stone wall. He could try to stay in the overslums, but the Slumlady's guards would eventually catch him and toss him back into the lower level.

If they didn't just outright kill him for inconveniencing them, that is. The undercity had just tossed him out, and going back there was a death sentence. The middle city—or merchant sector—was beyond the undercity and was the most amazing place in the known world. It was stuffed with trinkets, wonders, and artifacts that boggled the mind and enhanced lives. So they said, anyway.

The *upper* city was the home of minor nobility and temples to the Goddess, also known as the religious sector. The numerous and lauded blessings of the Goddess—such as healing and powerful miracles performed by her clerics—never reached down to affect the people in the slums.

The city center, home of the City Lady—the Queen—and her high-class nobility, was so well-guarded and walled off that no rumor about it could be trusted. There was simply no way to validate any information. There was talk of beautiful gardens and magical occurrences, visiting Elves and various races. Even *male* dignitaries, as far-fetched as that sounded. He sighed; Ramset would never know the truth for sure if his life stayed as it was.

Ramset was interrupted from his reverie and self-rumination as the squadron of upperslum guardswomen came around the corner. Trying very hard not to panic, he tucked himself into a doorway and tried to look as meek and innocent as possible. The squad passed by, but the very last woman in the column sneered at him and took a swing at him with the butt of her spear. He didn't try to avoid it or even mitigate the damage. That was a sure-fire way to get a *far* worse beating. Instead, he tried to appear thankful to her for letting him off with a single blow instead of breaking parts off him. She scoffed and walked away when he bowed, falling into step with the others.

Ramset released a shaking sigh of relief and continued on his way. Now he was meandering and thinking about trying to find a different way into the underslums. They circled the entire city after all, and one gang couldn't have control over the *entire* area! He walked as fast as he could over the rough gravel roads; his shoeless feet were tough, but sharp rocks still hurt. He was passing a small market area when he spotted it.

A... *rat!* A huge, *meat-filled* rat was sneaking away from the market with a gnawed-on apple core. Ramset's eyes followed the rat's path hungrily, and he reached down and slowly grabbed a chunk of rock from the ground. He threw the rock as hard as he could, and... success! The rock hit the rat, who gave a squeal of surprise and stumbled.

Ramset was excited for a moment until the rat turned its beady eyes on him and *hissed.* The large, fat rat scrambled toward him, and Ramset tried to back away. Sadly, the loose rock under him didn't cooperate, and he slipped. The rat was nearly upon him, so he grabbed a fist-sized stone in his hand and swung with as much power as he could muster. The blow stunned the rat for a moment—all Ramset needed as he grabbed the animal and wrenched its neck, snapping it with a wet **pop**. He stared at the corpse, and a rush of *energy* filled him with excitement. He was going to *eat* today!

A cheer startled him as a few onlookers congratulated him on his kill. One or two even exchanged small, copper coins. They had bet on his chances of killing the rat? Or... getting killed *by* the rat? Ramset felt somehow more dirty than usual upon realizing this fact.

"*Boy!*" A voice behind him made Ramset jump, swinging around with the dead rat dangling from his hand. He pulled it closer protectively; the rat was *his*.

Ramset looked up to see the largest, meatiest, most muscular *man* he had ever had the misfortune of being this close to. "Y-yes, milord?"

The man frowned down at him, crossing his arms. "Hmph. You did well there with that rat. You have quick hands, and the creature didn't suffer overly. Why did you attack it though? Do you just hate rats?"

Ramset looked at the carcass he was cradling, then to the ground. "This one is... hungry, Lord. This lowly one has nothing against rats."

"You must be from the underslums with that sort of speech. Should a' guessed from your... clothes." He glanced at the tied-together burlap that formed Ramset's barely important-bit-covering clothes. The man made a face. "Why are you in the upperslums?"

Ramset began to feel very nervous. Everyone else had moved on, and this man was interrogating him. Did he work for the guard? Could a *man* do that? He started to try to back away, but the man made a noise in the back of his throat and shook his head. "Look, kid, I don't plan to hurt ya. Y'er scrawny, and normally I wouldn't 'ave bothered to talk to a rat-eatin', little brat. However! The way you killed that rat intrigued me, and it looks like you don't exactly have *better* things to do today. So, we talk."

The man took in Ramset's wary gaze and sighed. "Here's the thing. The father of one of my apprentice butcher boys pissed off the wrong woman, and his whole family got themselves executed. He was always a little too squeamish to kill anything directly, so the poor beasts he worked on had to go through a lot of unnecessary pain. He wasn't trying to hurt 'em. He was just... inefficient. You though, I'm bettin' *you* have no qualms about killin' a beast or two and cutting 'em up? Say, if there is food and a place to sleep in it for you?"

Ramset's eyes widened. "My Lord... are you offering this unworthy one... a *job*?"

"Let's *not* get ahead of ourselves. I'm offering you a place to sleep and one meal a day to start with. You don't know the proper way to cut a beast up for meat or the cuts or grade of meat either. Abyss, you've probably never had a chance at *eatin'* good meat before if y'er planning on eatin' *rat*."

The butcher glanced at Ramset's thin form. "It's dirty, tiring, stinky work. If you can learn what I have to teach ya, you'll go from cleanin' up blood, scat, and innards to killin' and cutting up animals in a month or so. Then you'll get *two* meals a day and a set of clothes twice a year. Standard apprentice rate for the Butchers. Guild."

Ramset nearly swooned at the thought, "This one could get into a *guild*?"

The butcher chuckled. "You sure like gettin' ahead of yourself, lad. You'll get an introduction, but it'll hafta be your own hard work that'll get you in. You'll need to know how to strip down every standard animal we use, separate every usable bit out, and package everything up in a certain time frame. Do that, and you'll be a Junior Journeyman. Butchering is a *science*, not an art, and we have serious rules about progression. It is *possible,* though. I take it you'll come and work for me, then?"

"This one is unworthy of this–"

"Yeah, you can stop *that* right now, too. I can't have a timid, little underslum brat working for me. We work on a time limit. Meat spoils. No beatin' around the bush, nothing but answers as directly as you can answer them! Do you want the job?" The butcher glared down at him.

"This one– yes! I mean, *yes*, milord!" Ramset added belatedly. He was now staring at his torn-up feet, sure the butcher would move on.

"Good! Well, boy, from now on, you can call me 'sir' or 'Master Dylan'. What's your name, butcher boy?" Dylan quizzed the scrawny lad.

"This one's... that is, *my* name is Ramset." He told Master Dylan with a wince as he tried to suppress his habits.

"Eh, too long to yell in a hurry. You'll go by 'Ram'. That sound doable?" Ram wasn't going to do anything to upset the man, so he kept his mouth shut and briskly nodded. "Good, you're learning. Remember, Ram, a man learns and stays alive by keeping his mouth shut and listening. Making the laws and discussing important things are best left to Women, and if we forget our place for a moment... well. I'm sure you've seen the bodies. I listen to *them*, you listen to me *and* them. Got it?"

Ram nodded hurriedly. They started walking, Ram cutting his feet on the sharp stones to keep pace. As they got near an alley, Dylan grabbed his rat and tossed it into the darkness. It was caught before it hit the ground, and the sounds of a weak scuffle started as the people hidden by shadows fought for the treat. Ram looked noticeably down about losing his rat, so Dylan told him that as soon as he had a bath, he could have his daily allotted meal.

As they walked further, a foul odor reached out and smacked Ram right in the sense of smell. His face scrunched up as they continued, and he hoped they would soon be past whatever was releasing that foulness. Even with all of the benefits in mind, he began doubting his decision to become a butcher boy when they walked right into the building that was stinking up the entire block.

Dylan took a deep inhale and released a satisfied sigh. "Ahh, that's the stuff. Nothing like the smell of coming home to make you feel *right*. Here we go, lad. You go into that room and strip, get into the water, and scrub until all of your skin is raw. Throw your... clothes... into the fire heating the water. I'll find something that'll fit ya."

Ram stepped into the smallish room, uncertainly removing his clothes. Should he really throw them in the fire? What if this was all an elaborate prank by the butcher? He looked at the scraps of cloth in his hands, dirty and falling apart. He strengthened his resolve. He had a *chance* here! Even if it meant the worst conditions possible, smells that would make a skunk gag, or daily beatings... it would still be better than the assured death that awaited him in the underslums. The rags went into the fire, the oily material blazing high in the flames.

He stepped into the tub and sighed as the near-boiling water soothed his many aches and pains. The bruises stopped screaming along his nerves, and muscles sore from malnutrition and yet another night on the ground relaxed minutely. It was all he could do to tiredly begin rubbing at the accumulated filth on his body. He got to his tangled mess of hair, wincing as bugs tried to burrow into his scalp as the water washed over them.

After staying underwater as long as he could to try and drown the lice, he sighed and stepped out of the now-murky water. The air was cold enough that even with the fire next to him, he began shivering. Ram looked around for the promised clothing but didn't want to open the door and expose himself to whoever may be nearby. Just as he was starting to panic, the door opened, and the butcher stepped in.

"Alright, time to get out of there... oh. Good, I thought you might have been taking your sweet time lazing about." He watched as Ram scratched his scalp. "Oh, right. Hmm. No point putting on clothes yet if you're just gonna be getting them all nasty with bugs. Sit on that stool. We're gonna shave ya."

Ram sat down, nervousness running through him as master Dylan pulled several cleavers from his belt. "Not that thi– *I* mean to question you, sir, but... are those the, um, best tools for the job?"

"Hmph." Dylan moved close, pulling at Ram's thin yet shaggy hair. "Haven't even started working as a *novice* yet and you are asking questions more befitting a seasoned apprentice. You would typically be correct that a cleaver isn't that great for having a pretty hairstyle, but we are taking it *all* off... and I am an Expert."

He spun the blade in place, then lashed out and began hacking at the hair he was holding. Ram didn't flinch, his body too tired and apathetic to attempt panicking. His hair fell off quickly, each lock carefully tossed into the fire. Dylan then pulled out a smaller cleaver and ran it over Ram's head, shaving it clean with razor precision. All of the hair and—more importantly—the bugs burned. The smell of burning hair on top of the horrid stench of the slaughterhouse sent Ram's head spinning, and he nearly passed out.

"Easy there, boy-o. My, but you are thin, aren't you? And what an impressive series of scars and bruises you have collected. Piss off a guardswoman lately? That one looks a lot like the butt-end of a spear..."

"Just... too close to their patrol on a narrow street," Ram managed to cough out around his gritted teeth.

"Sounds about right. Wash again, then put on these clothes. They may be a bit big, but you'll grow into 'em." Dylan shook his head, waiting as Ramset scrubbed and put on the clothes. They hung off Ramset's shoulders like a tapestry on a wall.

"Dressed? Let's get some food in you. Today you'll have beef broth and bread, hmm... maybe noodle soup? We'll see how well your body accepts that. After that, I'll make some introductions, and you'll get to work. Until you can manage more, we'll set you up mucking out the holding stalls in the morning and evening. Midday, you'll work the squeegee and focus on getting all the blood into the drains. I won't make you haul the water for cleaning yet, but you will be mopping the floors with the apprentices."

Ram knew better than to question, so simply nodded his head and muttered, "Thank you, sir."

Dylan nodded and gently patted him on his now-clothed back. "It's hard work, boy. Do well and work hard, and someday, people may even come to get their cuts of meat from *your* shop. If you somehow get a wife who can afford it, of course. Who knows?"

CHAPTER TWO

Ram was led around like a sheep, being taught the layout of the building and meeting people in a whirl. Luckily, there were only five total employees, or Ram would have had a lot of trouble. There were two journeyman, Erik and John, as well as two apprentices, Chase and Hunter. Of course, there was the Master Butcher, Dylan. Ram was starting as a Novice, someone who had not yet been granted an apprenticeship.

Ram was being led to the stables by Chase when something tickled his senses. "Excuse me, Chase? Where are the women?"

The large, husky, yet muscle-bound, young, blond man glanced at him. "Why in the *world* would a woman bother to work *here*? They have far better prospects that don't force them to deal with blood and poop all day."

"I thought that a man couldn't be a business owner in the city...?" Ram mumbled, remembering too late that he should just be quiet.

"Well, Master Dylan's wife *owns* the shop, of course. She still isn't going to come here and *work* all day."

Ram paused a moment. "Oh. That makes sense, I guess."

"Stupid kid," Chase muttered. "Here is the shovel. Here is the pitchfork. Crap goes into the wheelbarrow, hay goes into the trough, there. Please don't mix that up."

"When the wheelbarrow is full," Chase paused and looked at Ram's thin arms, "or I guess when it is almost too heavy for you, wheel it to the opening to the sewers and dump or shovel it off. Make sure there is water running down there before you dump it, or it might come back up, and you'll have to clean it."

"How do I get water to *run?*" Ram nervously questioned.

Chase looked at him as if he were a moron. "You look in and make sure it isn't clogged? The river should wash everything away, but sometimes, it gets stuffed with scat. If that happens, you use that stick over there to poke at the clog until it floats away."

They walked back to the stable, and Chase gave him some more instructions. "Don't feed any animals in these stalls. We like to have as little to clean as possible, so we don't feed animals the day before we butcher them. Also, cleanliness is a big deal to Master Dylan for some reason. He says that if he can show that something he is doing is a *better* way of doing things, he could be promoted in the guild and become a supplier for minor nobles in the undercity instead of the overslums."

"He thinks being *clean* will make us have better meat, for some reason." Chase snorted and chuckled. "It's odd, but whatever Master Dylan wants, he gets. The boss is the boss. You need to bathe daily and wash your clothes. Someone can show you how to do that later, but I need to get to work. So do you."

Ram was left alone in the stable, his young and tired mind frantically trying to remember everything. He decided to get to work and began laboriously loading the wheelbarrow from the huge piles of feces. The first time he got it full, he started trying to move it to the sewer, only to realize that he couldn't budge the contraption. After straining with all of his might, he had to concede that the poo had won this round.

He had to unload nearly half of the excrement before he could get the wheels to begin rolling, and when he got it to the hole of the open sewer, he couldn't lift his handles high enough to tip the *stuff* out. Ram had to shovel half of it out again before he could lift the wheelbarrow at an appropriate angle to release its contents. They slumped out of the cart, plopping down into the water below.

He was already exhausted, but stubbornness and hope won out; he got back to work. Ram only put in enough to fill the small cart a quarter before wheeling it to the sewer. This went a little faster and allowed him to take small breaks from shoveling. Already, his hands were scraped, and blisters were forming from the unfamiliar work, but he powered onward. After the first few hours, he was moving so slowly and shaking so hard that he could barely lift the shovel. Master Dylan showed up just as Ram lost his hold on his shovel and it fell to the floor.

"Lazing about?" Dylan joked with crossed arms as he looked around the room.

Ram barely had the energy to defend himself. "No, sir, I've–"

Dylan held up a hand. "I'm sorry. I forgot that you don't have a sense of humor yet. I've been checking up on you. I know you've been working hard. I'm here because I forgot to feed you before you were set to work, and your meal is ready right now. Follow me."

Ram stumbled after him, body numb and tingling. With his deep bruises and long-term lack of proper food, he was barely able to force his tired muscles to obey him. Dylan made him wash his hands with a bar that smelled like smoke; then they walked again. Stepping into the office area of the building, his nose twitched as he smelled something non-foul for the first time in hours.

At the table was a steaming bowl of soup, filled with hearty broth and thick noodles. There were even small chunks of *meat* in there! He took a step closer to the food, then stopped, looking at Master Dylan. "Um. That's *all* for me?"

Dylan nodded, a touch of softness in his eyes. "Aye, lad. Don't rush to finish it though. No one is going to take it from you, so eat slowly. You might hurt yourself otherwise."

Ram limped the last few steps, then almost fell on the food. Only the fact that Dylan was watching him allowed Ram to maintain even a pretense of self-discipline. He had only gotten halfway through the meal when he couldn't eat any more. He stared at the food, urging his body to digest what he had taken in.

"Boy, don't get so worried. Stay there until you finish. There will be plenty of work when you are done, and you don't exactly need a lot of light to shovel *that* pile." Dylan patted Ram on the back, his massive hand able to rest on both of Ram's shoulders at the same time. "You only get one meal a day right now, so make sure to always eat it all. You will need the energy."

Ram nodded appreciatively. He gauged the fullness of his stomach. Surely he could get more in now, right?

"Another thing, if you finish your work, you are allowed to do whatever you want in your free time. There won't be a *lot* of free time, but we close the shop at the nineteenth bell or the onset of darkness, whichever comes first. If you want to be a *successful* butcher, you'll spend free time in that room when your work is finished." He pointed at a closed door.

"What's in there?" Ram eagerly hoped to repay the Master Butcher's kindness.

Dylan smirked. "It's a study room. In there, you will be taught how to read, write, and do your numbers."

A serious look appeared on his face. "The teachers are my daughters, and on a *very* rare occasion, my wife. I cannot stress this enough. If you want to remain here, do *not* piss off my wife."

Ram gulped and nodded. "I will try *really* hard not to."

"Good. I don't need to get whipped because she doesn't approve of my choice in a new apprentice. Add on the fact that I didn't *ask* her before bringing you here, and I am already on dangerous ground." Dylan patted Ram on the head. "Hurry and eat up, get strong, smart, and most importantly..."

Ram leaned in, paying rapt attention.

"...get back to work!"

Ram nodded furiously and started eating as fast as his body would allow.

CHAPTER THREE

Ram was back in the cattle holding pen, shoveling again. The food had done wonders for his flagging spirit, but it would be quite a while before his body had energy to spare again. His arms and back were burning as he lifted another load of scat on to the wheelbarrow. Ram lifted the handles, making sure it was still light enough to move before loading more on.

The light had begun to fade an hour ago, and no matter how much he felt the need to prove himself, this would have to be his last load of the night. Lifting the wheelbarrow with a grunt, he began maneuvering it into place over the hole. With a slurping *plop*, the excrement slid into the drain, flowing toward... wherever it went.

He sat down against the nearest wall, watching a small river of blood flow down a gentle incline from the slaughterhouse to the drain. Ram could not believe how much this place still stunk. Sitting down may have been a bad idea because he started to drift off almost instantly. As his eyes closed, a headache came on suddenly, and he started to see... odd *things* in the air. Attributing the odd lights to a tired mind, he barely noted the anthracite-black color that dominated the area drifting nearer to him at a constant pace.

"Well, good *morning*!" Ram's eyes flew open in alarm; the gangs had found him! No, wait. That voice belonged to... Master Dylan? It wasn't all a dream?

Ram looked up, seeing the hulking form of the butcher. He scrambled to his feet, "G-good morning, sir! I tried to keep going, but it got too dark to–"

"Stop all that chattering. You slept here all night? Abyss take me, I forgot to show you where to sleep, didn't I? Come with me." Dylan had an odd look on his face as he turned and began walking away.

Ram started to follow, but his muscles locked up and he fell with a startled yelp. Dylan looked back and grunted as Ram got to his feet. "Sleeping on stone after having been beaten and working your first day of hard labor? I'm not surprised. You'll take the morning off. You can work your mind in the meantime. Come clean up, and you'll start to learn the skills you need to be an apprentice butcher. Having the morning off won't be a common occurrence, but it was *my* fault this time. Dratted day *one*, and I messed up twice."

After showing Ram where he would be sleeping from now on—an *actual* straw-filled *mat*—Dylan made him take a bath before delivering him to the study room. Dylan paused before opening the door. "My daughter is in there. Mind how you speak. My wife is sure to hear about *anything* you do wrong. Treat her as an adult, even if your ages are similar. Remember that you are *just* a male, and as the daughter of a shop owner, she can have you whipped or worse without requiring permission from anyone. Even me."

"I understand, sir. I'm used to it at this point." Ram braced himself to deal with yet another woman who had the power of life and death over him, wondering how terrible of a person she must be for Dylan to feel the need to warn him about her.

Dylan opened the door, allowing a smell of lavender to pour out of the small office and mix with the scents of butchery. Poop, blood, and flowers. Yum. Fun times on the olfactory organs.

"Daddy!" A blur of golden hair slammed into the hulking butcher.

Dylan laughed. "Sunshine! I have a new student for you! Want to teach another boy how to help me out?"

"Boys are stinky! Why can't you find a *girl* who wants to learn from me?" the small girl pouted up at her father.

"I made him take a bath before we came here, just for you!"

"...Well, that might help a *little*. Bring him to me, then." She finished with an over-exaggerated exhalation of air.

Dylan's hand descended on Ram, pushing him into the room. "Ram, this is my daughter, Chandra. Make sure to listen to what she has to teach you. She is a wonderful instructor."

"You aren't even as tall as I am!" Chandra announced accusingly. "Look at you! No muscle, either!"

She looked at Dylan with a glare. "Did you ask mommy before bringing him here?"

Dylan coughed loudly and strode out of the room. "Good luck, boy!"

Ram stared incredulously at the man who had just thrown him to the wolves.

"Hey! I have to teach you, so let's get on with it!" Chandra snapped her fingers in front of his face.

"What do you know how to do? Multiplication? Sums? Writing? ...Can you *read*?" Her voice was getting more desperate with every head shake 'no'. Ram was flushed and embarrassed at his lack of knowledge.

"Well... at least you won't have any bad habits?" Chandra took a deep breath and looked for the silver lining in the situation. "I've never had to teach down to this level of basics before. Maybe it will be good for me? Make me a better teacher?"

She motioned to a chair and sat down on the other side of the small desk.

"I'm... sorry," Ram mumbled. "I'd like to know how to do those things, though."

"Oh, *really?*" Chandra looked at his serious face. "*Interesting.* Daddy brought me a butcher boy who actually wants to learn what I have to teach him, not just someone who wants to beat meat all day?"

"I really do want to learn," Ram promised earnestly.

"Why don't you just leave learning to whatever woman decides to keep you?" Chandra prodded with an unfriendly tone.

Ram was taken aback. He had heard this statement in various forms his whole life. "I just..."

Then he did something he hadn't since meeting master Dylan. He lied a little. "I *only* want to know so that I can do whatever job your father wants me to do. He has been so kind. I will do *anything* to repay him. He asked me to learn."

"That's... reasonable." Chandra thought it over for a moment. "Daddy *is* pretty great, isn't he? Fine then, I'll teach you. Here. This is a slate. We use chalk to write on it. This way, we can erase it and reuse the slate a lot. Letters are arranged in something called an 'alphabet'..."

Three hours later, Dylan came back, opening the door to Chandra shouting at Ram and slapping him across the face. "No, you *idiot!* 'C' is for 'cat'! 'G' is for 'goat'!"

"I'm sorry!" Ram apologized for the hundredth time since they had started. "I don't know why it matters! They look the same to me!"

"The 'G' has that little line! Look! If you can't see a little *line*, how can you make a precise cut along rib meat worth two silver!" Chandra bellowed at her cowering pupil as she raised her hand again.

Ahem Dylan coughed to announce his presence. Chandra looked over with burning eyes, which brightened as she saw him.

"Daddy!"

"Hello, Princess. How did he do?" Dylan chuckled as Ram looked at the open door desperately.

"Not... *too* bad, I guess," Chandra stated after thinking a moment. "He learned *most* of the alphabet correctly, and we started in on small words and sounding things out."

"I see the difference in those two now! I'll remember!" Ram promised, wild-eyed.

"You'd *better*," Chandra growled at him darkly.

Dylan took charge of the situation. "Ram, are you ready? I have soup for you, and there is a growing pile of offal that needs to find its way to the sewer."

"Yes, sir!" Ram tried bolting to the door, only to be caught and *looked* at by Dylan.

"You weren't going to leave without *thanking* your teacher for taking the time to instruct you... correct?" The Master's eyebrow twitched.

"Of course not! My mind was only on completing the next task!" Ram sputtered. He spun around and bowed at the golden-haired girl who had just been screaming at him. "Thank you for teaching me how to be an asset to your father."

"Come back anytime!" she called sweetly as the door swung closed.

The men were walking to the dining area quickly, and as Ram began eating... Dylan began laughing. "So, *ha ha*, how was your first, *ha*, learning experience?"

"Um," Ram sucked down a noodle quickly, "...terrifying?"

His answer made Dylan laugh even harder. "Ah, that's the good stuff."

Dylan wiped at his eyes. "I know it isn't fun, lad, but if you want to better your station in life, knowledge is the only way. How can you fill an order if you can't read it? How do you know if you are getting the correct coin for your goods? Only by learning before you *need* to know it."

Ram thought about these words as he slurped down a noodle. "Well, as scary as she is... I... I'd like to go back again soon then. If that is okay, of course."

"Good." Dylan grunted and rolled his eyes. "I need someone who has an *interest* in these things. The other apprentices *suffer* through their lessons, but I don't know if they are actually learning."

He glanced around. "I'll let you in on a secret, Ram. Only if you promise not to let others know, and I'll only tell you because you *want* to go back."

"...Sir?"

"One of the tests to become a journeyman in the Butchers' Guild is a *written* exam. You need to do calculations and read through contracts to find where you would be swindled if you signed." Dylan sighed mightily. "You only get two attempts to make journeyman, and you need to make those attempts within a month of each other if you fail the first one. Fail twice, and you can never get a higher position in the guild than an apprentice. Technically, you aren't allowed to tell apprentices about this requirement, which means that at least *one* of the boys working in my shop is bound to fail. Chase hates reading."

"Why are you telling *me* then?" Ram asked with great curiosity.

"Well, you aren't an *apprentice,* are you?" Dylan grinned slyly. "Seriously, you cannot tell the others. It would mean instant disqualification for them and a fine for me. This is for you to know, and that is *it.* Full stop."

"I understand."

"Good. You finished? Lots of work to do."

CHAPTER FOUR

Ram grunted as he made another quick motion with the squeegee. Watered-down blood collected in a wave as he pushed it away, though his foot still splashed in the knuckle-deep fluids.

"That's pretty good, Ram. Keep it up," Hunter assured him as he wielded his own squeegee.

"Quit coddling him, Hunt. He's barely affecting the puddle." Chase glowered at Ram as he worked to get the bloody water flowing toward the sewer hole. "*Ask* could have been done by now."

"Yeah, well, Ask is *dead.* How about you stop bringing him up?" Hunter snapped at his fellow apprentice.

Chase quieted for a while as they tried to clean out the room before all light faded. "He still shouldn't be here. He hasn't paid the fees."

Ram went still. "Fees?"

"Knock it off, Chase," Hunter growled warningly. "You know he doesn't have money. At least he is a hard worker. I haven't had to shovel crap in two days now. If you want to go do *that* instead of actually working with meat, *you* can make a complaint to the guild."

"It just isn't fair that *he* gets to be here for free while..."

Master Dylan poked his head in to look at them. "Life isn't fair, *Apprentice* Chase. If you have a problem with *my* decisions, feel free to come let *me* know about it."

The ominous phrasing and way Dylan seemed to appear and vanish randomly had Chase shivering as he returned to work *quietly.* It took another ten minutes, but the blood and meat scraps too small to save had finally been washed out of the stone room. Chase worked at guiding the fluid to the drain, while Hunter showed Ram how to add just enough soapleaf to the water they had boiling for it to lather correctly.

"Too much soapleaf and it'll take forever to clean the suds out of here, too little and the floor won't clean properly. Either way, Master will have us do it again," Hunter explained as he crushed the dried herb into the roiling water. As the water began to sud, they stepped out of the way and poured the huge pot out on to the floor. Soapy water sloshed against the walls, and some even poured down the slope without help. Hunter yelped as the water—luckily only *hot* after washing across the floor—flowed on to his feet.

"Heh. Always funny." Hunter chuckled as he handed Ram a mop. "Now, we scrub until the floor is clean, and then we squeegee it out again. It'll be dry by the time we start work tomorrow."

They got to it, and even Chase only glared a *little* as he rejoined them and began scrubbing. It was fully dark by the time the remaining water was out of the room, and an exhausted Ram was barely standing. Dylan came into the room and took a sniff. "You *think* it is clean?"

Hunter nodded respectfully, and Dylan harrumphed. "Well, I'll believe you, but if we need to redo it in the morning, *you* are going to have to do that instead of working on the chop-block. You okay with that?"

Chase spoke almost ritualistically, "Yes, sir. We have faith that you will find our work satisfactory."

Dylan nodded once. "Good then. Dismissed. Head to bed, or to study after cleaning up."

He walked away but hesitated for a moment. "Chandra is doing lessons tonight if that factors into your decision."

Chase and Hunter grimaced and started making their way directly to their beds above the cattle pens. Ram, though he was almost asleep on his feet, felt the need to improve his standing. "I'll go... if I'm allowed?"

"Hmph. Well, aren't *you* a glutton for punishment? It isn't like she won't have the free time to train you; the others tend to avoid lessons when she is around. She can work with you one-on-one, and you'll improve faster that way."

"I'll clean up and go over," Ram grimly promised.

Dylan laughed at his stony face. "She isn't *that* bad! Chandra is just a fan of corporal punishment for *any* failure. She really does know her stuff, though, and you will certainly learn *very* fast with her as your teacher."

Ram agreed with his words and went to clean up. He walked to the door of the study room, took a deep breath, and entered.

Chandra had her eyes half-closed and was staring at a glowing, purple flower. She didn't take her eyes off of it but was scribbling away at her slate the entire time. Ram coughed lightly, and she whirled around so fast that she almost knocked the flower over.

"What are *you* doing here?" she demanded, shocked to see another person in the lessons room.

"Um. I was told you would keep teaching me if I came tonight?" Ram edged back toward the door, just in case she got too violent.

"No one *ever* comes to my lesson nights." Chandra looked suspicious, then thoughtful. She glanced at the flower once more before setting her slate down.

"If you don't mind me asking, what were you doing?" Ram asked her cautiously.

"Hmm? Oh. I'm trying to find a use for this flower," Chandra responded offhandedly.

"What do you mean?"

"I'll tell you if you keep it between us?" She glanced at him. Ram quickly nodded. "I really like to... cook."

Ram stared at her, exceedingly confused. Women didn't *cook* unless they had no other choice.

"Don't stare at me like that!" Chandra demanded heatedly. "I don't like coming to this smelly building every day. I like things that smell good or are tasty! As a matter of fact, I want to open a restaurant someday."

Ram relaxed a bit. "Oh, well, I see, if you–"

"I want to be the *cook*, too!" Chandra finished triumphantly. Ram nearly choked as he thought about the idea of a woman *working* to make someone *else* a meal. Straight. Up. Outlandish. "Enough about me. Let's get to lessons."

They worked on his ability to read, Chandra making Ram read every word she wrote on her slate. It was slow going, and after an hour, Ram was swaying in his seat.

"Tired? Good, get out. I need to cultivate anyway." Chandra shoved Ram toward the door. He turned and bowed, thanking her, then paused.

"Cultivate?"

"Yes. I see you have graduated to three-syllable words," Chandra sneered at him.

"What is cultivating?"

Chandra paused, thinking a moment. "Oh, why not? It isn't like I'm going to break the law and show you how to *do* it. Cultivating is a way to draw energy from the world into you. It makes you stronger, smarter, and healthier. Also, *only* women can do it. That's the law."

"Oh. Well, thank you for telling me," Ram muttered, turning to leave.

"You want to see me do it?" Chandra smirked at him.

"No thanks."

Chandra glared at him. "Sit down! It's super boring, so stay here and talk to me when I need a break!"

Ram looked at her with pleading eyes, but she simply pointed at the seat and glared. He sat down heavily, grumbling softly.

"Be quiet. There aren't many plants in here, so I really need to concentrate," Chandra growled, adjusting her seating position.

The room went quiet as Chandra scrunched up her forehead in concentration. Ram sat around, waiting for her to finish. His head started to bob as the work of the day, and the warm fire next to him conspired to push him ever closer toward sleep. He blinked his tired eyes, and for a moment, he thought he saw a green haze moving from the plants into Chandra.

"Pretty," Ram muttered softly. Half-asleep, he looked around and saw multiple colors in the room, including a deep black that was leaking in from the cracks of the doorframe. He frowned, stood up, and weaved on sleep-laden feet toward the enticing darkness. His face moved closer until a wisp of the shadow entered his nose.

"Bleh!" He almost gagged as the scent of the butcher shop entered his nostrils. It had been well hidden by the plants, but he had taken a large nose-full somehow. He felt *very* awake now.

Chandra's eyes snapped open. "Hey! Are you trying to sneak out?"

"No, there was just..." He trailed off as he looked around, only seeing the normal colors of the room.

"You may as well just go." Chandra turned away, voice soft. "No one wants to be in here with me anyway."

"Sounds good, sleep well!" Ram started opening the door, but a feral-sounding growl from Chandra made him turn back.

"Don't you know that you are supposed to *comfort* a sad woman?" Chandra's eyes were blazing.

"I literally did not." Ram reluctantly closed the door, seeing his chances at sleep vanishing. "*Why* are you sad?"

"No one wants to visit me or learn from me," Chandra stated bluntly.

Ram rolled his eyes. "Do you mind if I speak freely? I don't want to get in trouble or get kicked out of here. Or whipped. If I'm gonna make you mad, I'll just be quiet."

She looked at him with cold eyes. "So long as you aren't intentionally insulting... go ahead."

"When your dad found me three days ago, I had just been brutally beaten by a street gang. They were going to kill me because I didn't run to them and turn in a loaf of bread I found on the street. I hadn't eaten for three days before that. I had no home, no work, no food, or friends. If I hadn't been taken in, I'd likely be dead right now." Ram raised his shirt to show the intense bruising that was blooming into beautiful, painful coloration.

Chandra's eyes were even larger than usual after being told this information. "Whoa. That's too bad, but I don't really see how it relates to this situation. You don't seem *sad* about it."

Ram looked at her incredulously. "I was trying to show you that *you* shouldn't be sad? You are upset because no one wants to *learn* from you? No one wants to learn from you because you scream and hit them for the most minor mistakes. *I,* on the other hand, have an actual reason to be upset, and I am instead working to better my position in life and doing everything I can to repay your father for his kindness."

Chandra looked confused. "I don't get it. You're just a boy. You are *supposed* to take screaming and beatings *stoically* and without complaining. Stop saying stupid things. Your situation isn't even comparable to mine. I *am* glad you realize that Daddy is great, though."

He looked at her, mouth open. He shook his head, unable to articulate how much her words upset him. "Um. Goodnight. Thank you for... teaching me."

Ram slipped out the door before she could say anything else, hurrying to find his bed. He lay on his pallet a short while later, unable to sleep though his body was aching. What was cultivating? It looked boring at first, but after he saw the colors in the air... he was mesmerized. It was *beautiful.* Why weren't males allowed to learn how to do it? Was that why women were so much stronger and smarter? Why they ruled men with an iron fist?

He sat up, frowning. Chandra had said that cultivating made women stronger and smarter. It was well known that a grown man could never defeat a woman in a contest of strength or skill, even though they were so much smaller than their male counterparts. Was *this* the secret? Cultivation? Ram had to find out!

CHAPTER FIVE

A hand shaking him woke Ram with a start. His eyes flew open as he swung his fist wildly in an attempt to hold off whoever was attacking him... Oh, it was just Chase.

"Wow. I am making Hunter wake you up from now on, you little psycho," Chase muttered as he rubbed his smarting cheek. "Get up. Daylight is about to reach us, and Master Dylan will be inspecting how clean we left the butcher room."

Ram nodded and hopped out of bed, quickly pulling on his clothes. Chase's nostrils flared, and he coughed. "Tonight, make sure that someone shows you where to wash your clothes. Master Dylan told us that if we don't wash them regularly, we will get sick."

Ram scoffed at the old husband's tale. "That's just a myth! An extra layer of dirt helps you stay warm."

Chase nodded wisely. "That's what I said, but he told me that women wash all the time, and we never see *them* get sick."

Ram considered his words, but he thought that he knew the *real* reason women didn't get sick.

"It doesn't matter, though. You need to wash properly, or he'll kick you out." Chase walked down the stairs, vanishing from sight. Ram hurried after him, nearly tripping as he walked down. They got into the butcher room just before Dylan and had to wait while he walked around inspecting every surface.

"Passable," he finally asserted, drawing a sigh of relief from the three waiting boys. He arched a brow and grinned. "Here is what you can do better *tonight.*"

He launched into an explanation of the issues he had found, moving from wall to wall and pointing out nearly imperceptible streaks on the floor. "Angle your squeegee more carefully, so you avoid leaving behind blood or soap as you did here. You are going to have to scrub this spot tonight to get this dried blood off."

He pointed out a few other areas, then finally turned to face them.

"What is our goal? How do we become Masters of our profession?" he demanded with crossed arms.

The two boys next to Ram responded in unison, surprising him, "By perfecting our skills and using our tools to their maximum potential."

Dylan nodded sharply. "This does not mean only our skills with the *blade*. What use are you to me if you are unable to fulfill the jobs I give to you? Ram, you are new here, but you have much to learn. You need to *pace* yourself better to ensure that you are building muscle and are still able to clean the stables each day before coming here for cleanup."

Ram nodded hurriedly, eyes wide as he waited for punishment, but instead of beating him, Dylan just turned to the others. "Chase. You told me that your work was satisfactory. I have found it to be *only* passable. Your word is your bond, lad. You need to ensure that you are able to assess your work and find faults correctly. Perfecting your skills applies to every aspect of yourself."

"Hunter, you left blood on your cleaver." The boy turned pale as Dylan continued, "Not only that, but I was informed this morning that you haven't been to a lesson in two full weeks. If your blade rusts, you will need to replace it *yourself.* A dull blade is a danger to yourself and those you work with. A dull mind is the same. Fix these issues, or prepare a new apprenticeship."

Dylan addressed the group as a whole, "Now, get to work!"

He turned and started walking toward the stables. "Ram, we brought in a few more cows today. They should be arriving soon. I am going to start teaching you how to look for signs of injury or illness that might spoil the meat. You don't need to worry about feeding them. We let them go hungry for a day before slaughtering them. That way, they have less weight to clean out."

Ram half-jogged as he tried to keep up with the long legs of his Master. "Yes, sir!"

"Chandra told me that you came to lessons last night." Dylan glanced at the glistening, bald head of the child next to him. "She says that you were able to learn the entire alphabet and begin on words already. That you seem to have a natural *talent* for learning and discussion."

Ramset didn't know where this conversation was going. "I'm just trying to do well, sir."

There was silence for a moment. "You seem to have a talent for thought, boy. If you want... I could likely get you a position as a scribe in a few months. It would be an easier life, and it can even pay well if you show a talent."

"Thank you, sir... but..." Ram hesitated. He didn't want to anger his new boss. "I'd rather stay here. If... if you are okay with that."

"Good, good." A large nod accompanied these words. "I am glad that we didn't scare you off too early. A loyal man is a trustworthy man. I feel that you will do well here, in time."

They stopped talking as a farmer slowly herded a few cows to the door. He looked up from under the brim of his straw hat. "You the butcher?"

"I am. Got some cows for me, then?" Dylan grinned at the slow-speaking farmer.

"Nah, these are chickens. Just fed 'em too much."

Dylan started laughing. "Ah, I walked into that one, didn't I? Mind if I look em over?"

"I'd be offended if you didn't! You need to see how much *higher* quality my beef is than the average farmer!" the man stated proudly.

"What do you do differently?" Dylan asked after looking over a few cows and shaking his head in admiration. "They really do look good, and from what I can tell, the meat seems fairly tender."

"Ah, right, come 'ere, lad. What we are looking for is bleeding or inflamed areas, loss of teeth..." Dylan talked for a few moments as he showed Ram how to guide his hands on the flanks of the cows.

The farmer waited patiently while Dylan talked before answering his question when he had his attention again. "New apprentice? Lucky boy. Now, my cows are fed from hay like the others, but I make sure that they don't drink from the river, only my wells."

"That, and each one gets a measure of grain each week. Helps fatten 'em up and keeps 'em lazy. Tender, tasty meat." He grinned a gap-tooth smile.

"Well, I can't argue with the results. The price though..." Dylan started haggling, trying to drive down the price, but was soon defeated by the farmer, who made only a small concession.

As the cows were led into the stable, Dylan and the farmer shook hands and planned on more business in the future. Ram waited until the man was gone, then asked, "Why were you so happy to pay that price? That was a *lot* of silver, wasn't it?"

"Good beef is worth it, and this is *great* beef. One of the other important things to look for to judge the quality of the meat is to see how *willing* the owner is to part with it for less than the price they wanted. If they go too low, there are only two reasons. They are a fool, or the meat is not worth the price they asked. Fools don't stay in business, and cheats could ruin *my* business," Dylan explained cheerfully. A *splat* announced the arrival of a steaming cow pat.

"Oh, looks like your workday has begun." Dylan chuckled with a smile. He walked to a different portion of the stable and led away a different cow. "See you at midday."

Ram got to work, scooping up the fresh turds and tossing them into his reeking cart. He worked quickly to empty out the individual stalls, then moved on to scraping out the room the pigs were kept in.

"Careful, lad." Ram looked up to see one of the journeyman butchers in the room. "Only go in the empty rooms. Those hogs haven't eaten in a day, and if you get into the midst of them, they will tear you apart." Ram looked over the chest-level fencing to see a sounder of hogs silently staring in his direction. He shivered as he realized he had almost opened the gate holding them in.

"Th-thank you!" Ram stepped back and bowed as low as he would to a woman.

"Hey, stop that! I work for a living. Don't bow to me." The man chuckled. "I'm John. You must be the new boy."

John had thick, curly hair and a beard so poofy that it hid his mouth entirely. "I specialize in pork meat, so I've had a long time to get used to how they act."

"All the same, thank you. I like not being eaten." Ram nodded once, then returned to work.

John watched him for a bit. "I can see why Dylan likes you. You're a hard worker. I appreciate you cleaning out the stalls. I've been doing it since the last new boy... left."

"Only doing what I can, sir."

"Hmm." John watched him for a moment longer, then started to help. "I've noticed the others avoiding this job now that you are on it. Fools... they could get so much more done if you were there to help them. They're neglecting strength training now as well."

"I don't mind the work." Ram actually felt more energized when he was working, something he had never expected.

"Well... just keep at it. Things will get better." They worked until the stall was empty. Ram continued working until mealtime, then kept going. He remembered Dylan's words and took smaller but more numerous trips to the sewer entrance. As evening approached, he helped clean the butcher room again.

The others left for lessons or bed after that, but Ramset had one more load of feces to dump. He got to the edge of the sewer and looked down, noticing that there was a large mass that wasn't moving. Ram grabbed the poop-poking stick and started stabbing down, but on the second poke, the lump *spoke*.

"*Stop that.*"

CHAPTER SIX

Ram was pulled off his feet and into the sewer entrance. How? He had no idea. One second he was looking down; the next he was standing in front of a wild-eyed man with white hair. "You? That's not supposed to happen for hundreds of... oh wait, you're a child. Is this where we meet? Have we met yet?"

"I...!" Ram was floating above the surface of the moving sludge. "I have no idea who you are! Please don't–"

"Blah, blah. Nice to meet you, little *Ramset.* I'm Egil." The man stuck out a hand, and Ram took it even though there was literal crap on it. "I'm going to be the one you credit with rescuing you! Oh... look at that empty center. Mmhmm..."

"What are you...?" Ram tried to pull away, but moving at all was as difficult as lifting a dozen cows.

"I'm going to be running a little experiment on you, *Ramset.*" Egil smiled brightly, in no way showing bad intent. "I've been playing around with Cores, memory stones, and dungeons recently. You'll make a nice distraction for me while I hang out in the sewer for a while. That silly organization is still trying to capture me, and I can't let that happen for..."

The man looked away. "I think it is thirty-two years? Sounds right. Anyhoo, you've been able to pull Essence to your eyes already... so let's set this to your vision. Sorry if this hurts!"

A... blade? Some kind of knife-shaped *something* appeared in Egil's hand, and he sliced open the front of Ram's left eye. Ram tried to scream, but a foreign pressure forced his lungs to refuse. Egil was muttering, but Ram wasn't able to hear what he was saying. Finally, a spark of *something* rushed into Ram's eye, and the pain vanished. In fact, the whole experience was somewhat hazy.

Ram blinked and sat up. He was on his mat? Hunter was about to shake him awake but nodded as he saw that Ram was up. They got to work, and Ram tried to figure out what that dream had been about. It was strange... Did everyone have dreams when they were well-fed?

He blinked as a cloud drifted over the sun. The entire area was filled with purple-tinged, black smoke. Ram rubbed his eyes and looked around. Nothing. Whew. He stopped rubbing his left eye and opened it again... The smoke was back. He could see all sorts of colors, but black was the most prolific for certain.

It was *everywhere*, but especially around the blood and poo that he needed to clean up. He was going to go talk to Master Dylan about it when a *huge* wall of black exploded out of the butcher room he was about to enter. In a panic, he ran in to see the butcher standing above a freshly-slain cow. "Ram? You need something?"

Ramset had no idea what to say. 'I can see death' would likely not be the right thing to announce. "Oh, I heard a sound and wasn't sure what it was."

"Cow mooing as it bled out, most likely." Dylan got to work. "You should get moving. I want half that pile gone before eating today."

"Yes... sir." Ram walked back to the pile and tried to ignore the smoke that he saw everywhere. He tried to avoid breathing it in, but it seemed drawn to him for some reason. Just before lunch, another odd thing happened.

Minimum threshold of Essence acquired. Initiating 'Seed'. Corruption purge has begun.

Hello, Ramset. Welcome to 'Cultivation Revamped'. Egil Noslen has created a cultivation method for you specifically, and it is time to begin. First, your meridians will be mapped to the Core fragment in your left eye, and the best methodology for progression will be determined. You are currently in a comatose state as corruption is ripped out of you.

There are two rules that you will follow at all times.

1)   You will grow as strong as possible in the shortest amount of time.

2)   You will never tell another soul about the Core fragment in your eye. If you do, your death will be more painful than anyone else can possibly threaten you with.

It is time for you to learn how to cultivate.

AXIOM
BY: DENNIS VANDERKERKEN

CHAPTER ONE

Ideas bloomed in the sproutling's thoughts. The plan was straightforward: make it to the cave, get the secrets, get home before morning meals. The old man just watched them with a pleasant joy as they put things together. He'd given them pieces of the puzzle, and even without being exceptionally prompted, he could tell they were solving the conundrum. They had wants just like any of the adults; using those to teach them sharp thinking was just good sense.

"Can we make it?" the oldest boy asked as he stole a look at the deep water. It looked awful dark even as the first rays of sunlight struck it.

The old man nodded with certainty. "You lot? Certainly. Myself? Maybe a few more times before I can't hold my breath long enough."

Their Elder did some stretches. "Here's what happens. Once you're deep enough, the water is going to pull you. Specifically, it's going to pull you down, and you're going to get caught in a force of water that feels like you're falling sideways. That stream spits you out into a cave. You're going to feel like you're going down, then up; then you're going to hit the ground while water is rushing past you in a hurry. *Steady yourself there.* If you go farther, you're back in the stream, and it will spit you back out over *there*."

He pointed farther to the next hill, the salt stream cutting that one in half as well. "It's only a tiny bank of space you'll have to move on—a wall to the left, crawlspace to the right. Crawl to the light, and you'll be in the cave."

A detail came to mind that he swiftly threw in, "Oh, don't eat the stuff that glows. Tried that. Couldn't tell what was real for a week. Do *not* recommend."

His voice trailed off and waited for follow up questions. The mousy voice called, "So... we just hold our breath?"

"Just hold your breath. There's no swimming against that current once you're that deep, so take a big one and keep your hands over your mouth once you lose your swimming direction. I would say it takes about... hmm. Maybe half a minute? To..."

He'd lost them. They had no idea what a minute was. "This long, I'll count in seconds."

He raised both his palms and moved his fingers one at a time until he'd moved every digit on both his hands three times. "Twenty to twenty-five fingers is normal, twenty if the pull is fast. However, so you're not surprised in the future, I've known it to take thirty. Thirty seconds is half a minute. A 'finger', if referenced directly, is one minute, and a 'hand' is five minutes because that's how many fingers you have."

The younger ones were afraid but couldn't stop the older ones who had eyes full of lust for adventure. The Elder noted their hesitation. "I'll go first. Ditch your robe. Just go in your pants. Extra cloth and weight really don't help."

He motioned at a spot near the pail for all the things to be dumped and dove right on into the darkness with a splash. The children could see him swim straight down for the first few lengths of a person, and then with a sudden movement, the Elder was pulled to the side and vanished into the black.

The youngest girl shuddered and was about to voice her concern as the oldest boy loudly plunged into the depths. Her words didn't ever reach her tongue as the oldest girl followed the

Elder. She turned in borderline panic to the younger boy, but he was filled with determination and taking deep, steadied breaths. He swallowed a big one and joined the other three. Now she was alone with the mousy boy.

"Maybe we... should not..." she almost whimpered the words as daring teeth were flashed back at her in a sizable grin. *Oh no.* He was going to go as well. No, she didn't want to be alone. The mousy boy took her hand and squeezed it.

"Together?" His expression one of confidence and excited wonder. Her hesitant hand squeezed in return. Fear melted away as something akin to butterflies in her stomach bloomed. She wasn't so afraid if she wasn't alone.

"Y-yes. *Together.*" In unison, they began taking deep breaths, and with a jump, they were gone in the stream as they swam to follow. The first gasp of air the youngest girl heaved as she broke the cavern's surface was met by a strong grip on her arm. It pulled her to safety as she sputtered. Hearing another set of gasps right behind her, she saw the boy too was snatched to safety. Holding their breath had been mostly successful, but at least two of them were hacking up watery coughs.

Support was ready for them. After a solid few breaths in the dim dark, they began crawling in the perhaps two-and-a-half-foot tall space in clear direction of some faint light. Once inside what looked to be a tall dome, they all pushed their backs to the wall, breathing deep and looking to one another with proud smiles. They'd all made it. Every last one of them. A round of chuckles went around the circle as the Elder managed a few words, "I would like to welcome you all to my little secret place."

The Elder raised his hands, motioning at the luminous, domed space. "It's safe to touch that odd glowing moss, but again, don't eat it."

Another series of half-laughs and chuckles did the rounds in memoriam to the courage it had taken to get here. The euphoria cut to pure silence as the Elder declared five names, "Lunella, Grimaldus, Tychus, Wuxius, and Astrea."

Everyone fell silent when the dome began to shudder, worriedly looking all around them as the walls thrummed and tremored. After what sounded like the thudding hooves of a stampeding herd passed above, the dome fell quiet.

"Well," the Elder's voice rose with apprehension, "it doesn't seem like the sky is falling on our heads. I'd say we're clear."

The oldest girl snapped her head sharply at the flouting Elder as he'd spoken with such nonchalance. Her emerald eyes stabbed him with greater force than her words, but that was one of the traits that made her such a delight. "You said all of that and just *hoped* the Fringe was going to let you get away with it?"

"Yes, *Lunella*. I just believed." He sounded certain. In reality, he'd absolutely rolled the dice on that one and would *never* tell them so.

The previously tense and miffed girl gasped as her hands went over her mouth. Was that *her* name? She *adored* it and was now trying to keep it together as her swiftly overwhelming emotions bubbled and fluttered. She hadn't expected to *actually* get a name for several seasons. This had been her gamble, and it paid off *wonderfully!*

The old man crossed his legs and swatted at wet pants; blasted cloth always got unpleasantly cold when he lingered here long. He'd bear with it. Pressing back against the wall, he saw her heartfelt reaction and extended his warmth with a delighted expression. "Do you like it?"

Lunella nodded through her crushing emotions; it was *beautiful*. The mousy boy chirped up and nodded as well but was thinking about something else with some concern.

"They all sound so *strong*. Does... does the Fringe have enough room for that many strong names?"

The Elder **humphed** at the notion, arms crossing. "The Fringe can come *complain* if it's dissatisfied at this point."

The retaliatory look in his eyes softened as it fell back on the poorly illuminated children. "I won't be around for many more seasons. I have many fond memories of this village. It has some great places and sights, but they're not what I love about it. The biggest secret I have is that what I love the most is *all of you*."

The kids felt fuzzy at the mention. "The joy you bring this old man with your clever little tricks and energetic playing around is a life of fulfillment I cannot describe. Watching you all grow has kept my heart beating. I might be a touch lazy, but waking up to find what trouble you're going to get into that day is a *hoot*. Your lives are what gave this old man the will to keep seeing just one more day."

He rubbed the sides of his arms to warm up a touch. "So, I thought, and I thought. If *I* was going to give the few minds who I treasure most in this world *anything*, it was going to be the best names I could grant. The lengths I wouldn't go to see you all healthy, safe, and in good spirits..." He paused to let out another rebellious **hmmpf**!

"Oh, the heavens would have to descend to rob me of my last breath before I would stop trying!" His hand softly laid on the head of the mousy boy next to him.

"Yes, *Tychus*. Your names are *strong*. They are filled with a purpose for you to choose and a depth of meaning that will likely take your entire life to uncover. With your names, I've granted you something *special,* something only the five of you have in the Fringe—a reason to live that *you* can choose. That's all I want you to do when I pass. Just *live* the way you want."

Tychus went wide-eyed. That had been the toughest sounding name! Why did *he* get it? He was small and unblossomed, an absolute *acorn.*

"*Tychus?*" He tasted the name.

"That's *you,*" the Elder affirmed with a pat on his head, "and Astrea is next to you."

Tychus tensed as the girl next to him needed immediate support. Having been holding his hand this whole time, Astrea was firmly crushing his grip, equally unable to keep her emotions in check. For her, this was less because it was a social implication and more because she now felt solidly included. The weight of the designation pressed invisible on her sternum, and the pressure made a cool shiver crackle over her skin. She was going to get through it. They were all here together, and that meant the world to her. Having Tychus' hand to crush *admittedly* also helped with coping a little.

The oldest and youngest boys were nervously exchanging glances, voices trapped in their throats. The Elder motioned at the youngest first to dismiss their uncertainty. "Grimaldus."

Then the oldest. "Wuxius."

"Do you like them?" The boys still had no words as the Elder returned palms to his knees, an eyebrow raising. The old man honestly wasn't sure. They weren't making a sound, and that made it *terribly* difficult for him to get any details.

"They love it," Lunella replied as she was wiping wet cheeks with the back of her hand."

The boys then agreed in a hurry.

"Oh, eh... Yes! I just don't know what to say," chirped Grimaldus.

"I just feel really *heavy*." Wuxius was nodding in firm agreement as he found his voice. "I just... It's so *solid*. I don't know what it means. The name just sounds like it's filled with more than I can get a hold of."

That statement was echoed by the others as well, and the Elder filled in, "Well, that's part of the point, isn't it? You'll grow up with this, you'll shape it, people will recognize your name based on what you've done and what you say. However, unlike a simple meaning, I've given you complicated ones."

His hands drew visualizations of his words in the air. "Another *secret* for you. Certain things in life may *look* complicated, but really, they're made from a large number of small things that are simple. Coming together, small things look like a big mess, as we're only used to seeing the whole. When you have a good grasp of the small things, the big one will suddenly make sense too."

"I've given you this weighty, unknown thing that you're probably not sure what it is or how to carry. However, little by little, you'll discover details that paint a bigger picture, and when you finally have all the pieces, you'll find the truth hidden in a small hole in the ground surrounded by people you love." The Elder's voice faltered, and he cleared his throat. He tried not to dwell on how cold and hazy he was getting. The chilled Elder did the usual handclap to clear himself of his thoughts and rubbed them together.

"Well, I'm freezing and starting to shiver; shall we go home and go eat?" His facsimile of a smile didn't get the expected reaction; the sproutlings had grown and were holding back sobs.

They had been so happy about their names a few moments ago; why the somber air? He had to relent and looked to Lunella since she was going to be the one to speak regardless. Sure enough, her tone was bleak as she asked with displeasure. "How long do you have?"

If it hadn't already been chilly, the old man would certainly have lost feeling in his fingers after this. They had assessed that the clock was ticking down, and he supposed it was better to give them time to come to terms with however long he had left. He maintained eye contact with Lunella and gave the dreaded knowledge with a clenched heart, "Maybe a season."

The kids winced and bit their tongues at this. He wasn't sugar-coating the pain and just hit them with bleak truth. The anchor of knowing was an additional weight they didn't want to carry, and it made them feel terrible. They didn't want him to leave either, but that *abyss*-cursed serene expression on his face told them he was content with the impending end.

Seeing them muck about had been a joy. These children were an alternate reality of a life he'd never been blessed with. What had been closest to this contentment had been ripped from him as a young adult. This world was cruel that way. Cruel and unrelenting in the wake of the eternal unknown. It was normal to fear and shy away from what you didn't understand. He grasped this well as he found his voice.

"I'll begin my final lessons shortly. I suppose as a preamble, I'd like you to keep hold of this. It's a bit of knowledge that I hold very close." He cleared his throat again, but it throttled in significant need of some fresh air. "You're going to make mistakes, and that's okay. You're going to fall, and that's okay. *Get up.* You're going to question yourself and wonder if you're doing things right. *That's good.* Keep asking!

When you make a choice to go forwards, don't waver. Only one choice is worth making, and that's the one you should live by."

The Elder leaned in, hands strong on his knees, emphasis carried on the provided wisdom. "Everything is either a choice you *can* live with or a choice you *cannot*. There is no reason to second guess; merely pour all your effort and being into the world you wish to see around you."

His back fell against the wall, eager to end it as he felt finished with the conversation. "I would have felt such regret if I didn't grant your names. Though, one day you will find that the best names are the ones you've chosen and made for yourself. Regardless of how long I have, if you fall and stumble, I'll come for you. I'll *always* come for you."

With a push to the floor, he was up and ready to go. "Now, let's go get warm. All of you first."

CHAPTER TWO

The Elder knew something was off as soon as he resurfaced. A smell in the air... it was *wrong*. His first breath of what should have been crisp air instead filled his tongue with the flavor of smoke. His hearing picked the muffled cries alongside the crackling *whips* of wildfire. Something was *burning*, falling... breaking.

The crashing tear of wooden supports caused a puffy *scrumph* as the unstable home collapsing on itself hit the ground and oppressed the senses. It also ended *several* muffled cries. This experience turned what should have been a peaceful morning gaggle of hungover groans into tortured screams.

The Elder had been the last to come back up through the stream, yet could not locate a *trace* of his young group through smoke so thick it forced his eyes to swell. The children had gone ahead of him, so the expectation was for them to be present when he resurfaced. A high-pitched screech cut through the rumbling, ambient mess of fire-wrought sound. *No*. He *knew* that voice! "*Lunella!*"

With significant effort, he dragged his old bones from the stream and on to the dry bank, worming his way from the water with all the elegance of a landed fish. His lungs burned; nasty smoke clogging the thick air made it all the worse. It reminded him of times he'd rather never recall.

It seemed that as much as he'd run away from conflict, strife with its endless reach had grasped him again. Life would not let him go silently into the night; it was here for the pound of flesh it was owed—or rather, from the rebellious voices that were dragged further and further into the distance, those of his *children*! The surrounding blares of activity made it a nightmare to determine who was where.

Accented, foreign screams echoed from the apiary as the crashing buzz of a destroyed hive split the air. A panic-fueled cry screamed out, "Bees! *Bees*!"

It wasn't any adult voice the Elder recognized, so that confirmed outside forces were at play. Total, howling disarray and fear sirened from uphill, so the Elder moved as fast as his feet would take him—which was admittedly rather pathetic and frustrating. He was *useless* like this! That his heart rate caused his hands to shake was nothing new, and old mantras chimed with military repetition in his mind.

Keep steady.

Keep moving.

Stay alive.

His shambled pace brought him back to the pile of robes the children had ditched. Creeping, wet cold still clung to his skin, and the cold-sickness was going to get his claws into him before his age did if he didn't bundle up. So, on went the robes, while a sack was repurposed as an anti-smoke face mask—a trick picked up in a desert long ago. He looked ridiculous and couldn't *begin* to care as his mind laid the foundations for action.

The Elder couldn't assess the threat. The amount of smoke meant the majority of the village was on fire, so this was a *raid*. His priorities in this battle boiled down to survival and retrieval of the children. That second objective was going to be difficult in his current state if there was so much as a toothpick-armed *weasel* in his way. He'd told the kids to stay alive. With hope, they would cling to those words. That's all he wanted them to do.

Stay alive.

Just stay alive.

Anxiety was squashed under absolute need as he throttled his worry and self-doubt by the throat. A *season* to live? No, old man! A *day* was fine! *One day* was more than *fine*, so long as he could see the safety of the children! The **clang** of metal clashing with metal put a hearty and swift dent in the chances of that plan. Thieves were bad; thieves with weapons were worse.

However, there wasn't a sword in the village? The **clangs** repeatedly rang from the wood storage direction, but there wasn't a... realization struck him like a brick. "*Choppy's axe!*"

The Elder then crumpled inwards like a potato sack as a pain spread from his stomach. A slung rock had struck him at speed and taken the wind right out of him, forcing an unexpected **ooof**! The earthy slam to the ground wasn't so bad, but it sure *felt* like it was. He remained there, unmoving. A crass voice called through the dense, smoky haze that hung low. "Hah, got another one! That's two hands for me in the lead!"

The Elder held his stomach with both hands but couldn't move, just gasping air with a soundless wheeze. "Looks like that one's not moving. I'm calling it *dead*, and a point for me!"

The same crass voice then gained excitement as it spotted moving prey. "Are those *runners?*"

"Yes, they are! Let's *get 'em!*" After a murderous laugh, the thudding impact of several boots promptly vacated the location. The vibration was so heavy that the Elder could feel it through the ground he laid immobile on. This pattern of footfalls felt incredibly similar to the... to the thrumming they'd experienced while in the cavern!

"*Abyss!*" It took at least a full minute for his breath to even out, and he was forced to hear the community around him burn to ash. The syrupy coughing of people choking to death filled nearby homes, only to be silenced as the buildings burned and collapsed down on top of them. Anyone who wasn't trying to run had attempted to hole up, and neither choice ended happily.

The Elder barely got to his hands and knees as a pained whimper cried from the logging section. It sounded like Choppy was in severe pain; pain that he couldn't understand. Infantile whimpers and sobbing, bubbling cries told the old man there was liquid in the boy's lungs. The familiar sensation of strained muscle twisted in the Elder's legs as he got up and forced himself to move on.

While he was certain an arrow whistled past his head at a certain point, he winced and ignored it. The old man found the woodchopper on his back with a face stained by pained tears. The Elder fell to his knees to support the lad, momentarily skidding to a halt. "I'm here, Choppy. *I'm here.*"

Firmly taking his calloused hands, the old man attempted to console his boy by being up close and personal. He could see the damage, and he knew the end was coming for this lad. A deep cut from the right shoulder raked down into the lung, but it hadn't been shallow where it vitally mattered. There was going to be no recovering from an injury like this, not even if the big man found immediate attention. The remainder of the woodcutter's short life was going to be agony.

The Elder knew Choppy wouldn't bleed to death from this wound; he'd choke on his own blood first—a fate he wasn't about to let the boy suffer. Choppy's good arm held the Elder firm as needing, glossy eyes cried for help as the boy stammered begging words, "*Gllrblpain*. Pain. *Glpain*. Hate pain. Pain."

This good boy had used his wood logging axe to fend off the invaders. A swift glance in either direction showed not one but *two* split melon heads. For all the harsh times the village had given this big lad, he'd always been *amazing* with his aim. From the angle, the axe must have gotten stuck in a spine. It seemed to be protruding from the slain raider, but the Elder had no time for that now. He slid forward and detested that he knew what to do.

A familiar, practiced grasp firmly took hold of the suffering boy's head, and the old man pushed a knee forward to press down on that wide chest. This was the kind of injury that left a man to suffer for as long as possible while still being fatal—purest suffering until the final gurgling took the agony to a crescendo, finally coming to an undeserved end.

"I know, my boy. I'm going to take the pain *away*, Choppy. I'm going to make it *stop* hurting now." The old man needed to suck in a breath, tearfully ignoring the bite of the smoke. "Hold me tight, *my son*. Hold me *tight*."

The Elder's voice was trembling, and his jaw was clenched shut. His eyes burned, and wet streaks lined down his cheeks. He had to do this for a prized child once *more*. His breath quickened, and his dry mouth swallowed to cope. The good boy did what he was told to do and clung tight. The psychological harm the Elder did to himself that next moment was unspeakable, as he shattered the happy illusion he'd built for himself over these many, many years.

The physical exertion was just... a simple...

Snap.

Chapter Three

"Alright, recruit. *Once* again, from the start." Armored fingers drummed with delicate impatience on the extended table in the salt village longhouse. This entire *mess* of a report had more holes in it than his favorite cheese, and Head Cleric Tarrean had not been able to acquire said cheese for *far* too long. He shook his head and forced himself to refocus. The bags under his eyes were reminiscent of crescent purple moons, and *still,* he couldn't take the liberty to rest; duty demanded the task be seen through.

His faith would carry him, as it always did, but this whole endeavor had been a repeated set of annoyingly convenient events. *Bothersomely* convenient. He went over how he just *knew* his superiors would be reacting:

'Where are the *raiders,* Tarrean?'

'Oh, I don't know! We have this intercepted vellum with a *surprisingly* detailed troop placement plan. Well, now we've arrived at the abandoned settlement, *Tarrean.* Where are the wanted men?'

'It appears that they're just taking their sweet time walking right over to us without a care in the world! Sure, we're already occupying defensive emplacements and are the wolf waiting for lost lambs to walk into our open mouth. Those raiders never saw it coming!'

'Why, Tarrean, where are we supposed to go from here. The map isn't very clear.'

'Recruit, if you look in the distance, doesn't that look like an awfully *large* funnel of smoke rising into the sky?'

'Why, *yes.* Yes, Head Cleric, we should rush to that position post-haste!'

'Tarrean, are we *certain* these are the raiders we thought they were? The last group seemed exhausted and in retreat.'

'Well, recruit, there's an awfully *large* number of buildings on fire, people screaming, and sharp, metal objects being stuck rather deeply into what seem to be awfully *innocent* people.'

Head Cleric Tarrean snarled and slammed his armored fist on the table, startling the man giving him a report into silence. Whoops. He hadn't heard a word the man had been saying. To top it all off, this mess was in the celestial-rejected *Fringe*. As if the history of this place wasn't *enough* of a nightmare for the Church!

Tarrean *almost* wished he could have just a sip of wine again, but his vows prevented him from such pleasures. The bridge of his nose received another squeeze, the shining metal of the gauntlet not injuring the cultivator in the slightest. A circular *go on* motion of his hands restarted the report. Acolytes and a Keeper were seated around the Head Cleric, pouring over stacked documents. Their gear was far simpler than his, though most of them had a weary expression that matched his own.

A new day was already starting to rise from the horizon, and silence laid on the wreckage that used to be the prominent village of Salt. Beams of sunlight funneled through the gaping holes in the longhouse walls, and a collective grunt heralded eyes being squeezed together to cope with the sudden brightness.

The next recruit in tow cleared his throat; ready to give a near-exact replica of the report with differences based *entirely* on the viewpoint of where he was at the time. Acolyte Tibbins fingered through the vellum to find the beginning of his report, and everyone worked to hold in a sigh as it began.

"As mentioned in the other reports, we found the settlement under *raid* rather than under *siege*. A poorly organized force arrayed itself against us and flung itself on our spears. The consensus I agree with—the intention was for a series of waves to greet us and that the utter lack of coordination altered that to a loose stream of individuals charging into a defensive line. Our casualties were minimal, and according to Acolyte Jiivra's more knowledgeable report on the matter, entirely due to an uncommon venom coating the arrows our squad was attacked with."

"We caught the effects too late since the poison was crystal clear and just made the arrowheads look shiny, which caused affected troops to not pay attention. The majority of the village was on fire before our arrival, and it seems that the idea was to pillage and burn." Acolyte Tibbins drank some water from a recovered local cup and retraced his fingers to where he was on the report.

"Losses for the village are... borderline *total*." The young adult motioned a thumb behind him to the still figures lining makeshift resting spaces along the wall.

"Recovered individuals of note are two old people. The catatonic woman hasn't spoken and was found seated in frozen horror at the head of this very table. As of yet, we have not found an explanation for why the *longhouse* is one of the few buildings not burned to the ground. From the stains on the floor, we can easily put together that people were executed here, but the old lady appeared to have been spared. From the complete inability to communicate, we are guessing that she was made to watch the ordeal."

"This also led us to think that we could not locate the leaders of the raiding force because they were simply not part of the main assault and escaped during the confusion while our forces were tied down with consecutive attacks. Cowardly, to be sure, but there was no doubt of that. We did find carriage tracks, but any more effort on our considerably exhausted forces was essentially impossible. No chase was given."

He flipped a page, took a breath, and continued speaking, "The other individual of note was an old man in a dark blue robe. Keeper Irene found him still breathing next to the body of a deformed man that had a sizable gash in his chest and shoulder. It is the Keeper's opinion that the man was spared due to being partially obscured and having the appearance of someone already dead. His breathing was found by accident when she was prying bodies apart for proper death count."

"Based on the high quality of the cloth, we've concluded that this must be one of the Fringe Elders. So, per the plans of the ecclesiarch, he is likely who we need to speak with pertaining to the *greater effort*. He has as of yet not woken, and while basic aid has been provided, we have no idea what state he may be in when he wakes up. Acolyte," the young adult's eyes bulged, and he needed to take a strained breath as he saw his own name noted, "*Tibbins* is responsible for the wellbeing of the Elder until a positive outcome can be reached."

A pleading look was in the Acolyte's eyes, but his superiors were too laden with their own burdens to reconsider his plight. Defeated without any words, Tibbins continued, "Almost no bodies under burned and collapsed buildings could be recovered. The few we *did* find were indicative of having received crippling injuries rather than directly lethal ones."

He swallowed and rasped out more of the report, "Being burned in their homes was *intentional*. Consensus is that the additional cries of help would distract us from pursuit. To my great regret... I must report that this was a fairly successful ploy, and no actual adults were recovered. However, we found no bodies nor remains of *any* children. With the depth of the discovered tracks, we are of the opinion that the children were *taken* rather than slaughtered."

Vellum rustled as he'd gotten to the bottom of that section, needing to flip to the next page. "Temporary encampments are being erected, as our forces require rest. Morale is low from being so close to the scarred zone, though merchant intelligence indicates it has been locally renamed to the 'Salt Flats'. Updated documentation shows that history past a few hundred years has been entirely forgotten or *wildly* misunderstood."

"Is *it* still dormant?" the tired commander inquired, wanting *that* off his chest *now*, as he hadn't heard this part of the report before.

The Acolyte calmed his worries. "Yes, Head Cleric, the scar is not expanding. The current state of the flats matches the scriptures."

Relief washed over the group.

"Good. It would have been a *horror* if that dungeon woke up again. Can we safely conclude no deaths were on the scar itself?" A different, more wizened Acolyte nodded, *older* vellum embossed with golden text unfurled to compare with fresher notes.

"Yes, Head Cleric, that is correct. No casualties were incurred on the flats, so there is no chance of the calamity coming to pass." The Acolyte received a stern nod from the commander, who chuffed in reply.

"Excellent. While that is good to assume, we must be *certain*. Establish a forward base rather than a temporary encampment. We cannot allow the possibility for these raiders to let misfortune come to pass due to their *blithering* ignorance!

Tibbins, you're in charge of making the Fringe Elder agree to let us stay here."

"I don't care how *inane* some of the requests may be; the rules are *twisted* in this place, and we need *both* verbal and written consent... as far as I'm aware. So, if he wants to ride a *pony*, fetch the blasted horse! *Don't* come to me with requests for permission; just get it *done*. Bill it to Keeper Irene, have it added to the expenses tally. If it's *truly* egregious you may ask or, better yet, decline. Still... make him happy with us."

The hand of the fifth Acolyte down the bench rose. The Head Cleric snarled at being interrupted, "What is it, Mandell?"

The heavy accent of the Acolyte gave away his centralized heritage. "Sir, I don't understand. Why would a purely celestial dungeon waking be a *bad* thing? The majority of us have major affinities that align! From initial reports, I thought this place would be ideal for cultivation in addition to our daily chants and prayer."

Irene turned to give the Acolyte a leer, but couldn't fault the young man for not knowing. Her tone was motherly, though cutting. "May I, sir?"

The request to her superior was waved off with a, "Do as you please."

Irene's chair *squealed* on the floor as she turned herself to face the recruit. "In ordinary circumstances, yes, you would be correct, Acolyte. Unfortunately, this dungeon doesn't operate under the common behavior we generally expect from dungeons. It does not align with the reports we cross-referenced from the Adventurers' Guild, and even the *scriptures* refer to what happened here in the past as '*The Great Scarring*'."

"This is why we've been referring to the salt flats as '*The Scar*'. This particular dungeon is strange in several ways." She lifted her gloved hand to keep count on her fingers. "The scriptures say that at least a hand's worth of centuries ago, a celestial dungeon awakened here. Not developed slowly; not came from the heavens. It just... *woke up*, and *pop*... it was there."

"Not only was no one ever able to locate the core, but clerics at the time couldn't figure out if it even *had* one. Instead of building in layers, applying clever traps, or adding what we've come to expect as the usual gambit of monsters, those aspects simply *never appeared*. This dungeon only did *two* things, beyond absolutely *ruining* hosts of armies and emptying entire coffers of nations."

All the Acolytes, while tired, had latched on to Irene's words with rapt attention. "The first thing—and the only *confirmable* thing that this dungeon did—was flatten every bit of area it could spread to. On this flattened area, sporadic amounts of highly desirable resources would slowly accumulate as the tides came and went."

"The tide—to this day—remains one of the great mysteries of the Fringe. There is *no* major body of water nearby, and the mapped rivers simply do not provide the amount of water that comes and goes as the scriptures describe. Over the next few days, we will be able to generate an updated account."

"One of the rare Mages in those days described the phenomenon as watching a great beast breathe during slumber. As people died by the droves over the pursuit of scarce, rare resources, the dungeon grew—and grew in *width* only. It snaked across the landscape, and wherever its rising waters touched... the earth slowly flattened to a very *specific* depth. In certain places, it split like the roots of a tree. Up north, the pattern seems designed more like an infection rather than any cohesive pattern, while down south, there's nothing but straight lines and right angles."

A hand rose again, but she was just getting to the point and was sure she would answer the query before it was asked. "The *second* thing the dungeon did—something we're still not *certain* about it actually being responsible for—is a phenomenon that we frequently see in celestial cultivators that don't keep a proper balance."

"Every warrior, *every single one*, who stepped foot on the salt flats... slowly lost their sanity and the ability to see reason. They began claiming the land and resources as *theirs* and seeing themselves as superior regardless of established hierarchy. They also gradually physically withered when they failed to be present on the landscape the scar '*owned*.'"

Irene pointedly motioned to the Elder in the blue robe. "Eventually, you end up looking like *that*. We actually have fairly detailed notes on the subject, which involves internal corruption problems. So, Acolyte Tibbins, please *do* take care to not let his corruption consume him before the Head Cleric has what he needs."

Tibbins nodded with a salute. This part was following orders; he could do that. Mandell still looked confused; he didn't feel his question had been answered. "While that is certainly unfortunate, why would that prevent this area from being a good source of Essence for us to cultivate with? Our prayer certainly provides, but why would already present celestial Essence *not* be beneficial?"

Irene had to think for a moment but was decently certain she had the answer. "It is *very* beneficial. Had there not been a hidden trap that caused people to lose their minds, I would agree with you."

She squeezed the tips of her fingers together. "The issue comes from the *interaction*. By taking, we also give back. Any Essence we fail to refine fully returns to the dungeon. Unlike in a common dungeon, Essence density here is *always* low. A place where additional Essence suddenly depletes because of, say, the presence of a dozen cultivating clerics? Well, that may awaken a cycle we *very* much wish to avoid."

"The scripture is also *clear* that the Core was never found. The scar is vast, and worst of all, the spread of Essence is *incredibly* even. So using the adventurer trick to follow the path where Essence density is thicker to locate the core is *unfruitful*."

"Scripture says that the Mage in the area proclaimed the dungeon *dormant* rather than dead. Specifically, when its expansion fully ceased after years and years of the Church and the Guild deterring people from entry."

"The region isn't named 'The Fringe' due to some landscaping design. It is named such because this very scar brings someone to the *fringe of sanity*. Delusions of grandeur and grand heroism are recorded to have been declared by cultivators rapidly rising in rank. Their intent to do well and invoke the best for us all was devoured and overshadowed by this place. It is one of the *well-kept secrets* the Church does *not* want the populace to be aware of."

"Could you *imagine* the rumors? That a celestial dungeon, a gift of the celestial above, drives people *insane*? Makes them commit great acts of violence in the name of what they consider to be right? The Church prizes and relies on its relationship of goodwill, its values of great virtue, to remain in the hearts and minds of the people. The Fringe is one of those secrets that has been obscured with misinformation to soothe the minds of those who don't *want* to know. This place isn't on the map because the Church *does. Not. Want. It.* To *be* on the map."

She put her finger down hard on a fat book. "The scriptures complain for an entire *volume* of notes and complaints that not a *single* bastion or permanent stone building could be erected! If there was any semblance that something *important* was here, permanent structures would have given it all away. A *full chapter* is devoted to disgruntled scribes going on and *on* about how movement was constant and tensions were *always* high!"

"Not only did they need to keep themselves from venturing into the scar despite the glint of prizes clearly visible in the distance, but they had to keep everyone and *everything* else out as well. Why do you think we still haven't seen a single monster? Eradication was *widespread.* As you must have clearly noticed just by glancing, the scar is utterly *massive.* The manpower and coordination that took made fully devoted scribes complain. *Fully. Devoted. Scribes.* Were... complaining." She trailed off with a soft sigh.

"I have never seen a scribe complain about *anything* in my decades with the Church, and these are *written* accounts." Her finger repeatedly pressed down *hard* on the volume. The importance of her words was not difficult to discern, even for the tired. Irene leaned forward in Mandell's direction. "Do. *Not.* Cultivate. While. In. The. Scar. Near *might* be fine, but certainly not *in.* Is that understood, Acolyte? All of you, in fact?"

Mandel's stand and snap to attention was textbook. His chair screeched back, and in an instant, he was in the official salute position. "Yes, Keeper, sir!"

The others gave mumbled responses. Irene let Mandel be at ease and return to his seat, handing the reporting back over. "Acolyte Tibbins, please continue."

Tibbins had lost his place on his report vellum and scrambled to find his lines again. The reporting continued for another hour until a fresh recruit announced himself with the news that temporary camp was set up. The meeting was dispersed, and the priests went to rest as a guard rotation of the least exhausted was set up.

The camp was sizable. Four dozen clerics had been housed in tents with only a handful remaining in the longhouse as the construct was not considered structurally sound. As soon as the majority of them had acquired some much-needed rest, the *real* work would begin.

CHAPTER FOUR

The Elder continued rising from the depths of the small coma he had been trapped within.

"You win this one as well, shiny sky orb." The old man kept his eyes closed after stirring from slumber. He had opened them only to find a ceiling he didn't often see. A spike of light sunk right into his sight, and the chorus of complaining voices was wholly unfamiliar. He *sort* of heard most of it but didn't pay real attention—he wasn't able to.

Illusions and ghosts played across his senses, and he instead vividly experienced the memories of past conversations as if hearing them for the first time. He knew all the words of the conversation; he heard the retorts and quips that would lead to some juicy gossip. The giggling of children came and went with the usual swiftness as they swirled across the floor, carried by a haze on an unseen wind. In short, reality fled from his mind.

The unwelcome was truth pushed aside, and the old man's mind found nothing but shards with no idea how to put it all back together. Why bother? His imagined conversations of warm nights and welcoming stew were rudely interrupted by words and flashes that suggested that the village burned down. A pang of discomfort struck the inside of his head, and the old man found it best to relieve the pain by remaining still. Swiftly, long-past conversations and warmth returned with the obscuring certainty of steam. The haze lazily veiled over once more and was welcomed dearly.

"*Losses of the village are borderline total.*" A hollow distortion of the speaking voice reached him. The pang of discomfort returned with greater strength, and the misty haze blew apart as a strong gust sundered it. The laughter in his thoughts wavered, the emotions and ability to express repressed as grief found no foothold on the shattered glass shards in his unwilling mental state.

No, no, no. He didn't want to be *here.* There was just nothing left.

"*The children were taken rather than slaughtered.*" These words rang like a gong through the empty halls of his mindscape, painting chaotic color over and over on unseen walls. *Hope* arrived on screaming wings. The Elder felt overwhelmed. Unreal, ghostly steps approached from the other side of his closed eyelids as again he sunk ever deeper into malaise. A fall ended when you hit the bottom, and for the Elder, that was in a space between madness and self-reflection. It was time to save his mind. It was time to give someone else the reins.

Dizziness struck even though his body was unmoving. The Elder's view altered drastically as he meandered through an imagined hallway of memories. The scenes replayed in sudden flashes, and he fully experienced the images and accompanying scents and tastes. They bombarded against his mind with each additional step. Another step, and another, and one last one were taken before the familiar and comforting rasp of a whetstone reached his ears.

Scrape

A large flame was centered in this stable mental space. Moving towards the burning representation of his will to live, the old man that came into view near the fire had a considerably stronger back—a younger back. *His back,* from many years ago. The large fire licked at the dry, wood-shaped memories in the center, burning through everything with all the time in the world, sampling the flavors of ancient happenings soon to be forgotten.

Many more figures surrounded the fire, and they *all* appeared as younger, more youthful versions of him. All of 'him' was obstructed in a partial or complete, snowy haze that obscured their individual features. They were the reflections of his old self, the blurring corruption on them a representation of aspects long forgotten and traits willfully abandoned. He wasn't those people anymore. Those identities. Not completely.

Scrape

The whetstone personality paused sharpening its weapon, prompting the Elder to step forth and join the circle. He seated himself on one of the many cut stumps as darkness and blackened doors surrounded him. He recognized the whispers coming from behind those chain-closed barriers. They contained all of his regrets. His many, *many* regrets. The doors strained and shook inwards, threatening to burst even as he watched.

"I didn't expect that I would ever use *this* philosopher's trick again," his wordless voice spoke to nobody in particular. He was talking to *himself,* after all. There was no need to explain himself. This place was purely to accept that once again, he'd *failed.* The little crevice in the mind was the best imagined space he could construct to cope and convince himself to try again. You didn't become a philosopher and *not* make tricks to protect yourself from infinite existentialism. When you come to the realization that you know nothing, your world has a tendency to fall apart. There had to be stability, even if it was fabricated.

"*I* can't do this anymore." The current perspective's hands folded together and tearfully sighed, head dipping low in shame. It took willful effort to right himself again. He turned on his stump and faced the next empty seat to relinquish more than a mere question. "Can *you?*"

Slowly and with deliberate intent, a copy of his current appearance formed on the stump. An exact replica of his current voice replied in kind, "I believe *I* can. *I* can find the way."

The original nodded and asked, "Where did *I* go wrong, old friend?"

The copy slowly stood, and the perspective shifted. Focus faded from the eyes of the original and instead saw from the eyes of the new copy. "Nowhere, *Elder*. You did everything right, and we all know well that you can make no mistakes and *still* lose. That's not a weakness or a failure. That's just life."

The abandoned original remained seated on the stump. His time was over, and his mind needed to go elsewhere to move on. "What will you do?"

The new perspective folded his hands behind his back, adopting a slightly hunched posture to answer his own question from the version which had passed the torch. "What we *chose* to do. What we learned over all these years. That we hold to the *ideal.* That we make the decisions we will *not* regret. That we always, *always* hold promises to those dearest to us."

He laid a hand on the Elder's shoulder. "It has been a pleasure and a *privilege* to have *been* you, Elder. I *loved* the life you gave us, free of what we were used to doing."

Another door sprung up and immediately revolted as regrets exploded to life behind it, only to be plastered against the darkness and fade into obscurity. "I am *no longer* an Elder, and I believe I am the first one that will *accept* the regret. Because in this breaking I've realized... *grief* is the price we pay for love."

The Elder nodded at the new perspective and laid out his last question. He was fading, losing active consciousness as the new mentality gained it. "What will you do?"

The fresh outlook rolled his shoulders behind him. "I am going to get my children back if it's the *last* thing I do. It is *high* time we break into the details of an old tidbit we weren't supposed to hear, *old friend.* We can pretend to not be aware of that conversation out there all we want, but those voices are openly talking about Essence. That means they are *cultivators.*"

The new perspective shared a knowing look with the version of himself that had paused using the whetstone. "It is high time we discover how they live so *long* and attain that time for ourselves."

The whetstone version of himself smiled like a fox, turning the blade over to show regretful, carved words etched deeply into the other side: '*This good man never goes to war again*'. This version of him had his mind broken in a desert long ago. His doppelganger put the whetstone down, gave a small salute, and proudly closed his eyes. He fuzzed over and began to fade.

The new perspective was adapting, restructuring personality traits and priorities. Major components of the personality of that time were being rejected, obscured, denied. Similar to the personality present from the war, several others became blurry. A few vanished from the bonfire scene altogether as their values and beliefs were fed to the fire, never to be considered in a decision-making process again.

When the new perspective looked back down to the Elder, half of the old man was a sketchy imprint of what it had been. A younger, more vibrant personality had cleared up significantly. His haze near the beginning of the circle was almost fully cleared. It was both necessary and thrilling to possess the blind will to go always forward. "I retreat no more. I hide no further."

"I'm going to need a new name." With a powerful movement of the old man's hand, '*never*' was blotted out and erased from the blade. The new perspective turned and, with unwavering steps, strode away from the bonfire. His voice trembled, then gained an unyielding quality, the core trait from which the fiber of his being was now constructed. "*Again.* Again, we go to war. "

CHAPTER FIVE

The mental space collapsed into kaleidoscopic memories behind him, and every step forward pulled forth ideals, beliefs, and remembrances. This path he now walked was a recollection of all he'd done and was again *willing* to do. Memories knit together, and the new perspective opened his arms wide, walking straight ahead as he took his first step on the path of pain. No more gates to lock his agony behind. Blackened doors burst through their chains, and a deep breath was taken as he affirmed himself.

"I am neither Elder nor old."

"I am the weight of all my experiences and the incarnate will of the path which I now walk."

His hand snatched out and grasped a recent remembrance, slowing only to place the memory of Choppy's death before him. The boy had never deserved that, and it hurt to keep it in mind. Sadness and a clutched heart squeezed the space of his surroundings. With the acceptance of impending suffering, he took a step into the memory to make it part of his being.

Crushing lamentation struck him immediately as he looked to the light, willing himself to leave the convenient lie his mind had constructed to protect his sanity. His real body convulsed, and his eyes snapped open. It was at least high noon by the time he came around, and aged fingers gripped the sheets as the first of many howls rang from his throat. His face was once again stained with tears as he immersed himself in loss.

Survivor's guilt beat him without mercy as he worked his way through the fugue that entrapped him. One last time, the old was relinquished, and someone new was born to carry the torch. He had never ascribed to the idea that a person always remains that same person. People change, *dramatically* even, in times of crisis. He could never understand why others couldn't grasp that this wasn't the slightest bit odd.

He'd seen it *countless* times after a war.

Great loss.

Great grief.

Great love.

It all *changed* people. *How* they thought and what ideals they held. *Who* they were, and how they saw the world. His physical outcry had several clerics by his side in an instant, ready to steady the uncontrollably weeping, old man.

Some had no idea what to do, and others ushered them out of the way as Keeper Irene waltzed her way through and violently waved the rests of the priests off. Her voice was brisk and cutting as she dismissed them. "Why are you all standing around gawking like a foolish bunch of art historians? Fetch me water and fresh cloth! This man is in *severe* shock and requires immediate tending. *Where* is Acolyte Tibbins? Isn't this *his* duty?"

Irene had the old man supportively weeping into her neck while the majority of the thin figure slumped over her shoulder. She clearly had a great deal of experience handling uncontrollably weeping children. Her attentive hushing resounded with gentle care, soothing what in her eyes was just another big baby. She found there to be little difference between the very old and the very young, having had to take care of both.

"Tibbins!" Her words were as welcoming as they were grateful, the bony burden swiftly handed over to the Acolyte. He was soon holding the inconsolable Elder upright. As soon as Irene was free, she gave Tibbins a strong '*it's your problem now*' pat on the shoulder and walked off. Irene might have been good at this, but that didn't mean she *wanted* to deal with it. She had *scriptures* to tend.

Nothing the Acolyte said or did appeared to have the remotest impact. Sure, he succeeded in making the old man drink down some water, but this was an ordeal the young Acolyte still needed to learn to deal with. It took several hours for the heaving to slow down. Only then did Tibbins again attempt to reason with the man, who he was currently convinced was completely out of his mind. Granted, he could not blame the behavior.

"My back hurts," was the first set of cohesive mumbles he heard from the bleary-faced, old man.

"Sir, my name is Acolyte Tibbins. Do you remember yours?"

The old man pathetically groaned in response, "*My back hurts.*"

Tibbins had honestly run out of patience. The taxing hours had taken the goodwill right out of him with the unexpected and unwanted nursemaiding. Still, the man was his charge, so he used those strong cleric muscles of his to lift the aged old log with all the difficulty of bench-pressing a feather. Tired eyes squinted through the sunlight as the old man saw a long set of tents set up in a familiar order. "Ah. *Clerics.*"

He recognized the orderly campsite immediately. It was *meant* to be memorable, after all—the place you run to when you're injured and trying to survive. Each was a higher quality than a common healer's tent. The tent he was carried into, to his great chagrin after his most recent thought, was an *abyssal* common healing tent. Still, the cot he was laid on was significantly better than some sheets on the floor with bedding crammed under it. This was a resting place for the sick and had a much greater degree of comfort to facilitate that rest.

"*Sir*, do you remember your name?"

The old man blinked, taking hold of the words. Recent memories were filtered and parsed. He was a new man after his mental shift at his campfire, so he needed something *new—* something he could hold on to that was neither the ordinary nor similar to any previous *unordinary* name.

"Art..." the old man pushed a hand into his face, kneading skin together, "...Orian?"

He was grasping for ideas based on something vague a womanly voice had recently said. Art... historian? It was always healthy advice to listen to a good woman, and thus, he pulled his ideas from the recent experience and released his face. Expression clearing, he extended a hand in greeting to Tibbins. "*Artorian*. A true pleasure to meet you, cleric but truly unfortunate *circumstances* for it."

A weak smile slowly built upon his aged features, his voice slowly blooming with confidence as it all came together. "Yes. It is decided. My name is... *Artorian*."

AFTERWORD

We hope you enjoyed Essence! Since reviews are the lifeblood of indie publishing, we'd love it if you could leave a positive review on Amazon! Please use this link to go to the Essence: A Divine Dungeon Anthology Amazon product page to leave your review: geni.us/Essence.

As always, thank you for your support! You are the reason we're able to bring these stories to life.

ABOUT MOUNTAINDALE PRESS

Dakota and Danielle Krout, a husband and wife team, strive to create as well as publish excellent fantasy and science fiction novels. Self-publishing *The Divine Dungeon: Dungeon Born* in 2016 transformed their careers from Dakota's military and programming background and Danielle's Ph.D. in pharmacology to President and CEO, respectively, of a small press. Their goal is to share their success with other authors and provide captivating fiction to readers with the purpose of solidifying Mountaindale Press as the place 'Where Fantasy Transforms Reality.'

Connect with Mountaindale Press:
MountaindalePress.com
Facebook.com/MountaindalePress
Krout@MountaindalePress.com

MOUNTAINDALE PRESS TITLES

GAMELIT AND LITRPG

The Divine Dungeon Series
The Completionist Chronicles Series
By: DAKOTA KROUT

A Touch of Power Series
By: JAY BOYCE

Red Mage: Advent
By: XANDER BOYCE

Ether Collapse Series
By: RYAN DEBRUYN

Wolfman Warlock: Bibliomancer
By: JAMES HUNTER AND DAKOTA KROUT

Axe Druid Series
By: CHRISTOPHER JOHNS

Skeleton in Space Series
By: ANDRIES LOUWS

Chronicles of Ethan Series
By: JOHN L. MONK

Pixel Dust Series
By: DAVID PETRIE

Artorian's Archives: Axiom
By: DENNIS VANDERKERKEN AND DAKOTA KROUT